Revenge

Bill Ward

Copyright © 2013 Bill Ward
All rights reserved.
ISBN: 149237735X
ISBN-13: 978-1492377351

CHAPTER ONE

Christmas was fast approaching. Not that Tom was feeling very festive as he hurried down Sloane Street, past the fashionable designer shops, towards where he'd parked his car. A sharp cold wind caused him to pull the collar of his old brown leather coat tightly around his neck. It had a rather worn look, not unlike its owner. In truth both had seen better days.

He lowered his head and focused his eyes just a few feet ahead on the pavement, to escape the worst of the biting wind's force. He drew small breaths through tightly clenched teeth, protecting his lungs from the frosty night air. He could just glimpse, out the corner of his eye, the shop windows screaming out their messages of goodwill, their brightly lit decorations illuminating the pavement. No doubt a lot of creative thought had been put into designing those windows, in an attempt to grab the attention of passing pedestrians.

It wasn't just a result of the cold weather that Tom didn't linger to look closer at what was on show. Even though he didn't have many to buy presents for, he couldn't afford to shop in this part of London without taking out a second mortgage on his home, or more accurately speaking what would be in fact a third mortgage. And Christmas or not, he had more pressing financial challenges than just buying a few presents.

His bank had seemed to take delight from pointing out to him that, even before the further recent plummet in house prices, he had no remaining equity in his house to secure any additional borrowing.

He hated the way banks always made him feel like Oliver asking for more food. He had laughed at the suggestion he could meet with one of the bank's business advisors, who somehow might be able to help. Tom knew from previous experience that would probably be someone much younger, who had never owned a business, or worked in the real world outside a bank. He had replied as politely as he could that perhaps, given the bank's recent performance, they might have greater need of his advice. In truth, given the amount of sarcasm in his voice, he wasn't actually all that polite.

He fondly remembered the days when he could pop into his local bank and have a chat with a manager he had known for years, and who shared a common interest in racing. Now it was a call centre and an impersonal secure message informing him of the bad news. Tom was certain if he treated his customers with the same contempt exhibited by the banks, he would soon have no customers. The problem was everyone needed a bank and they were all as bad as each other.

As a result, presents this year would once again have to be measured more by the thought than the value. Not that that was an entirely bad thing. It was more in the original spirit of Christmas and he actually quite enjoyed shopping for presents on a budget. Out of necessity he was creative in his selection of presents and generally it was appreciated by the recipients.

A heavy overnight frost had been the prediction and for once it seemed the weather forecasters would be right. That in turn was expected to lead to at least a week of snowfalls and icy roads, which in turn would bring chaos to Britain's eternally ill prepared transport system.

It would also inevitably result in horse race meetings being cancelled and for someone who owned a small betting shop, which barely provided an adequate income at the best of times, any reduction in turnover could only be viewed as impending disaster. Thus, despite generally enjoying Christmas, he wasn't feeling very festive.

While the big betting shop chains thrust every form of slot machine at their customers, Tom's clientele were mostly true horse racing aficionados, who gathered to share a coffee in the company of likeminded fans of the sport and debate who would win the next big race. Neither did they bother betting on the laughable virtual racing now beamed to shops.

Even the coffee he provided was free of charge and if there was no real racing, then there was little revenue. It wouldn't be so bad if it was a one off occurrence but over the last couple of years, there had been an increasing number of such occasions, resulting in a loss of revenue. The success or otherwise of running a betting shop was beginning to be far too dependent on the whim of the weather gods.

Tom moved at a brisk pace, encountering very few pedestrians going in the opposite direction. Anyone with half a sense was at home with the central heating on full blast. Tom had been willing to gamble on the bad weather not deteriorating further and had ventured out to meet his brother for dinner in a very smart Knightsbridge restaurant, owned by a famous television chef. In truth he hadn't cancelled because this year it was his brother's turn to pay and trips to swanky eateries at someone else's expense were rare treats.

The food had lived up to expectations. Dishes with unpronounceable names had tasted amazing. Indeed this pilgrimage they both made annually, on the first Friday in December to celebrate Christmas and keep in touch, had been a truly pleasant evening. For at least a few hours he had been able to forget about his financial plight.

Colin was ten years his junior. Unplanned he'd presumed but their parents weren't the type to be asked such a question. Father had spent his life in the army and believed in firm discipline and doing things by the book. An expression Tom found faintly ridiculous, as he was sure no such book had ever been written.

By the time Colin was born, Tom was already in the English public school system. While the army posted his father around the world, Tom was packed off to be a boarder at a Prep school in Berkshire. It wasn't an experience he remembered with any affection. He learnt to be independent and self-sufficient but to his mind the austere surroundings had not been a suitable replacement for the family home.

He spent most of his school days playing sport at every opportunity and avoiding academia. In the sixth form he was almost expelled for running a book on the Derby, which paved the way for his future career. That he only scraped through his exams was the result of an absence of studying, rather than any lack of intelligence. He could work out the probability odds on any poker hand by the time he was eighteen.

He was in his second year at Portsmouth University, doing a Business Studies degree, when both parents were killed in a car accident. Colin went to live with their Aunt in North London but despite regular holiday visits, the age gap meant they had never really been close. Sadly, a few years earlier the Aunt had also passed away, leaving them with only each other as close family. That was when they had instigated their annual dinner, to ensure they didn't lose touch. Now Colin was a successful young something in IT frequenting Michelin starred restaurants and Tom was a regular at his local Indian on Tuesday nights, when they did their special offer of everything you can eat for a tenner.

Tom wasn't in any way jealous of his brother's success in the corporate world. Even financial security wouldn't be enough to induce him to spend all day behind a desk staring at a computer screen, or at least not a screen that was used for writing computer software. Tom often spent hours staring at a screen playing poker on one of the Internet sites but it would never occur to him to think of it in the same terms. Anyway, financial security could only ever be a transitory state, as there would always be the poker and the horses to challenge any risk of having stability in his life.

It was rather like the search for the Holy Grail. Pursuing financial independence by gambling gave meaning to his barely controlled addiction but in all honesty he couldn't imagine life lived anywhere except on the edge. The result of a close photo finish, or the turn of the river card when all in for a lot of money, left you in no doubt you were still very much alive.

For a long time he had wondered why the last card dealt in a Texas hold 'em hand was called the River anyway? He knew he'd felt like jumping in a river a few times, when that last card dealt had yet again not delivered what he needed, and turned to the internet to discover it's history.

The river card supposedly got its name from poker games on river boats. Often cheaters would deal a hidden fifth card from their sleeve to better their hand. When caught, the cheater would be thrown into the river. Tom often wondered if he had lived a hundred years earlier, whether he might have been a river boat gambler, although he couldn't imagine ever being a cheat. He could see no pleasure in winning anything if you had to resort to cheating.

Colin had announced over dinner that he and Liz were trying for a baby, so there was every possibility of Tom becoming an Uncle, in the not too distant future. Tom greeted the news with a certain degree of apathy. He had nothing against children, quite the opposite but Liz so strongly disapproved of his lifestyle that he doubted he would get many chances to play the role of Uncle. Liz had made it very clear from their first meeting that she did not approve of gambling and gamblers. The frosty reception she gave him, when they did rarely meet, made the current weather seem innocuous by comparison.

There was a regular open invitation to visit on Boxing Day but that was one of the busiest racing days of the year and he was needed in his shop. He suspected Liz knew that and it was the only reason he received an invitation. And if he wasn't needed in the shop, he knew he would instead be at Kempton Park, to watch the racing not sharing the day with Liz's look of disapproval.

Tom turned left towards the back of Harrods and hoped he might yet avoid the worst of the freeze on the drive back to his small detached home on the edge of Brighton. He would normally have preferred to take a train into London, especially with Colin buying the wine, but he had spent the afternoon visiting his accountant, who worked from home in a very nice house on the edge of Slough, which was virtually impossible to reach by train.

There was also the possibility of trains being delayed or cancelled, if the weather deteriorated further, so he'd settled for driving. At least there was little sign of traffic in what was normally a busy part of town on a Saturday night. The only vehicle about was a large noisy beast, owned by the council, moving slowly up the road and disgorging grit from its bowels.

The famous store was closed but he noticed a small group of people emerge from one of the rear entrances. Hands were shaken and then one person quickly returned inside the store. That seemed to leave one broad man and two women, although he couldn't be one hundred per cent sure, as they were wisely wrapped in large coats. They hurried across the road. All three were laden with bags displaying the store's well-known logo. Privileged shoppers, Tom thought to himself. Perhaps even someone famous. He'd heard before of the store opening exclusively just for film stars and celebrities to be able to shop without the crowds.

Out of curiosity, and seeing they were headed in the same direction, he accelerated his pace a little. He was only about fifty feet behind them but couldn't distinguish whom he was following, although he had decided it was one man and two women by the way they walked. He felt a tinge of disappointment when, after going only a very short distance, the lights of a nearby Mercedes flashed, announcing the group ahead had arrived at their car.

Tom almost jumped out of his skin when the two men suddenly appeared from out of the shadows and he simultaneously heard the explosion of a gun and saw the man accompanying the two women fall to the ground.

Scarcely able to believe what he'd seen, he quickly ducked beside a parked car, while up ahead at least one woman was screaming. He rested his back against the side of the car and drew slow deep breaths to try and combat the sense of panic he was feeling. He was fairly sure he hadn't been seen but was listening intently for any sound of advancing footsteps.

His focus went back to the woman who was still screaming. He couldn't just stay hiding and ignore her screams. Crouched low, he snatched a quick look from the rear of the car. He could see one man standing with his hand extended, pointing a pistol at the two women, while the other man was pulling one of the women towards an open car door. She in turn was resisting and the second woman was pulling her in the opposite direction to the gunman. Both men were simultaneously shouting at the women, swearing at the one to let go and at the other to get in the car.

Tom returned to safety behind the car. For an instant he wondered if a movie was being filmed but there had been no cameras. He felt his heart pumping at a hundred miles an hour and was worried it was going to explode out of his chest. He recognized the feeling and fought to stay calm. But this wasn't just the turn of an important card. He forced himself to once again breathe steadily and focus.

He fumbled inside his coat for his mobile phone and with an unsteady hand managed to dial 999. "A man's been shot and they're trying to kidnap a woman," he said quietly but clearly, not wishing to attract the attention of the gunmen. "Back of Harrods and hurry." The woman at the other end of the line tried to ask further questions. Tom cut her off with a firm and slightly desperate, "Please hurry." Then repeated, "They've already shot one person."

He risked a further glimpse. The sound of another shot made him jump. It brought the tug of war to a halt as the second woman collapsed to the ground. Tom had observed the rose emission of blood and fragments of skull, exploding from the back of her skull, and knew with absolute certainty she was dead.

The callous bastards, he thought, placing his phone on the kerb, careful to leave the line open. Shooting the man had been bad enough but now a helpless woman as well. Seething with anger and using the parked cars for cover, he managed to move within about twenty feet without being seen by the killers.

He had no idea how he could help but at the same time knew he had to do something. They were too busy to have spotted him and he knew surprise was his only chance of success. He didn't like the odds and wished he'd had more of his father's army training, as he sprung from behind the last of the cars that afforded cover. A year in the army cadet corps didn't prepare you for this type of encounter.

Twenty feet became ten then six. He charged the man manhandling the woman into the car, as he was closest. Just as he launched himself, some sixth sense made the man turn towards him and Tom saw the look of horror on his twisted face.

In something akin to a rugby tackle, he hit the man sideways on below the shoulder with his full thirteen stone. As they both fell to the ground, Tom was grateful to hear the thud of the man's head as it hit the hard pavement.

He rolled off the motionless body beneath him and sprung to his feet as fast as he could. He knew the second man, the one who had held the gun, was to his right and as he looked in his direction, he saw the open-mouthed look turn to anger and then the gun arm turn in his direction.

Tom was winded from his efforts and though his mind told him to move fast, his body was slowed down by too many years of inactivity. He made a half-hearted effort to lunge at the killer but knew he'd never make it in time, when suddenly the man was knocked off balance by the remaining female victim, who hurled her bags through the air like someone used to throwing the hammer in an athletics competition. The killer raised his arm to fend off the shopping bags and that gave Tom the extra time he needed to once again throw himself forward at the man's legs, in another crude attempt at a rugby tackle.

There was no repeat thud of head on pavement this time but there was the sweet sound of metal bouncing across concrete as the killer lost his gun. Tom felt the man beneath him kicking out trying to get free but at least for the moment he was pinned to the ground.

Tom was tempted to simply roll away and hope the killer would make his escape but there was also the other scenario in which he ran nowhere but instead found his gun and shot Tom for being so bloody stupid as to interfere.

As a man used to having to calculate odds for a living, he decided to err on the side of caution. He lashed at the killer's head with his fists and tried to pummel his kidneys. Still though the man continued to try and break free. Where the hell were the police when you needed them? Or at least a passerby who might help. Probably running in the opposite direction, if they had any sense. Exactly what he should have done.

The killer was ever more desperate and Tom realised he'd made a grave error in letting his head stray too close to the killer's. He saw the head butt coming but, interlocked as he was, he could move very little and felt the full force of the blow on the bridge of his nose. As he saw the killer intended to deliver a repeat blow, he decided it was better to roll away and make for where he'd heard the gun fall.

He hadn't anticipated how groggy his head felt and once he moved his weight off the killer, it was him who was quickest to rise to his feet. Tom was on the receiving end of a vicious kick that connected with his knee and halted his attempt to get to his feet.

The killer was smirking as he moved in to deliver a further kick, when suddenly the crisp night air was shattered by what Tom knew intellectually was a shot but didn't understand who was doing the firing. A second bullet passed close to him but just as he was about to dive for cover, he realised he was not the intended victim. The killer beside him fell to the ground clutching at his stomach. Tom spun around to see the woman standing there with pistol levelled at the man on the ground.

"Don't you fucking move," she screamed hysterically in an American accent.

Tom glanced at the body on the floor and though no expert on the matter, it appeared to him there was no chance of the killer moving, with the amount of blood that was gushing from his middle. Tom looked back at the woman who was shaking and seemed in a state of real shock. Gently he walked towards her and took the gun from her hand.

In the distance he could at last hear the sound of an approaching police siren. He felt an icy cold envelop his body as the adrenalin rush subsided and the chill wind combined with the shock to make him feel very weak. He also had the metal taste of blood running down from his nose, via his top lip and into his mouth. He wiped away the blood on his sleeve and walked over and checked the condition of the first man he'd tackled, who was showing no obvious signs of life. He felt for a pulse and quickly found one.

He glanced again at the wounded man who was clutching at his stomach and moaning. Tom had no intention of going any nearer to check on his welfare. Frankly he hoped he was in a lot of pain. He took a few steps back and watched both of them, fully prepared to use the gun he was holding if necessary.

The woman came up to his side. He put his arm around her shoulder, in theory to comfort her but needing the support just as much himself. He looked closely at her for the first time. She was wearing a long purple coat that shouted out quality and designer. Her head was wrapped in a furry hat of the type he associated with Russians in cold winters. Or at least they wore them in Doctor Zhivago. The hat covered her forehead and framed her face. She had high cheekbones that gave her a slightly oriental look or was it Slavonic. Striking green eyes shone out from perfect skin. Dark brown hair fell to her shoulders.

His first thought was that not only was she beautiful but also slightly familiar. Then the evening produced yet another seismic shock, when he recognized who he was comforting. There was hardly a person on the planet that wouldn't recognize Melanie Adams. Her face regularly adorned the front covers of glossy magazines and her latest film, where she once again played the sexy love interest, was still breaking box office records.

He gave a weak smile of support and wondered what the hell had happened to his quiet night out, as a police car screeched to a halt nearby. Two uniformed officers jumped from the car pointing guns at him and shouting instructions.

"Drop the weapon and get down on the ground," the first policeman commanded.

Tom glanced back at the killers to see which of them still had a gun.

"Put the weapon down and get on the ground," the policeman

repeated.

This time Tom realised the instructions were being shouted at him. He remembered the gun in his hand and suddenly felt very uncomfortable. Christ the bloody fools think I'm dangerous. He extended his arm sideways and gently placed the gun on the ground.

"Move away Miss," the second policeman barked.

Tom first knelt and then prostrated himself on the cold hard ground. He'd seen it done in films but never thought he'd be doing it himself.

"Don't be so stupid," Melanie screamed at the policemen. "He saved my life. It's them you need to arrest." She pointed at the two injured men.

The policemen moved forward. The first one carefully picked up the gun. The second was warily inspecting the bodies that now littered the ground.

"It was me who called you," Tom explained, turning his head sideways to meet the gaze of the policeman. He could hear the second policeman in the background on his radio asking for assistance and ambulances.

Melanie Adams was obviously not easily intimidated. "Do you recognize me?" she asked the policeman, moving close enough to elicit a positive nod of the head. "I'm telling you that these two men attacked us. They shot my bodyguard and my assistant." She pointed out the guilty. "And this man saved my life. Now please let him get off the ground." Her tone suggested it wasn't a request she expected to be denied.

"OK Sir, you can get up," the policeman agreed somewhat grudgingly.

Tom gratefully got to his feet. Further sirens could be heard approaching. He turned to Melanie and said simply, "Thanks." He could see the last of her strength was draining from her and tears were forming at the corners of her eyes.

"Carol wasn't just my assistant, she was a good friend," she explained. Then as if realising the enormity of what had transpired, she started to shake and uncontrollably sob.

CHAPTER TWO

In the smoke filled back room of an old terraced house near the centre of Belfast, four men were sat round the table. A threadbare carpet covered the floor and there were no material signs of the power the four men could wield throughout Belfast and the North. They constituted the Brigade Staff of the Provisional Irish Republican Army or IRA as they are more often simply called. It was early Sunday morning and no one had had the time or inclination for breakfast. Their appetites had been ruined by the previous night's news.

"Who the fuck's responsible for this?" the Chief demanded, bringing his fist down hard on the large wooden kitchen table, causing coffee cups to jump from their saucers and spill their contents over the side.

It was his house where they were meeting. He wasn't a big man physically, of only average height and with a wiry frame but he was known to be a tough bastard. It was a reputation he had been happy to cultivate over the last twenty five years. It had been a long time since anyone challenged his authority.

In the eighties and nineties there had been rivals but through a mixture of good luck and some good judgment, he had survived when many others ended up dead or in jail and almost by default he had been left in unchallenged command. Some said he had the luck of the Leprechaun and lived a charmed life. Others less politely just referred to him as a lucky bastard but not within earshot.

For sure there had been some near misses, such as in 1987 when he was due to sail from Libya on the MV Eksund carrying a huge supply of arms from Colonel Gaddafi back to Ireland. At the last minute he had stayed behind for further negotiations and he had indeed been lucky, as the Eksund was intercepted by the French Navy while in the Bay of Biscay. There had been four shipments before the Eksund, which weren't intercepted, so he would have considered himself bloody unlucky if he had been on the ship. Once he had the power, he had no intention of letting it go and had always been ruthless in protecting his position. Now fifty five years of age, he gave no hint of relaxing his iron fist rule.

He hadn't yet shaved this morning and a dark stubble covered his face. His equally dark hair was uncombed and scruffy. His clothes were thrown on in haphazard fashion, the green shirt not sitting comfortably on top of the blue jeans. He had large ears that would be the first feature picked up by a caricature artist and his face was lined with deep crevices. He had dark piercing eyes that conveyed menace as he stared in turn at each man, challenging them until they averted his gaze.

"This wasn't fucking sanctioned," the Chief continued angrily. He took a long drag on his cigarette to calm himself. He knew he smoked too much. Too often, like this morning, he relied on nicotine for sustenance.

"You know Maguire's always been a head case," one of the others volunteered. He was the tallest man sat at the table. "He always had too much of a taste for blood. And the lad with him was Pat Murphy's son."

"You're responsible for operations," the Chief snarled. "Did you know what they were fucking planning?"

"Course not," he responded quickly, wishing he'd kept his mouth shut in the first place. "After Maguire's last bank job went wrong we told him to get over there and lie low for a bit."

"Well he made a grand job of that," the Chief replied sarcastically. "Killed two people and tried to kidnap Melanie fucking Adams no less. Might as well have been the Queen. Now he's frigging dead and the Brits will think we fucking planned this! We need damage limitation and we need it fucking quick or else."

One of the men who had so far remained silent spoke. He was the only one dressed smartly, wearing a dark suit as he would be going straight to Mass once the meeting was finished. "What do we do about the Murphy boy? He had a nasty concussion but he knows enough to drop us right in the shit. If he starts talking the bloody Unionists will have a field day. It would give them the perfect excuse to break the agreement."

"He wouldn't talk," the Head of Operations said with conviction.

"We don't fucking know that," the Chief interjected. "He knows he's a dead man if he ever came back here so he'll trade."

There was silence around the table for a few seconds while each contemplated what the Chief had said. It was broken only by the sound of a baby crying in the next room.

"We need to take young Murphy out and quick," the Chief instructed.

"They'll have him stashed away safe. We'll never get near him," the final man in the room remarked. He wore horn rimmed glasses with large lenses and thick, heavy frames. He was a little younger than the others.

"You're job's intelligence," the Chief came back quickly. "Someone must know something. Squeeze every frigging contact we have." Then he shouted at the top of his voice, "Will you shut the young one up. I'm trying to have a fucking meeting in here."

There was no immediate end to the baby's crying but the sound receded and then the front door could be heard closing with a loud bang, after which there was silence in the house.

The man responsible for intelligence broke the silence. "They may well have jumped ship to the Real boys. They've been working hard recently trying to convince a few of the younger or wilder sorts to join them."

"We are the fucking real boys," the Chief shot back with venom.

"That vermin calling themselves the Real IRA is just taking the piss. And even they aren't stupid enough to try and kidnap Melanie Adams. It makes no fucking sense."

There was again silence broken only by the Chief noisily slurping on his coffee. "Get Connor on the case," he continued. "Do whatever it takes to shut Murphy up and get ready for the shit to hit the fan when the press gets their hands on this. We need to distance ourselves from Maguire. And remind our boys that if we hear of anyone talking to the competition, they'll be spending the rest of their lives in a wheelchair and taking their meals in liquid form through a straw."

It was just after four in the morning before Tom made it home. By no means a castle, but it felt reassuring to be back and shut the front door on the rest of the world. A world that now seemed a lot more dangerous than it had when he last left the house. He had lived in the same three bedroom detached house close to the racecourse, looking down over the town of Brighton, for twelve years. The location next to the racecourse had nothing to do with his gambling way of life. It was simply a more affordable area to live but it did seem appropriate and it was fun in summer to be able to attend an evening meeting and stagger home after a few too many beers. The outside of the house was nondescript but over the years, and with the help of poker tournament winnings, he had radically changed the interior. He had found a Polish builder who worked hard for a very fair hourly rate and used him to knock down walls, to extend the size of the kitchen and the living room. The result was a modern bright home that often surprised visitors with its spaciousness and style.

Tom loved living in Brighton. He thought of it as a mini London on sea but unlike the Capital everything is squeezed into a small area. He enjoyed the vibrancy and creativity that was evident all through the year. There was never a shortage of things to do. He particularly liked the large choice of live music venues and the comedy clubs.

And of course he was a regular at the Casinos.

In the summer there would be a variety of Festivals that fought for his attention. What he liked best though was the cosmopolitan nature of Brighton. It is the Gay capital of the UK and a huge tourist destination, whether for hen and stag parties at the weekend or for family holidays in the summer. Diversity is welcome and expected by the inhabitants. He doubted he would ever live anywhere else.

Earlier, he'd sat in the back of a police car while ambulances and further police cars arrived, all with flashing lights and sirens blaring. Soon the scene was flooded with a mixture of uniformed and plain clothes officers. He could see Melanie Adams sat in the back of a different car.

He watched them all going about their business, then after a while one of the senior uniformed officers approached and spoke to him through the open car door. When the officer said would he mind going back to the police station, to help further with their enquiries and make a statement, he wasn't entirely sure if he had the option of refusing but in any event would have chosen to go and get it out the way.

He'd already refused the offer to go to hospital, pointing out that there would be no permanent damage, just severe bruising to his forehead and knee. He'd dismissed the idea he might have concussion and convinced them he would be perfectly capable of providing a lucid description of the night's events, especially while everything was fresh in his mind.

Once at the police station, he was sat at a metal table in a sparse room and kept waiting twenty minutes, although in the meantime he was offered and accepted a hot mug of tea, which was delivered by a perfectly friendly female officer in uniform. Finally, two interviewing male officers in plain clothes patiently went over virtually Tom's complete life history, before honing in on the evening's events. They questioned his every detail and then cleverly would ask the same questions in a different way a short time later to check his answers. He recognized what they were doing and trying to spot their traps kept him alert and helped fight the monotony of the protracted questioning.

Tom recognized the double questioning was not specifically an indication they didn't believe him but a professional need to be one hundred per cent accurate. The media were all over this case and there would be no career for anyone who made even the smallest error.

Tom had to laugh out loud when one of the officers asked how well he knew Melanie Adams! Not as well as he would like to he was thinking but such flippancy seemed out of place. The way it had been asked, there was the hint of an implication something was amiss about the night's events and maybe he and Miss Adams had a relationship.

Realising laughing wasn't really an appropriate response to the questions, he gathered his composure and with a straight face simply stated he knew her as well as anyone else who had seen her films but no more than that.

When the officers were finally satisfied and brought the interview to an end, the senior one shook his hand and praised his actions. They'd done the official bit. That wouldn't be on the record but it meant a lot to Tom. Then he was brought more tea while his words were transcribed into a statement for his signature.

When it came time to leave he was surprised and pleased when his mobile phone was returned. While sat in the police car, he had remembered that he had left it on the ground and asked the officer to find it but wasn't sure he would do so. As he tucked it in his jacket pocket, he reminded himself not for the first time, he needed to keep a copy somewhere of the two hundred numbers in his phone.

On the journey home he realised just how much his knee hurt and was thankful he drove an automatic. The thought occurred to him that it was fortunate for Melanie Adams that he had decided to meet his accountant and drive to London. On balance he decided he also was pleased he'd driven. Okay, so he'd been in the wars and scared to death but the outcome had been positive enough to leave him with quite a feeling of pride.

There was also the thought he may have used up all his luck for the foreseeable future and perhaps poker should be avoided for a time. The wind buffeted against the car and he focused on driving extra carefully. He had no intention after what he'd survived of finishing the night as a traffic casualty.

The house was freezing cold as he never wasted money on heating the place when he wasn't actually there. Despite the late hour, on the way to the kitchen he turned the central heating up to maximum. Resting on top of the fridge he found the bottle of Metaxa, the neighbours had brought him back the previous summer, from their Greek holiday. It wasn't his favourite drink by a long way, which explained why it was still half full after so many months but the large measure he poured was downed in one and sent a fiery warmth flooding through his body. He poured a second drink and headed straight for his bed with the remainder of the bottle.

It wasn't surprising he slept like a baby and didn't wake until ten. He'd taken three paracetamol before falling into bed but as he awoke their effect had worn off and his head was thumping. The Metaxa probably also contributed to the sore head. At least the house was warm.

He found his knee had stiffened as he climbed out of bed and was generally feeling decidedly ropey. But despite the combination of pain he was feeling good about himself. It was a bit similar to staying up all night winning a particularly important poker tournament. He was completely knackered next day but there was a euphoria that came from the achievement.

He showered and looking at himself in the bathroom mirror wasn't overly impressed with what he saw. Certainly not film star looks, he smiled to himself. He regularly looked rather tired and all of his forty-two years of age. Patches of grey were starting to emerge from his normally chestnut brown hair, especially around the ears. The bags under his eyes were testament to too many late nights and too much stress.

Today though there was the unwelcome presence of a large swelling above the bridge of his nose, which was turning blue where he'd been head butted. He was not a pretty sight.

As he surveyed longer, his only comfort was that being exactly six feet in height he was at least able to carry some excess weight without looking obese. The only slight damper on his spirits was when he opened the medicine cabinet and remembered he'd finished the paracetamol before going to bed.

Weekend mornings were nearly always spent at the same small coffee shop in Patcham, on the outskirts of Brighton, as you approach from the North. The expected snow had not yet arrived but it took Tom several minutes to remove the heavy frost from the windows of his old BMW. He had a small garage but could never be bothered to use it and thus paid the price on frosty mornings.

The neighbour across the road waved a greeting and seemed about to cross the road to engage in conversation, until Tom shouted out he must rush and quickly jumped in behind the wheel. Tom wasn't feeling like polite conversation or explaining the bruising on his face. He suspected he was going to have to explain to a great many people, over the next few days, how he came about his injuries but right now he needed some coffee and hot food.

He gave a small thanks to the car's designers for its reliability, when it spluttered into life at the second turn of the key. In years gone by, he had had more than one car that didn't like the cold and it was a lottery whether they would start on such a morning.

He was pleased to find the road had been gritted and the journey was only a minute or two over the normal ten. His knee was feeling much better and he could drive without hindrance. It wasn't the décor of the cafe that prompted him to pass several others on route to reach his destination. The walls were painted a gaudy gold colour and covered with prints of famous French Impressionists. No one would ever be able to say it was tastefully decorated. In fact, Tom imagined the style would not look out of place in a Paris brothel, though his experience of such places was strictly limited to his imagination.

He initially sat at the first vacant table but then found a strange feeling compelling him to instead choose a table at the back, where he could observe everyone entering the premises. He knew he was being foolish and couldn't quantify his concern but felt better once he'd moved. So is this what it's to be like for the rest of my life, he thought; scared of normal everyday situations for no good reason.

Tom spotted mostly familiar faces as he surveyed the various tables at which people were gathered. They were a predominantly male group, which suggested that like Tom they lived alone. One or two met his gaze and nodded a greeting. A mixture of nationalities and cultures brought together by great coffee and freshly baked pastries.

The café was run by a Lebanese family who had fled their country many years ago. Rafiq the father baked; Zaina the mother ran the service counter and two children served the tables. They all worked very long hours but they always had a warm smile of greeting. Tom was used to hearing conversations in several languages and this morning was no different.

Despite the bad weather or maybe even because of it, he knew that come the middle of the day seats would be at a premium. The clientele were not generally early risers. Once seated however they would linger for hours over their dark coffee, food and conversation. Tom loved the animated vibe of the place and had been returning regularly for longer than he could remember.

He had picked up a newspaper as he entered and having ordered a latte and a full English breakfast turned his attention to the headlines; MELANIE ADAMS IN FOILED KIDNAP ATTEMPT. He'd expected to find the story on the front page and in that respect wasn't disappointed but the large photo of Melanie, he felt entitled to think of her now in first name terms, still came as something of a shock. He read the article with some amusement as it described how an unnamed passerby had intervened and bravely risking his life, had tackled the gunmen.

He glanced around to see several others engrossed in the story.

Weird, he thought, that they are all reading about me but don't know I'm sitting next to them. A quote from Melanie had indeed been unequivocal in claiming he had saved her life and she would eternally be grateful to him. He was a bit surprised to see she had already spoken to the press. The last he'd seen of her she was fighting back tears sitting in the back of the police car. He'd then been driven back to the police station to make his statement and he'd seen no sign of Melanie Adams, so assumed she had been allowed to go back to her hotel.

As he turned the pages there wasn't much information about the two attackers, although a source close to the police was credited with admitting they were known to the authorities. The paper had no doubt that the motive was kidnapping, rather than terrorism, given that she was one of the richest women in Hollywood.

There was lots of background information about her life and career, which to Tom highlighted how uneventful his own life had been by comparison. He had read the article for the third time and was about to turn to the racing pages, when it hit him that quite possibly the previous evening would turn out to be the luckiest evening of his life.

He contemplated how fate worked. If it hadn't been Colin's turn to pay this year and if he hadn't chosen a restaurant in Knightsbridge then Tom would never have been in the right place at the right time. This story would be major news for some considerable time and the one thing he knew for certain, was that the papers would be willing to pay handsomely, for the privilege of printing his version of events. Blimey there might even be appearances on television and a book.

Okay, slow down, he said to himself. He needed some advice and Cliff Maxwell was the man who everyone always seemed to use in these situations. Tom hurriedly finished his breakfast feeling much better about life. This might just be a memorable Christmas after all.

Geoffrey Miller had been Head of SO15, the Counter Terrorism branch of the Met, for three years. He had worked in Special Branch for many years and when it was merged in 2006 with the Met's Anti-Terrorist Branch to form SO15, he had continued to prove his worth until eventually being promoted to run the new organisation.

He considered himself a proper old fashioned policeman. He had joined the force straight from school. He didn't have a degree and not been on any fast tracked career path. He didn't wear flashy expensive suits but then he thought that those who did often put style over substance. He would be the first to admit he didn't dress stylishly. He never had done. He liked to wear simple off the peg blue suits purchased at high street chains.

He kept his grey hair cut short, preferring to visit his local barber once a month rather than any expensive hair salon. Being of average height and build, he knew he looked very ordinary to anyone who met him and sometimes he had been able to use that to his advantage.

He was thrifty by nature and the glasses he wore for reading were purchased from various supermarkets, rather than expensive opticians. But when he had a criminal in his sights, he was terrier like in his dogged determination to pursue him until he brought him to justice.

His career had flourished as a result of his undeniable successes and he had climbed steadily through the ranks. He could be blunt and wasn't afraid to tell it how he saw it, which meant he wasn't universally popular but he didn't mind. He was at the forefront of tackling terrorism and upsetting the occasional person was the least of his worries.

He was a methodical man with an eye for detail. He had little time for politicians and their desire for instant answers. You could get instant coffee and most other things nowadays but not police work. It was painstaking attention to detail that produced results and it usually took time and lots of manpower, everything politicians loathed. Do more with less he was repeatedly being told. The problem was that no one had bothered to tell the terrorists there was a financial crisis. His budget had been slashed but at the same time the threat from terrorism both abroad and internally was increasing.

He tried to remain phlegmatic. He was in his fifties and not too long until he could retire with a decent pension and take a lucrative job consulting in the private sector. He was already being wooed by a couple of large companies. Both had taken him out for a very expensive dinner in elegant surroundings, which were meant to impress and succeeded.

He knew a couple of ex coppers working at one of the companies and they were both doing well and spoke highly of their new life. Apart from a shiny new office with a secretary, it had been explained to him he would be able to work half the time for more than twice the money. He didn't need a degree to work out that was a good deal. So soon he would hand over the reins to some unlucky bugger who would inherit a world Miller barely recognized any longer.

Mary, his wife, deserved to know he would be home at the same time each day from work and they could plan an evening at the theatre, without the worry he would suddenly be called to some urgent matter. He had messed her around for the twenty five years they were married but she had rarely complained and brought up two children almost single handed at times.

Victoria and Cassandra were now both at University and it would soon be time to take the round the world cruise, he had been promising Mary for many years. She was desperate to see all the great historical sites of the world from the pyramids of Egypt to the Great Wall of China. They had seen most things in Europe but the rest of the world was still unchartered territory.

He considered Mary to be the intellectual half of their relationship. She read proper literature as he liked to call it and watched documentaries on a wide variety of subjects, while he mostly preferred a crime drama or gangster film. Despite their differences or maybe because of them, they had enjoyed a good marriage and he was well aware he had leaned very heavily on her support over the years.

Perhaps, closer to home, retirement would also allow him to get to see the end of some of those gangster movies he so liked watching but which were so frequently interrupted before the end by an urgent phone call. His favourite was The Godfather but anything with De Niro or Jimmy Cagney, was also high on his watch list. In his time he had made more than a few criminals an offer they couldn't refuse! He would have liked to be an old fashioned policeman fighting gangsters alongside Eliot Ness in the thirties in America. A much less complicated world where there were good guys and bad guys. Today the lines between good and bad were far more blurred.

In all honesty though, he didn't have too many regrets about the direction his life had taken. He recognized most successful careers were built on sacrifices in other areas of your life and that was true not just within the police force. At times he had struggled to maintain the balance between work and the rest of his life but it had also brought its rewards. He had been able to wake up each day looking forward to the day ahead. There had been no boredom from repetition. Every day was different. Sure there was stress and he was challenged sometimes to his limits but that was because he cared about what he did. And at the end of each day he knew he had really made a difference.

He recognized he lived a privileged life. Through his job he had often been exposed to the darker side of life. Many people were struggling just to exist, often through no fault of their own but because of where they were born or who had brought them into the world. He was one of the lucky ones. He had a nice house in a beautiful part of Surrey. He had a great family and the knowledge his pension would be significantly better than most people had to get by on, in their retirement. The knowledge of how fortunate he was drove him even harder in his work.

Miller had been notified of the bungled kidnap attempt as soon as fingerprint checks identified Maguire and Murphy as known IRA terrorists. They both had long arrest records and even longer lists of probable crimes, which had never been proved. Miller felt almost nostalgic as he read the dossiers from Belfast. It had been quite a while since Irish terrorism had been a part of his daily life. They had been difficult times but friendships had been formed in adversity, which were still as strong all these years later.

His views on Ireland had changed a little over the years as he learned more about the problems and role England had played in their history. Mary had pointed him to a history book written by an Oxford professor, which explained the potato famine of 1845 and how the landed English gentry had been largely responsible for the death of a million men, women and children, and caused another million to have to flee the country. It was the Catholic farmers who had suffered most.

When Miller was younger everything seemed black and white. The terrorists that formed the IRA were just vile murderers to be hunted down. As he grew older, he realized most things in life were actually a shade of grey. Since he had left Ireland and understood more of the history, he didn't have any greater sympathy for the IRA but understood better how they had come about and flourished in their community. There can be no greater motivator for evil than a huge sense of injustice.

He had ventured back a couple of years ago to visit Cork, something he couldn't have dreamed of doing a few years earlier. He'd even kissed the Blarney Stone at Mary's insistence, as she felt he needed to gain a bit more of the gift of the gab. Where the legend originated that kissing the stone endows the kisser with the gift of the gab is uncertain. Many of the stories recount how the stone was taken to Scotland and in 1314 Robert the Bruce presented it to Cormac McCarthy who built Blarney Castle, to thank him for his support.

Miller hadn't realized what it would entail when he agreed to visit Blarney Castle. He'd climbed to the top of the castle and then had to lean over backwards on the parapet's edge to reach the stone, while holding on to two iron rails. He had felt a bit foolish but millions of others had gone before him and Mary was insistent.

He understood she was hinting that too often he kept his thoughts to himself and could seem quite introverted in company. It wasn't really the case. He just preferred only to speak when he had something worth saying. He found all too many people prattled on for ages, without ever saying anything worth hearing. He wasn't convinced kissing the stone had made any difference but it was a good story to share over dinner.

Miller had known many fanatics over the years. They had always come in many guises, from animal rights to anti-nuclear protesters and the IRA but nowadays they were all secondary to the overwhelming threat posed by Al Qaida. Whatever the terrible danger presented by former terrorist threats, at least you knew they weren't willing to walk into a crowded public place and blow themselves up for their cause. Even the vilest IRA terrorist had wanted to awake to read and gloat over newspaper reports the next day.

It had also been far easier to infiltrate IRA cells or develop a network of informants. Al Qaida took conviction to a whole new level. Their religious fanaticism made them difficult to penetrate. So did the reality that it was virtually impossible for anyone white, which was still the predominant colour of those fighting terror. With their wealthy Middle Eastern backers, they also had the finances to globally attack America and its supporters including of course the UK. Miller had known most of the IRAs leading figures. Known where they lived and worked. Though they seemed terrible dark days at the time, he had learned that everything was relative.

Miller was, to say the least, surprised that prominent IRA members had been carrying out such a crime on the mainland. Since the latest ceasefire the IRA had become the new Mafia, involving themselves in every crime imaginable. Everything from Bank robberies to extortion were commonplace and today they seemed more interested in filling their coffers with the profits of dealing in drugs, rather than changing the political landscape. He expected to find them being run by an Al Capone or even a Don Corleone clone in the not too distant future but so far they had shown no desire to transport their crime wave to this side of the sea.

Miller read the IRA statement saying that they were not involved but admitting the two men had once been members, who had been banished for failing to follow orders and abide by the Good Friday Agreement. Miller remembered 1997 and the agreement by both sides to disarm as if it was only yesterday. They had gone out drinking to celebrate something they had worked many years for and he thought would signal an easier life but that hope had been short lived, as the following year the Real IRA had carried out the Omagh bombing, killing twenty nine people.

He was inclined to believe the IRA statement, as targeting Melanie Adams would attract a great deal of unwanted focus on their criminal activities and further alienate their American supporters. Too much public violence and bloodshed would undoubtedly adversely affect the business of making money. If, as he suspected, the statement was true, then he had to smile at the thought of the leadership running around desperately trying to cover their arses and apportion blame to each other. It might at least temporarily divert them from their normal life of crime.

He adjusted his glasses and also read the press release from Sinn Fein, the republican political party, which condemned the attack on Melanie Adams. Miller had to smile at how times had changed. Sinn Fein was the new definition of political correctness. They had one or two senior figures who Miller knew better from their days as IRA activists.

Miller considered the worrying possibility that Murphy and Maguire had joined one of the splinter groups such as the Real IRA or Continuity IRA. Over the last year, Belfast had seen the first sectarian murders for many a year and a general escalation in violence. One huge bomb had been found before it could be detonated and there was a real concern amongst the intelligence community that the breakaway IRA dissidents were trying to drag the country back into terrible times.

There was always the constant threat of the troubles spreading across the sea and the Real IRA had recently been making a lot of noise about wanting to blow up London's bankers but so far it had remained just a threat. However, to Miller's way of thinking, this had more the hallmarks of a crime based on greed, rather than a carefully planned terrorist action. Melanie Adams was no banker and would make no sense as their first target on the mainland. That probably meant it wasn't the Real IRA or any similar group and as it was almost inconceivable the IRA themselves were transporting their crime wave to the streets of London, it was probable Maguire and Murphy, had indeed become greedy renegades and were acting alone. Anyway, that would be the gist of his initial report to the impatient Home Secretary on Monday.

What really interested Miller was the opportunity to interrogate Eamon Murphy. His father was a life-long IRA enforcer and a nasty piece of work, who had crossed Miller's path more than once. It had never been possible to pin anything concrete of a serious nature on him and the couple of times he had been arrested, the only witnesses had suddenly developed a terrible loss of memory.

He had been put away for bits and pieces but Miller knew he had done far worse and escaped justice by intimidating the witnesses. Even if a particular individual was strong minded enough to want to testify no matter what, they usually had wives, children, family that would be threatened and the witness would know they weren't idle threats. A visit from Murphy's associates would normally be sufficient. Murphy was a man to be feared. The successful prosecutions were where there was a crime witnessed by members of the police or CCTV evidence.

Miller knew the son had followed in his father's footsteps but by all accounts he was only a pale imitation of his father. For some years now, Miller had been spending most of his time behind a desk in London, so there was none of the personal animosity he felt for the father. However, young Murphy could still be a mine of information and whether there was a ceasefire or not Miller was intending to go digging in a big way.

There were many puzzles from the past that he might be able to help solve. In particular, Miller remembered all too well Brian Potter, a colleague who had been captured and terribly tortured. It was almost certainly an act of revenge for Potter killing a prominent Republican in a gun battle. Potter hadn't died quickly and the memory of being first to find his body had stayed with Miller ever since and still sometimes Brian appeared in his dreams, blaming him for not finding him sooner. Miller felt guilty, though in rational analysis he knew he had done everything possible.

What nagged away at him was the belief Brian had been taken as the result of a betrayal by someone from within the force. Someone had known where Potter would be at a very specific time and passed on that information or otherwise the IRA had got very lucky. Miller knew which was most likely. He had wanted revenge for Brian's death and in the immediate aftermath of finding his body, if they had found the culprits, he would have happily taken a literal eye for an eye. He had led one of the most thorough investigations he could ever recall but no one had been brought to justice. He would be able to retire a happy man if he could now find those responsible.

Melanie Adams had returned to her hotel suite suffering from complete physical and mental exhaustion. She had sat staring at the telephone for what seemed an eternity, trying to find the strength to call Carol's sister Annie. They had met twice briefly, which wasn't much of a basis for now having to tell her about the death of her sister.

It had been the most difficult thing Melanie had ever done in her life and took the last of her strength. Carol had devoted a large part of her adult life to following Melanie everywhere and making life smooth for her. Melanie could only guess at the sacrifices that had entailed.

She knew Carol had never found love and Melanie was feeling guilty that had partly been her fault for keeping her so busy and never spending very long in the same place. Their relationship may in theory have been that of employer and employee but over the years they had become friends as well. Carol was like family and would be sorely missed not just for her amazing organization skills but for the evenings they spent together, in various hotel rooms, watching old movies and pigging out on popcorn and chocolate.

Her sister had not surprisingly taken the news badly. At first not even believing what she was hearing. Then she was crying and kept wailing, "It can't be." Her husband Jack had taken the phone from her and Melanie had confirmed the news, filling in more of the details. She made him promise to call her if there was anything she could do to help and then left them to their grief.

Next Melanie had called Gerald, her agent, and related the night's events. He had offered to take the next flight, which she deemed unnecessary but they did agree a statement for the press. He was also going to arrange for new and increased security though as she remarked, it seemed a bit bloody late for that! He made one last protestation that she shouldn't be alone but that was exactly what she wanted.

When she put the phone down she realised she really had no one else she needed to call that mattered. It had been that way for a long time. She was an only child with no special man in her life, no close family and precious few real friends.

Her father had died just after his fiftieth birthday, from lung cancer. She was twenty three at the time and couldn't remember ever seeing him without a cigarette in his hand. Her mother had died five years later also of cancer but Melanie suspected her broken heart had played a part. Her parents had been inseparable and she had never really moved on from the loss of the love of her life.

Melanie had no siblings and family consisted of just a few cousins she had barely seen since her childhood. It had been a happy childhood and she missed her parents terribly. The worst thing was that they weren't around to enjoy the success she had achieved in the last ten years. She knew they would have been proud of her and she would have liked to have given them something back.

The press endlessly speculated about her private life, linking her romantically with every man she went within ten feet of but there had been no one serious for over a year now. Even that last relationship was barely deserving of the title. Less than a year spent with someone who owned a property empire and was continually pushing her, to introduce him to celebrity friends who might want to buy a house. She came to realize he was more interested in being known as the boyfriend of Melanie Adams and having his picture in the papers, rather than actually caring for her. It was about par for the course of her love life.

Her earlier flings with actors had not fared any better. They always seemed to put her second to their careers. Where were all the good honest guys? Or was it impossible for someone in her position to meet someone who could love her for the person she was, not for being a world famous actor who could further their career.

It wasn't as if she had unrealistically high expectations. Looks were nice to have but far more important was honesty and a sense of humour. Unfortunately her agent didn't help matters by encouraging the stories about her and her leading men. He saw it as good publicity but she hated the lies that were printed in the celebrity columns of newspapers. She didn't understand the fascination strangers had with reading about her imaginary love life. She was an optimist by nature but finding a true soulmate seemed a very long way off.

She rebuked herself for starting to feel sorry for herself. She may be alone but she was alive and still had a future. It was Carol and her bodyguard who deserved her sympathy. Melanie wasn't very religious but she did think of herself as spiritual and believed there was something further after death. She was once again thinking what that something might be, when sleep eventually arrived with the help of a second pill. She had taken just one the night before to deal with the effects of jet lag but this night she knew at least two were required.

When she awoke there was the glimmer of a possibility it had all been a bad nightmare but turning on the television dispelled that hope. She moved about her room not knowing what to do. There was no Carol to go through the day's timetable. No Carol to tell her where she had to be and at what time. She recognised she lived a privileged life. One where a team of people worked endlessly to ensure everything in her life went smoothly. But even so and despite all her wealth, the previous evening had seen her life torn apart.

She felt no sympathy for the man she had shot and whom the police informed her had died in the ambulance on the way to hospital. He had fully deserved his end and she felt no remorse for her actions. She was just pleased that her upbringing had included being taught how to use guns by her father and hunting had been a regular summer escape when she was young.

She was born in Pittsburgh but her family had a cabin in the mountains of northern Pennsylvania and it was there her father had taught her about guns. He would hunt deer in particular and though her appetite for the sport dwindled as she left her teenage years behind, the familiarity with weapons remained.

In one film a couple of years earlier, she had played an FBI agent and the film's young Director had insisted she spent some time at a shooting range, so she looked like she knew how to handle a gun, for the various shooting scenes. She had surprised herself and the Director by how much she remembered and the film had been another great success.

She still owned the cabin but hadn't been up there for several years. She had gone once since her parents died to sort out effects and one other time with a casual boyfriend for the weekend. It had seemed wrong to be there without her parents and the weekend hadn't gone well. He had expected a fun filled wild time. She had been moody and thoughtful and shortly after, their brief relationship had fizzled out.

Melanie was in London to promote her new film and knew there was an endless round of meetings with the press arranged but they now seemed incredibly unimportant. Especially as those meetings would inevitably require her to recount time and again the previous night's events, which would make for a groundhog style nightmare.

She wanted to get out of London as soon as possible. She wanted to be home in Malibu with familiar sights and sounds. She wanted to walk along the sandy beach and feel the warm sea wash up on her feet.

She snapped back to reality. She needed to focus. The one appointment she knew she did have to keep was with the police inspector, to give a more detailed statement. She realized that shooting someone dead, even a low life kidnapper, required thorough investigation. He was sending a police car to pick her up at eleven. She told the desk not to put through any phone calls and ordered coffee and newspapers from room service.

Melanie wondered what would have happened if the guy who had introduced himself as Tom hadn't come along. Would she now be tied up and locked away somewhere terrible. Maybe even buried in a coffin, she remembered that happening to one kidnap victim. Would they have cut off an ear or a finger to prove they had her captive? Her imagination ran riot until finally she told herself to get a grip. Tom had come along and fortunately for her he had been willing to get involved. She knew that back home most people would have thought first of self-preservation and stayed clear of the danger. Maybe it was different over here?

Though she had employed security and bodyguards for several years now, she had never contemplated having to deal with anything more serious than over enthusiastic fans, likely to crush her in their desire for an autograph. She'd been lucky and she had a life to live. In fact she had three lives to live. She needed to think about others not herself. She started to make phone calls. A good start would be to find out about the bodyguard who had been killed. She'd only known him twenty-four hours but it was her fault he was dead and the least she could do was help his family.

It was late Sunday evening when Brendan Connor received his instructions from the Chief. He wasn't surprised to receive the orders. He'd heard about the fuck up across the water and it was at such times he was often called for by the Chief. It had been that way for many years now. The bigger the problem the more likely he was to be needed. He was known to be reliable. He got the job done, whatever it was.

At forty six years of age he knew it wouldn't be that way for ever. He didn't have the same speed of his youth and he'd given up going to gyms many years ago. He was just over six feet tall and had an average build. His skin was blotchy and his nose a red colour that pointed to years of excessive drinking. He wasn't by any means an alcoholic, as he never fancied it early in the morning but he liked a regular drink.

His reputation deterred most people from ever thinking of crossing him or lying to him. When he asked a question he expected to receive an honest answer. He was ruthless and the passing of years had made him even more so. Strike first was his motto. He allowed nothing and no one to get in his way. He knew that was what the Chief liked about him and why he entrusted him with the most important tasks.

He packed a few clothes and bought a cheap airline ticket over the Internet. He was used to living out of suitcases and making trips at short notice. It had been the case for over twenty years, ever since he'd left the family home in Turf Lodge.

He wouldn't be able to say when he first started hating the Brit soldiers and everything they represented. He'd inherited the appropriate gene from his father and his father before him. Hatred and food were served up in equal proportions at the Connor dining table as he was growing up. While he was still in short trousers he'd joined the other kids from the estate, in throwing stones at the soldiers and shouting for them to piss off back where they came from. He had little interest in schooling. He learnt all he needed at his father's knee.

A little older and he was running messages before progressing to keeping watch while others pulled the trigger. He'd been a good learner and barely past his twentieth birthday they'd let him shoot his first soldier. He remembered the feeling of pride reading about it next day in the paper. He'd been told not to tell his Da or anyone because of the constant fear of touts but over breakfast, when his Ma was in the kitchen, he'd given a hint and seen the look of pride and approval in his Da's eyes.

Then came the news from Gibraltar. The murdering SAS bastards had shot his friends dead in cold blood without any warning and them not even being armed at the time. Operation Flavius they'd called it and the papers had made the SAS bastards sound like bloody heroes.

He had never forgotten or forgiven them for that. Any opportunity to strike at the SAS was particularly welcome. One time he'd had the chance to be part of a team that interrogated a captured Brit. He was Special Branch not SAS but there was little difference. They had made him suffer big time. He'd squealed for his mother like a baby.

After Gibraltar, even worse had followed, when the bloody loyalist Stone burst into the funeral and killed three more friends and injured dozens of others. From then onwards his mind had been set and he'd grown over the years to become the Chief's most trusted man. His expertise nowadays was in cleaning up messes. He couldn't go shooting Brit soldiers any longer but there was still plenty to keep him busy.

He knew the Murphy boy a bit. Knew his father better. They weren't friends. Paid not to have too many friends in his line of work. If it was possible to silence the kid then he was confident he was the best man for the job. He wouldn't particularly enjoy it because the kid's only crime was aimed at the Brits and Connor hated the Brits.

He didn't like politics and he wasn't really into the new ways of doing things. Hitting at the Brits on the mainland was good news as far as he was concerned but orders were orders. He understood you had to follow orders. Couldn't just do whatever you bloody wanted.

After his work was done he'd be taking a trip to the sun. He looked forward to that. He could do with a holiday. He'd chase some skirt and drink too much Guinness. The thought sent him to bed a happy man.

CHAPTER THREE

Samantha Murphy, or Sam as she was known to everyone except her parents, was lying in bed thinking about the previous twenty-four hours. The terrible news had been followed by an uncontrollable desire to get smashed, which in turn had led to ending up in this bed.

She'd had a blazing row with her Da when she announced she was going to go see her brother. He'd warned her to keep well away from him. She'd been around long enough to know her brother was now as popular as a pigeon crapping on your car. He'd gone out on a limb with that bloody Maguire and the boys would be after him. The Brits would make his life shit and his Da wasn't willing to get off his arse to help his only son. To her way of thinking that meant she was all he had.

She turned to look at the man asleep beside her. She felt nothing for him, and was shocked not by that realisation but by the knowledge that it had been irrelevant to the enjoyment she'd had last night. She wasn't the world's most experienced lover but she'd sampled enough to know when it was good and it had been bloody good. Not least because unlike so many men she had known he wasn't just focused on his own cock and actually cared about what she wanted. They had been at it for hours and when he finally let her sleep, she was exhausted but also completely satisfied in a way she had rarely experienced before.

Perhaps the difference was he was just a little older and more a man than the usual boys she played with. Or perhaps it was the line of coke he'd taken in the bathroom when they arrived back at his house. She had declined his offer to share but only because she knew mixed with the drink, it would leave her feeling completely wasted the next day and she didn't want that.

She certainly didn't make a habit of picking up strangers and screwing the hell out of them but she might rethink her ideas in future. The large bed and empty house helped. At home you too often spent most of your time being a contortionist in the back of cars. Either that or you snatched a quickie while everyone was out the house, hoping your Ma or Da wouldn't return early.

It confirmed again she was going to have to get a place of her own. Twenty five was too old to still be living with your parents. Problem was, it was all very well behaving like this so far from home but back in Belfast she'd soon get a name as a slut.

Everyone knew everybody and in particular most people knew her Da. He wasn't what she would call a modern thinking father. He was a hard man to please. She didn't doubt he loved her but he still often treated her like a child and boyfriends were never taken home. It would be all right if it was someone her Da approved of but it was her view that anyone he approved of, she wouldn't want to go out with.

She definitely didn't share her parents definition of what made a good catholic girl! She wondered what Father Thomas would say next time she went to confession. She enjoyed shocking the good Father and even an edited description of this was definitely a ten on the Richter scale for shocks.

She glanced at the bedside clock. It was early but time to be going. She gently extricated herself from under his arm and slid from beneath the sheet.

"Where're you going?" the man asked sleepily.

She leaned back and kissed him surprisingly tenderly on his

forehead. "Go back to sleep. I have a plane to catch."

He turned on his side and pulled the blankets up around him. She kissed him again on the cheek before quietly making her way out of the bedroom, her bare feet sinking deeply into the luxuriously thick, soft pile of the carpet.

For once he hadn't just been another bloke trying to impress her with a load of bullshit and really must have had his own IT business to support such a great house. Another time and she would have given him her number and hoped to see him again. He was even decent looking! He was definitely boyfriend material but right now she didn't have time in her life for a boyfriend. Anyway, she knew where he lived and liked to drink. She could always find him.

She went downstairs to the lounge and picked up some of her clothes from the floor, which earlier had been discarded in frenetic haste to get naked. She knew she wasn't stunning looking but she had a very fit body and with the help of makeup an acceptably attractive, if slightly plain face. Her best feature was the long legs she had inherited from her Mother.

From a young age she had been the school and district cross country running champion. She didn't run competitively anymore but was a regular jogger and hours at the gym ensured she had a flat stomach and toned muscles. Anyway, as far as she could remember the bloke was so plastered he'd have shagged anything half decent.

It had been a right crack. He had money to buy champagne and even if he was showing off, Sam hadn't cared. He wanted her and she needed somewhere to spend the night. She stood for a moment remembering how good his body had felt. How masculine and strong, and for a second considered going back to bed but her head was thumping, her mouth dry as the Gobi desert and she did have a plane to catch.

She laughed when she realized she couldn't even remember the bloke upstairs' bloody name. She noticed his jacket on the floor. She checked the inside pocket and found his wallet. She helped herself to his last eighty euros. He wasn't exactly living on the breadline and it would come in useful. The driving license reminded her he was called Danny. She went back upstairs and had a quick shower. She poked her head back in the bedroom one last time. Danny was soundly sleeping.

She gathered up her bag and let herself out the front door. In three hours she would be in England and despite the mother of all headaches she knew it was the right thing to be doing. She knew with absolute certainty her brother would do the same for her.

Tom had spent the morning at the office of the highest paying tabloid newspaper. He had been a bit surprised at first they wanted to meet on a Sunday but the story was hot news and they were very eager to publish the story in Monday's paper. The price agreed was one hundred thousand pounds for an exclusive story. Cliff Maxwell had done all the negotiating and definitely earned his ten per cent fee. He already knew everyone at the paper and had warned Tom before the meeting not to say anything. Tom was more than happy to keep quiet as he was definitely feeling outside his comfort zone.

One of the journalists showed him around the offices, explaining how everything worked, while Maxwell went off into an office with a couple of suits from the paper. By the time Tom returned, the price had been agreed and a contract was being produced for his signature. He was very pleased with the result as he would have been quite happy with half the sum.

Tom then spent three hours being interviewed by two reporters. There were photos taken and hands shaken and then he found himself standing on the icy pavement, wondering what to do with the rest of the day.

He had left his betting shop in the capable hands of young Ben, who made up in enthusiasm what he lacked in experience. In truth Sundays were always relatively quiet in the shop. He remembered fondly when there was no racing on Sundays and shops weren't even allowed to open. Now it was a seven day a week business. But opening longer hadn't increased revenue. Punters only had so much money they could spend in a week. Now it was spread over seven days instead of six.

The advent of Internet betting had badly hurt turnover and he might get out the business altogether and invest his new wealth in a completely different line of work, perhaps a restaurant. People still went out to restaurants to eat. You couldn't eat over the Internet.

The obvious thing for Tom to do was take the underground to Victoria and a fast train back to Brighton. He could be home within two hours. However, an idea had been gelling all morning that was much more enticing than the cold house that would await him. He telephoned the Imperial and asked for Melanie Adams's room. The operator responded in a slightly irritated voice, which suggested he was far from the first to want to speak to her, that Miss Adams wasn't taking any calls. He left a simple message saying he'd called and asking her to call him back on his mobile.

As he put his phone back in his jacket, he felt the need to pinch himself to check he was awake. He had just telephoned Melanie Adams and he'd actually expected her to take his call. Was he completely bonkers! Certainly a couple of days earlier the idea would have been absurd.

Tom decided to go for yet another coffee and hang around for an hour in the warmth, on the off chance she did return his call. He found a branch of his favourite coffee chain and chose a large skinny Latte and a small Pannetone. The choice of a skinny Latte was a habit developed some years earlier when he had dallied for a short time with a health nut of a girlfriend, who found it abhorrent he had full fat milk. The girlfriend hadn't survived long but he still drank skinny Lattes.

He recognized it was yet another anomaly in his life, as he made no other attempt to watch the calories he consumed. He received a funny look from the girl serving which he put down to the swelling and bruise on his face. He tried his sweetest smile and made a joke of his appearance, which elicited a friendly response that she'd seen worse.

He found a seat looking out onto the road. As he drank the Latte, he remembered his brief fling all those years ago and realized there had actually been quite a few girlfriends, who had just had walk-on parts in his life. At times it seemed he had made some spectacularly bad choices. He knew a number of people who had turned to the internet dating sights but felt that was a sign of desperation and he wasn't yet desperate. Or at least he wasn't going to openly admit to being so. Anyway, if he went on the internet his first inclination would always be to play poker rather than search for a woman.

He reckoned the cold weather was partially responsible for the place not being very busy and he passed some time calling his brother and updating him on events, alleviating the risk of his suffering a heart attack reading the next day's newspaper. Maxwell had warned Tom that he had one day left of anonymity and then his life would never be the same again. Even sitting having a quiet cup of coffee would be difficult, as the press and public were likely to intrude in every aspect of his life for the next few weeks.

Colin had been completely flummoxed by the news and thought Tom was joking at first but once he realized he was being serious, then he wanted to meet for dinner, so he could hear all the gory details, as he put it. Normally Tom met up with Colin in London but with all the recent trips he'd been making up to town, he suggested that for a change Colin come down to Brighton. There had been a brief pause while Colin considered this revolutionary idea but his eagerness to learn more from the horse's mouth about Melanie Adams, overcame his normal reluctance to venture down to the coast. As Colin worked in Piccadilly, only two stops from Victoria on the underground, a tentative agreement was reached that Colin would leave work early, which Tom understood to actually mean that he would leave on time, and Tom would collect him at Brighton station at seven on Wednesday evening. That Colin was able to make all these arrangements without first checking with Liz, came as a considerable surprise and gave Tom some hope his brother may not be quite as under her thumb as he had always believed.

Tom picked up the copy of the Racing Post he had purchased from a newsagent close to the café. For the first time in a very long time he spent some time scanning the classifieds to see what horses were being advertised for sale. He had always liked the idea of owning a horse and come close a couple of times to buying one from a local trainer he knew. Each time he had decided at the last minute, he couldn't really afford the monthly costs to keep the horse in training, even if he could afford the capital outlay. His new funds would allow him to buy at least the back leg of a racehorse as part of a syndicate. It was an idea worth pursuing further. At the very least, having a horse in training would lead to him meeting other owners and that might provide valuable inside information to horses expected to win.

Nothing immediately caught his eye, so he looked at the betting offices for sale. Maybe he should expand his business and build an empire that he would then sell for millions to one of the big high street chains. He laughed out loud at the thought. No chance! One shop was hard work. Two would be impossible.

His drink was finished and he was just beginning to doubt the wisdom of not going straight home when his phone vibrated. He didn't like the mindless ring tones most people used to disturb your peace and always switched to vibrate so as not to disturb others enjoying their coffee.

He didn't recognise the number and his simple "Hello," was delivered more in hope than expectation.

"Hi, is that Tom?"

Tom was pretty sure that the distinctive American accent could only belong to one person. He felt a little nervous and cleared his throat before answering. "Yes this is Tom."

"Hello, it's Melanie Adams. Sorry I didn't take your call, only the phones are going mad. Seems like every newspaper in the world's been trying to get me."

This is insane, Tom thought. I'm actually speaking to Melanie Adams. "I just wanted to check you were OK? I'm actually in town and was wondering if perhaps you'd like to meet up for a coffee or something?" He suddenly felt very foolish. Did he really expect her to rush out to his coffee shop to share a Latte with him?

Before she had time to reply he added, "I wondered if you knew anything more about Friday night's events?" He waited to hear her excuse for not being able to meet.

"I'd really like that," she responded without hesitation. "I've been feeling guilty all day that I never really thanked you properly. Why don't you come by the hotel? I'll tell them to expect you."

Tom took a deep breath before answering so he didn't sound as nervous as he was feeling. "OK. I'll be in there in about half an hour, if that's all right?"

"Looking forward to it."

Tom pressed the end call button and stared at his phone for a second. That was surreal, he thought. I just spoke to Melanie Adams and she invited me over to her hotel. Not a bad day all in all. Ninety thousand pounds richer after paying Maxwell's share and now mixing with one of the world's most beautiful and exciting women. All my Christmases seem to have come at once. Life doesn't get much better than this.

Brendan Connor had checked into a small hotel in Bayswater. It's one of London's most cosmopolitan areas, with a large number of hotels and Connor always felt at ease amongst the many different nationalities that live in or visit the area. It is a good place for someone to hide in the open.

The Chief had given him license to use whatever means necessary to get to young Murphy. That meant he could contact the Chief's top informant on the mainland, who went by the name of Jones and squeeze him for the information he needed.

Jones was too valuable an asset to overuse but he worked for the Security Service and had been foolish enough to be entrapped with an underage girl, when on assignment in Northern Ireland. She had been carefully chosen and though she had said she was eighteen, she was in fact only fifteen. Cameras had been hidden in the hotel room and the photographic evidence was explicit. Jones faced the loss of his career and time in prison or occasionally providing intelligence.

There was a point where Jones was asked to provide information that he knew would lead to a colleague being kidnapped by the IRA and that could only result in a terrible death for the individual. Jones had at first refused to help, preferring to face the consequences for his time spent with the girl but then he was shown the evidence of his subsequently passing information to the IRA. There was again a film and recording. He was now facing a charge of treason and any jail sentence would be significantly longer than for the sex with a minor, so he had caved in and provided the necessary details.

After that, there could be no going back because he would be facing a murder charge. Fortunately for the Chief, Jones had since flourished in his career and with each promotion came access to even better information. Connor had never met him before and doubted Jones was his real name but the Chief trusted his information and that was what mattered. Connor knew he was going to need some inside help.

Connor arrived early at the meeting point in Hyde Park. He'd been growing a beard for a couple of days and now had quite thick stubble. He wore old jeans and a thick blue overcoat favoured by country folk. He looked as unremarkable as most of the others in the park. He sat on a cold bench, from where he could see the bronze statue of Peter Pan with its squirrels, rabbits, mice and fairies climbing up to Peter at the top and waited for Jones to arrive. Fortunately, given the freezing temperature, he didn't have to wait long.

The man approaching matched Connor's image of a city banker. He wore a blue pin stripe suit under a long navy coat with a bowler hat on his head. There was no exchange of greetings. Connor had no time for anyone who would mess with an underage girl and wasn't going to waste words. Both men's eyes revealed what they thought of each other. Neither was there out of choice.

"We need to find a way of getting to Murphy. I need to know his whereabouts and any plans to move him," Connor said.

"You won't be able to get near him," Jones replied disdainfully, in the upper class tones of someone educated at Eton and Oxford.

"Just get me the fucking information I need and leave the rest to me," Connor said in a tone that didn't invite discussion.

"I'll see what I can do," Jones responded unenthusiastically.

"You better do better than that. I need results or else…" Connor let the threat hang in the air.

"I don't respond well to threats," Jones snapped.

"You make me sick," Connor sneered. "We know how to deal with the likes of you back home. You get me what I want or you'll end up behind bars and they don't like your sort inside." He knew he was laying it on a bit thick but it had the desired effect.

Jones turned paler; any fight draining from him at the thought of what would await him should he not comply. He didn't like showing emotion. And he certainly didn't like this terrorist criticising his lifestyle and making threats. He would have to call in favours. There were a great number of people owed him favours over the years and he stored them away like a camel does water until needed.

"It will take twenty-four hours," Jones said in an even voice. He had no wish for any further confrontation.

Connor turned and walked away. He knew Jones would come through with the information. He had no choice.

When Tom asked at the front desk for Melanie Adams's room, he found he was indeed expected. The receptionist almost came to attention as he pointed Tom towards the elevators and told him Miss Adams was in the Presidential suite, which was situated not surprisingly, on the top floor. As he stepped outside the elevator he saw a door to his right with two large men standing guard outside. Tom gave them his best smile as he approached and introduced himself.

"I'm Tom Ashdown. Miss Adams is expecting me."

The first man gave a small tap on the door and in the same movement opened it. "Please go in," he said indicating for Tom to enter.

As he entered the suite Melanie came towards him with a broad smile of welcome. "Hi Tom. It's good to see you again. I'm so pleased you called me."

Tom went to offer his hand in greeting but she ignored it and instead put both her arms around him, gave him a gentle squeeze and kissed him lightly on each cheek.

"I owe you so much," she said, breaking the embrace.

Tom barely managed to speak he was so stunned by the magnificence of the room in which he stood. "Actually it's my brother you should thank," he responded. "If it hadn't been his turn to pay for dinner, I would never have been there." Then seeing Melanie's slightly quizzical look he added, "It's a long story," regretting his original explanation.

"Well you were there and I'll be forever grateful you were."

Tom cast his gaze around the room. The sheer size of the place was the first thing to hit you. Then the opulence of furnishings reminded him of something from a royal palace. He wondered how many real Presidents might have stayed here as guests.

"Wow," was all he could find to say. "This place is amazing."

She smiled and glanced around her. "Guess it is kinda nice, though after a while one hotel room is much like another."

This is nothing like the hotel rooms I know, he thought. For a start there was no bed. He was standing in a huge living room with magnificent centrepiece of a fireplace. Around the fireplace were sofas and chairs. At the other end of the room was a dining table with six chairs. Heavy drapes hung at the windows. What he thought to be Persian or at least oriental rugs were on the floor. A large mirror with an ornate gold frame hung over the fireplace. Lighting was provided by two chandeliers and magnificent pictures were on the walls that looked like they might be original masterpieces. He couldn't imagine anything in the room would be a copy.

He felt the room wouldn't be out of place in the White House or 10 Downing Street. He wanted to regain his composure a bit and not act like the star struck idiot he was feeling. He'd stayed at some nice hotels in his time but this was a whole notch higher.

"How are you doing?" he enquired. Then added, "You look great."

He suddenly felt foolish telling Melanie Adams she looked great. The whole world knew she looked fantastic. But she did seem in much better shape than when they last met. She was wearing simple blue jeans and a white polo neck sweater that combined to give an appearance of casual sexiness, which many would aspire to but very few could achieve. As far as he could recall she was in her early thirties and he was as besotted by her as every other man who had seen her films.

"I'm doing good, thanks," she responded. "How are you though? That bruise looks real nasty."

"Looks much worse than it feels," he answered dismissively. "I'm thinking of auditioning for Quasimodo."

Melanie relaxed a little and smiled. "I'd say you're a cert to get the part but I'm not sure that's what you want to hear. Would you like a drink?"

"A scotch would be great, thanks."

Melanie moved towards a bar in the corner of the room. "Throw your coat somewhere and have a look around, while I fix the drinks," she invited. "There's a truly amazing bathroom over there." She pointed to a door on the other side of the room. "There are two bedrooms as well."

Tom did his tour of the suite and returned to find Melanie with a faint smile on her face. Probably because his jaw was on the floor.

"That's nothing like any bathroom I've ever seen," he remarked. "I don't know what you're used to in the States but over here we'd consider that more of a leisure centre. Are those taps real gold?"

"I think so."

"Do you think they unscrew easily?"

Melanie handed Tom what appeared to be a very large measure of scotch in a smart crystal tumbler. He was glad to see she had included a liberal amount of ice. She had poured a glass of white wine for herself.

"I've tried a couple of times but they're not budging so far," Melanie replied with mock seriousness. "Shall we sit?" she asked, moving towards the centre of the room where two very plush sofas faced each other, separated by a large marble coffee table. He sunk into the sofa opposite Melanie and managed to resist the urge to put his feet up on the table.

"I'm very sorry about the two people who died," he began. "Had you known them long?"

Melanie sighed. "Carol had been with me years. The bodyguard just twenty four hours." She seemed deep in thought as they sat silent for a few seconds.

"I'm sorry," was all Tom could think to say. "Actually I owe you a large vote of thanks for almost definitely saving my life," he continued. "I was in over my head with the man you shot."

Melanie snapped out of her thoughts. "Nonsense, it's me who owes you the thanks for saving my life. If you hadn't come along I hate to think where I'd be now."

"To us then," Tom toasted, raising the glass to his lips. "Do the police have any new information?" he asked, as he tasted his whisky and recognised it for a very expensive malt.

"Actually I learned more from reading your newspapers. Your police aren't very forthcoming. Incidentally, did you see this morning's papers say those two men were known to be members of the IRA? What the hell did I ever do to the IRA?"

"If it was the IRA it's going to cause a huge political stink," Tom answered. "Talking of newspapers," he continued rather sheepishly. "I feel I should tell you that I've sold my version of events to the press. Actually it's why I'm in London today. Frankly, business hasn't been good and I need the money." He felt a bit guilty but at the same time didn't because after all what would Melanie Adams ever understand about being short of money.

"Tom, I have no problem with that. And really it's none of my business. I hope you got a good price. The way I see it, if it wasn't for you I might be dead now. At the very least I wouldn't be sitting here drinking wine. So I'm happy whatever you choose to do."

Tom felt a certain relief. He knew he didn't exactly need Melanie's blessing for what he'd done but he was glad to receive it nonetheless. He recognized his actions could be interpreted as making money out of other people's misfortune and he didn't want this fledgling friendship destroyed before it had got off the ground. The truth was he had gone ahead anyway before speaking with her, so the reality was his selfish financial needs were taking priority over everything else.

"Cheers," Tom toasted, raising his glance. "To the future." He was feeling more relaxed in his surroundings.

"The future," Melanie concurred. "Talking of which I hope you're going to let me take you to dinner tonight? How about The Fig Leaf?"

Tom was struggling to maintain any sense of reality. It certainly wasn't reality, as he knew it, to be in Melanie Adams's hotel suite sharing a drink and discussing whether to eat at what is arguably London's most exclusive restaurant. He normally existed on a diet of takeaway cholesterol or the occasional homemade pasta dish. He decided he would stay in town to celebrate. His cheque would take a few days to clear but his credit card would just about sustain a night in a hotel, though not of the calibre of the Imperial.

"Don't you have to book The Fig Leaf weeks in advance?" Tom asked.

"They always manage to squeeze me in," Melanie replied with a slightly mischievous smile.

Foolish of me, Tom thought. Of course they would always find space for Melanie Adams.

He was pleased with himself for having decided to wear his only smart suit to London for his earlier meetings. Somehow he'd hoped it would convey an image of success and increase the price he received for his story. He reasoned that if they knew he was desperate, they would be tougher negotiations. As he would happily have accepted half what he received, he reckoned his suit must have done the trick. In future he would refer to it as his lucky suit.

He wasn't overly superstitious but like most gamblers he didn't mind giving lady luck a helping hand. Of course it would eventually lose its magic so he would wear it sparingly when he really needed a big win. Then again, maybe with his new found wealth such occasions would no longer arise. That thought only stayed in his head a second. He didn't try to delude himself there wouldn't always be occasions when a run of bad cards or horse results would leave him in need of a win. It was his karma to live life this way and he accepted it as such.

As Tom sat on the sofa contemplating dinner at The Fig Leaf, he felt he was stepping across the threshold into a new and exciting world. One inhabited by the likes of Melanie Adams. His suit was okay for mixing with the rich and famous but he gave himself a reminder to be on best behaviour over dinner.

He knew he had a tendency to drink a little too much wine given the opportunity, especially if someone else was paying. Alcohol in turn often had the effect on him of fancying the nearest reasonably attractive woman. He had no delusions that Melanie Adams would be remotely interested in his charms, so sensible drinking would be the order of the night. Embarrassing behaviour was definitely not on the menu. On which thought he smiled inwardly that at least he'd so far managed to resist the urge to ask for her autograph.

CHAPTER FOUR

Sam Murphy had never been arrested for any crime in her twenty-three years of life. Thus she had been able to move confidently through passport control, without fear of her name coming up on any computer screen. She gave her best smile to the man seated at the desk, who returned the smile slightly half-heartedly, like someone who is overworked and still has a long shift ahead. The bad weather had caused her flight to be delayed two hours and she was just pleased to have landed, before any further deterioration in the weather caused Heathrow to shut down completely.

  She remembered how as a kid, once a year, they would take the ferry to Holyhead as a family and after three hours feeling sick on a ferry rolling around in the sea, they would spend hours longer getting to their destination, whether it was Liverpool or London. She'd hated those journeys. Thank God for being able to fly, even with delays.

  On her previous visits to London she'd been able to stay with cousins but given her current circumstances decided she needed to keep away from anyone with ties to back home. Otherwise her father would soon get to learn her whereabouts and that could cause a right stink.

  The previous afternoon she'd booked into a small and shabby hotel in Ealing, which though on the west edge of London, is served by good mainline train and underground connections. The hotel was cheap and met the minimum requirements of having a working shower and a Television.

She had asked to see the room before agreeing to take it, not wanting to part with her money till she was sure of what she was getting. The young man on reception had reluctantly shown her the way to the second floor room, making no attempt at conversation and probably expecting her to have wasted his time, once she saw the small room and drab furnishings. But after checking the shower and telly worked she said she would take the room and they returned downstairs to register. At which point, his demeanour completely changed and he seemed to notice her properly for the first time. He managed a smile and asked if she knew the area, offering to take her for a drink later when he finished, to show her around.

She thought it was probably an approach he regularly tried on young single female visitors. Although how many of them there would be in a year was questionable. She might have been up for it on another occasion but was genuinely feeling knackered and needed some sleep. She had done a bit too much partying before she left.

Downstairs there was a small breakfast room and an even smaller bar. Everything she needed in fact. She initially paid for two nights in advance. It wasn't the type of place that gave you credit.

Then she'd visited a local hairdresser and had her shoulder length blonde hair cut in a new shorter style. The male stylist had renamed her "darling" and asked several times in a very camp manner whether she was sure she wanted to cut so much off, which had made her smile. She hoped it wasn't because of any concern on his part about his ability to do a good job. She thanked him for his concern and assured him she knew what she was doing.

She'd decided on the flight over it was a good idea and once her mind was made up, it was rarely dissuaded from a course of action. Next she'd found a chemist selling a hair dye that would transform her into a brunette. The end result was that she doubted her own father would recognise her if they passed on the street. She liked her new image. Even if she said so herself, she looked hot!

The rest of the day had been spent in fruitless phone calls trying to establish where the filth was holding her brother. She hadn't expected them to tell her but every time she irritated one of the coppers she spoke to, she saw it as a small victory. She was assured that her brother was in good health and being held at a secret location for his protection. She was eventually given the name of the solicitor appointed to defend him and had arranged to meet with him this morning.

On the way down to breakfast she stopped at reception to pick up a newspaper. They were laid out on the desk and one immediately caught her eye. The headline read; EXCLUSIVE – THE MAN WHO SAVED MELANIE ADAMS. There was a picture of a smiling man underneath.

She took the paper into the small dining room and studied it while drinking coffee and eating some toast, although it made it difficult to digest her breakfast. Sam stared at the photo loathing the man and burning an imprint of his features on her memory.

She had no problem with Melanie Adams she realized. She had done nothing wrong. In fact, she quite liked her films. What the hell had they been thinking of, trying to kidnap her? That bloody fool Maguire had been leading her brother astray again.

She drank more coffee and thought about her brother. How he must be feeling all alone at the moment. He was going to have to spend a lot of years in prison, maybe his whole life. There would never be any chance of amnesty for this. She needed to see him so he knew he wasn't alone.

She returned to the photo in the newspaper. Think you're so bloody clever don't you Mr Tom Ashdown, she said to the picture. When will you lot ever learn to keep your noses out of our business? The article did all but give his address. He'd be easy enough to find and when she did find him, she would make him pay. Of that she was certain.

Sam's thoughts turned back again to her brother and happier times.

She loved her brother but she'd be the first to admit he wasn't at the front of the line when they came to handing out brains. But he was there for her when she needed him.

She remembered the time aged seven when she came home from school crying because Micky Rourke had taken her sweets and when she tried to stop him, he'd pushed her over and she'd grazed all her leg. It was her big bruv who had gone straight round to Mickey's and come back home with some new sweets and a promise Mickey would never hurt her again.

She'd seen Mickey on the way to school next day and he'd crossed the road to avoid her and from then on she always felt safe, knowing she had a brother who would protect her. What her brother never discovered was that she made Mickey's life hell for the next three years of school. It had been subtle, not Mickey's style of brazen bullying. No, she had gained her personal revenge on Mickey every time she stole one of his books from his satchel or passed rumours amongst her friends of his disgusting habits.

The best time was putting a large fly in his sandwich. It didn't matter he never discovered the additional filling. She had sat staring at him with a huge smile fixed on her face as he enthusiastically munched away. Poor Mickey had never really understood why he became so friendless and continually so unlucky.

Sam knew she was different to her brother. Everyone always said so. She was used to hearing, "you're the smart one in the family." Growing up she'd thought to be a nurse when she left school but changed her mind and after studying languages at University, she'd found she had a passion for travel but no real idea what to do for a career. A succession of short-term jobs confirmed she couldn't face getting up every day to go to an office and spend eight hours behind a desk.

It was her brother who suggested there were opportunities within the organization for someone to travel, who could speak fluent Spanish and French. Her Da hadn't been happy when she went to him and told him she wanted in. But he knew how stubborn she could be and eventually agreed to make the necessary introductions.

For the last two years she'd travelled to Spain and South America to make arrangements for shipments of everything from arms to drugs. She never carried drugs herself and didn't count an occasional joint as really using them. She knew the money they made was put to good use and under the guise of working for a travel company, she finally got to indulge her passion for travel.

Sam finished eating and took the newspaper to her room. She tore out the picture of Tom Ashdown and folded it in two before placing it inside her purse. In truth his image was already irrevocably implanted on her mind. She knew from the article he lived in Brighton and ran a betting shop. After her meeting with her brother's solicitor, she'd hire a car and pay a visit to the seaside.

Tom wasn't entirely sure why he was surprised he'd had such a great evening. As he awoke in what was called the Royal suite at the Imperial he felt sure he must have been dreaming. The suite wasn't the size of Melanie's but it had all the same grandiose style and quality. This last couple of days was certainly creating unforgettable moments.

He recognized the signs of a near miss of a hangover. He had a dry mouth and tiniest degree of queasiness in his stomach but was thankful for the absence of a headache. He put it down to the quality of champagne they had drunk all evening. When Melanie had first suggested champagne and he'd readily agreed, he hadn't anticipated them drinking two bottles of Cristal. Perhaps the way to avoid a hangover was always to drink very expensive booze. Only drawback was that you would be bankrupt in very quick time. Then he remembered more clearly that they had had two bottles of champagne at the restaurant but when they came back to the hotel they had enjoyed nightcaps in the bar, which in his case extended to almost half a bottle of vintage port.

He'd enjoyed being able to have a really fantastic gastronomic experience without worrying about the cost. And he'd felt no pangs of conscience that Melanie was paying for everything. In fact with his new found wealth, it was probably the first time in his life he could actually have afforded to pay a bill of such magnitude. She didn't let him see the total but he knew it was more than a thousand pounds as the champagne alone was five hundred pounds a bottle, though it was by no means the most expensive bottle on the wine list.

He had been handed the list, which was many pages long, by the waiter, and was perusing it very unsure what to order when Melanie suggested champagne. He liked a bottle of bubbly, especially when he was celebrating as he was tonight so was quick to agree and turned to look at the list of champagnes. It was again a long list and he was pleased when she asked if he would be happy with Cristal, as it was her favourite. He'd never tried it but knew it was very popular with celebrities and concurred it was a good choice. Of course, he would have agreed that anything Melanie Adams suggested was a good idea.

It had been an eye opening experience to accompany Melanie to dinner. More a case of how the other point one per cent live rather than the other half! From the moment they had arrived at the restaurant they had been treated like royalty. Melanie took it as the everyday occurrence it undoubtedly was for her. To Tom it seemed there was extra warmth in the greeting "it's good to see you," which was extended to her by all and sundry. When she informed the Maître D' that Tom was as she put it, "the knight in shining armour who came to my rescue," he also was quickly elevated to superstar proportions.

Tom had been pleased to see she enjoyed her food. He hated picky eaters and had half wondered if she would be on some trendy Californian diet or perhaps a vegetarian but she matched him course for course. He had a theory that women who ate heartily were best in bed. It didn't mean he particularly fancied large women. In fact quite the opposite. It wasn't so much the quantity of food they ate but not being fussy that made them in his experience a great lover. A good appetite was a good appetite whether it was food or sex.

He wondered what Melanie Adams would actually be like in bed? Well he was never going to find out so decided it best not to dwell on the thought too long. He already knew from her films what she looked like naked. Some of the images that flashed in his mind were slightly disconcerting.

Tom had visited great restaurants from time to time including with Colin but The Fig Leaf with its three Michelin stars was probably the best place he'd ever eaten. The combination of the surroundings, service and food was unsurpassed in his experience. Of course, having Melanie Adams as his dining companion had also made the evening very special.

Before leaving the hotel for the restaurant they had mutually agreed to ban any further discussion of the events that had brought them together. A cloud would naturally enough hang over the evening. Melanie had lost her good friend and it would be at the forefront of her mind for a long time to come but they had set out to enjoy a dinner that was a celebration of life, in a way that perhaps only people who have recently escaped death can do. So they wouldn't dwell on those innocents who had been killed.

They were not being callous or disrespectful to their memory. Tom had thought of the saying, life goes on. A somewhat tired cliché that he wasn't going to repeat out loud but ever since losing his parents, he had understood that to be the case.

He had asked a few questions about the films Melanie had appeared in and was surprised how down to earth she was. She didn't take her film roles very seriously, pointing out that they were never likely to win her an Oscar, although she lived in hope. They did however earn her millions and she was quite happy with that trade off.

Tom had imagined a superstar actress to be somewhat different. When asked, he identified his favourite movie as The Cincinnati Kid and laughed at her rebuke that he hadn't chosen any of her films. She hadn't seen or even heard of the film but he explained it was the story of a poker player, a passion he shared. It starred Steve McQueen who she did know and having been released in 1965, she pointed out she wasn't even born then.

Her choice was Gone with the Wind. She admitted to being a romantic at heart and wished she could have played a lead role in such an epic. Tom told her he thought she would make a great Scarlett O'Hara. He was pleased he had seen a few of her films and could say he had genuinely enjoyed them.

Conversation flowed freely with the champagne and Melanie made him laugh hysterically with her impression of a cockney but he wasn't entirely surprised she didn't get the part in the remake of My Fair Lady.

They had talked a little about their childhoods and parents. Melanie had been unequivocal about how great her parents had been and how much she missed them. They had worked hard to give her everything possible when she was growing up and she had nothing but positive memories. Dad had been an accountant and mum worked in a library. Her Dad may have taught her how to use guns but it was her mum who introduced her to literature and drove her twice a week to the drama classes that would eventually lead to her future career.

Tom had described his own childhood with less enthusiasm but he recognized it could have been a lot worse and in their own way his parents had also done their best for him. When explaining why he travelled so much with the army, his father had taught him that you couldn't just ignore people in trouble, whether it was a country or an individual. That had stayed with him and was probably subconsciously the reason why he intervened to help Melanie, when he knew many others would simply have called the police and stayed hidden behind that car.

At some point, Melanie admitted to never having really been very close to getting married but was still hopeful, as she did want to have kids. That, as it always did, had struck a bit of a raw nerve with Tom and he'd explained about Alex. They had married in their early twenties and been madly in love but by the time they reached thirty they had drifted apart. She was a thrusting barrister working all hours and committed to her career. Alex worried about how to win her next case. He worried who was going to win the three thirty at Ascot.

Tom wanted children but it was never the right time for Alex. One day, in the face of his pleading that it was the only hope for their marriage, she had agreed to stop taking the pill. She wasn't desperate to have a child but was willing, for his sake, to accept pregnancy if it happened naturally. Their lovemaking had lost its spontaneity years before and usually occurred after a couple of bottles of wine but he'd made a concentrated effort for a few months and their sex life improved although she didn't conceive. He wasn't too concerned as he knew it could easily take a year or more but when he found the packet of pills in her bedside draw, he didn't even bother saying anything.

He presumed she wanted him to find them, so he took the hint and their sex life gradually went back to the old routine. Alex began having to stay more nights in London for important cases and less than twelve months later she announced she was leaving him. He wasn't surprised to later find that she had been having an affair with someone at work for a considerable time.

Despite Tom's initial protestations there were no tears. It had all been terribly civilized and they quickly reached an amicable agreement on sharing what they'd accumulated together over ten years. A sad indictment of two people living separate lives under the same roof. They had little in common and thus nothing to dispute the ownership of, not even their CD collection. Their music tastes were completely different. He was a fan of heavy rock and opera. She liked everything else.

Ten years on from Alex and there was still no sign of anyone special on the horizon. In fact the longer he went without a serious relationship the less important having one seemed to be. He enjoyed female company and there had been a succession of brief affairs but nothing serious.

He and a friend had tried speed dating in a hotel in Brighton one time. Actually they more stumbled across it when out for a drink. A woman approached them in the hotel bar and asked if they would like to join in as there had been a shortage of men turn up to the event. The woman who was organizing the event saw they were uncertain so offered to buy them a drink if they would take part and never the types to refuse a free drink they had accepted. The woman buying the drinks had been quite attractive and so Tom had made the incorrect assumption the women looking for dates would be the same.

He had found it very strange that you had just three minutes with each girl. After explaining for the fourth time what he did to an uninterested female sitting across the table, he had realized speed dating wasn't something he would try again anytime soon. He announced he was going to the toilet but instead headed straight for the exit. His friend had seen him leave and quickly followed. He recounted the story to Melanie which made her laugh.

Melanie told Tom how quite early on in her career she recognised that she was in an industry where relationships are notoriously difficult to maintain given that you could spend months apart on film sets. Her famous friends had consistently proved her right. As she was an old fashioned girl at heart and only wanted to walk down the aisle once, she admitted she couldn't see herself ever marrying an actor, preferring to go out with someone sane as she put it! The problem was that she spent ninety per cent of her time with actors and rarely met anyone remotely normal.

There was no shortage of dates however, and when challenged she coyly admitted that flings with her leading men were not entirely uncommon, although not as frequent as reported in the press. After all what was a woman to do by herself for weeks on end on a film set in the middle of nowhere. Then she'd added that someone needed to invent batteries that lasted a lot longer and they'd both laughed noisily enough to attract the attention of nearby diners.

He was pleasantly surprised by how at ease Melanie seemed to be in his company. She seemed most unlike a Hollywood star. There was no arrogance and no hint of being a diva. She was pleasant to all the staff and smiled warmly in response to the couple who approached the table and asked for her autograph. She seemed a very nice human being and he felt a tinge of guilt that he had ever thought she might be anything less.

The subject had changed to work although Tom refused at first to recognise that what Melanie did was work! She had been quick to point out that twelve-hour days in a jungle full of creepy crawlies did indeed constitute work, especially as the biggest creep had been her leading man.

Tom explained that he owned a betting shop, which was not making much money because of the trend towards Internet betting. That of course was only half the truth because even when the shop did make money, he usually managed to lose it at the casino. She imagined that a betting shop would be a license to print money, as she had never won anything when she very occasionally went racing. He suggested that he would take her one day and she agreed that would be fun.

Melanie described her sporting passion as football which caused confusion for one moment until Tom realised what she meant and pointed out she was referring to American football not football. Tom enjoyed watching what they agreed to call Soccer to save confusion but had never followed any one specific team, although recently he had made a few trips to the new Amex stadium to see Brighton play. Tom was mostly a fan of the big tournaments when he would avidly watch England play. Melanie seemed surprised to learn the USA had a half decent soccer team and several Americans played in the Premier League.

Melanie's football team was the Pittsburgh Steelers. She had gone regularly with her Dad when she was young and still went whenever filming commitments allowed. Tom had watched a few games on television over the years but never been to a live game, which news was immediately met with an invitation to see a match from Melanie's private box. She also offered to take him to the Super Bowl if they made it to the final, which she assured Tom was a real possibility.

Tom wasn't a great fan of what he'd seen on television, as he didn't like the start / stop nature of the games but a trip to a Super Bowl would be a great sporting occasion. He liked the way Melanie became animated and excited about her team. Tom felt the same way about going to Cheltenham or Royal Ascot.

Melanie had refused to hear of him staying anywhere other than the Imperial and he found it difficult to argue with her logic, especially after the vintage port, that it would be nice to have breakfast together. For a second he had kept a straight face and then Melanie had realized what she'd said and looked a little aghast at the idea. This in turn prompted Tom to mock her for making the idea of sleeping with Quasimodo seem so horrific and they had both fallen in to a further bout of laughter.

Melanie had organized the suite and asked for it to be added to her account. On reflection Tom thought it was not unreasonable that she should be paying for the whole evening, though it was an unusual experience. He didn't feel there was any sense of his abusing her hospitality or taking advantage of the fact he'd helped her out. She was a fantastically wealthy woman and wanted to say thank you, so he would graciously accept and in a day or two life would go back to normal and Melanie would no doubt return to the States.

The alarm call that awoke him had been ordered for eight o'clock, which Melanie had suggested was a bit early but he had pointed out he really did have to get into his shop today, to check the staff hadn't run off with his money. He wasn't serious of course but it was unfair to leave Ben shorthanded for another day, even if some of the meetings were getting cancelled because of the weather. Melanie was going to meet with the press, whom she had so far kept at arm's length but they were clamouring to hear her side of the story and she had a press conference organized for two o'clock.

Tom had some poached eggs on toast with a side order of bacon but Melanie admitted to feeling a little more delicate and settled for toast and coffee. He noticed how everywhere Melanie went both men and women looked at her and wondered if it was because of her looks or her fame. It must do strange things to your mind he thought. She seemed not to notice but Tom found it a little unnerving and decided on balance, he probably wouldn't like to be a film star.

"Could you get me a part in a film?" he suddenly asked. "Preferably one opposite Julia Roberts that involves some intense love scenes."

Melanie laughed. "I'll introduce you to Julia sometime." She drank some coffee then looked up. "Love scenes aren't much fun you know?"

"You certainly wouldn't get me undressing in front of millions of cinema goers," he agreed. The images of Melanie naked in a couple of her films had occupied his mind more than once over dinner.

"I'm lucky because I have complete control over these things nowadays. I haven't had to do a real nude scene for several years."

"But I saw your last movie. And frankly saw quite a lot of you too!"

"Not really you didn't. That was mostly body doubles. Certainly they weren't my breasts or my ass."

"That's not right," Tom exclaimed. "I paid good money to see your breasts not someone else's," he continued, feigning indignation. "I could probably sue you under the trade descriptions act."

"You're mad," she succinctly remarked.

The more time Tom spent in Melanie's company, the more he found he really liked her. Sure there was a bit of physical attraction as well but that was just added spice.

"Completely bonkers I have to agree," he admitted. "Would you like to go racing later this week? There's a meeting at Kempton on Friday evening." Melanie had told him over dinner that she would be heading back to the states at the weekend and Tom wanted the chance to see more of her before she left.

"Sounds fun. As long as you promise I'll win."

"The only tip I'll give you is to ignore whatever I tell you will win. That will narrow the field down for you." Recent luck had led him to believe his selections amounted to highly valuable information for anyone looking to pick a horse to finish second.

"Are you finished?" Tom asked.

"I think I'll have a bit more coffee. You get going if you need to."

"You certainly do enjoy your caffeine."

"I'd tell you it's my only vice but I'd be lying."

Tom got up from his chair and leaned forward to kiss Melanie on both cheeks. "I'll call you about Friday. If you change your mind let me know in time, so I can invite Julia or someone else!" Then he turned and headed for his room, turning back at the entrance to the dining room to look at her and remember the moment. He couldn't be sure when or if he would ever have breakfast again with Melanie Adams.

Connor had arrived early at the park for his second meeting with the Brit. It was another ice cold day in keeping with his mood and he hoped he wouldn't have to wait around long. He didn't fancy sitting on the nearby bench and freezing to death so walked in a wide circle around the meeting spot. A few hardy types had braved the freezing cold to stretch their legs. Everyone walked with a purpose though; no one was just taking a lunchtime stroll for the sake of it. On a warmer day the benches would be filled with office workers eating their sandwiches but not today.

Connor had telephoned the previous day to the Head of Operations in Belfast and updated him about his first meeting with Jones. He had promised to go straight to see the Chief and update him. It wasn't easy to telephone the Chief directly at home, especially regarding the most delicate matters, as it was always assumed someone was monitoring his calls. Connor wanted to know from the Chief what limits were there on his actions. He knew it was important to the Chief to silence the Murphy boy but was it truly at any cost, as he'd first suggested. Connor knew those words had been spat out in anger. And it hadn't been the right time to question what the Chief said.

Connor was an expert shot and normally that was sufficient for his work. However, what if the only way to guarantee a result was to detonate a car bomb as Murphy passed. That had always worked well in the past but such unrefined methods were no longer considered acceptable. Semtex going off in a public street inevitably led to a risk of widespread casualties. There was supposed to be a cease-fire in place. Connor made it very clear to his contact he needed the Chief to spell out very precisely what was acceptable.

Connor spotted Jones hurrying towards the meeting point, which given he was carrying more than a few extra pounds, was quite an achievement in itself. Connor intercepted his path by coming up behind him. "I'm here," he said simply but it was enough to make Jones jump, which had been the intention.

Connor came straight to the point. "What do you know?" he said brusquely.

"Let's walk," Jones said, but it sounded a bit too much like an order for Connor's like. "More private," Jones added encouragingly.

Connor immediately found himself having to walk faster than he liked, to keep pace with the man. A bit of a bloody ex soldier's march, he thought.

"He'll be up before the judge tomorrow," Jones said. "A two minute appearance in court to hear the charges. Then he'll be remanded in solitary until his trial."

"I need to know routes and time."

"He's in court at four." Jones reached into his inside coat pocket and withdrew some folded paper. "I've marked the map," he explained, as he handed the paper to Connor. "Give me a number where I can reach you in case they change the time or anything."

Murphy had brought with him a compliments slip from the hotel, detailing the address and telephone number.

"I'm staying here," he said, thrusting the slip towards the Brit who glanced at it before folding it neatly and placing it in his pocket.

"I hope you're not planning anything too wild," Jones cautioned. "It would be totally unacceptable. We don't want mayhem on the streets of London. Neither do I want to see innocent people harmed."

"A very touching speech. Now why don't you just bugger off?" It amused Connor to emphasise the word bugger. They had Jones on film with the fifteen year old who had encouraged him to enjoy her however he wanted, just don't make her pregnant.

Jones saw no point in responding. He understood the innuendo. He wanted to be away from here as soon as possible. Being around this terrorist made him feel unclean as everything about Ireland did nowadays. For him it was a place synonymous with death and despair.

The people who lived in the North deserved what they had created. A little piece of hell on earth in his opinion, inhabited by more than one devil. He did though want to know how many terrorists there were running around London. He didn't want their troubles soiling where he lived.

"What backup do you have?" Jones asked.

"That's my business."

"You bloody Irish are all the same."

"Know a lot of Irish people do you?"

Jones looked surprised by the question. "Enough," he answered.

"Only I wondered where you'd gained your in-depth understanding of the Irish people," Connor said sarcastically. "Was it from fifteen year old girls or did you actually meet some adults?"

Connor didn't know too much about Jones time in Ireland apart from how he had been trapped. He assumed he might well have been responsible for the death or imprisonment of old friends. He remembered the soldier like march and wished he could have Jones in the sights of an Armalite, rather than be doing deals with him. He did though enjoy winding the Brit up.

"I need to be going," Jones said impatiently. "Do you have something for me?"

Connor took out an envelope and handed it to Jones. Though they had Jones by the short and curlies they always paid him for his information. Connor would have preferred not to but he didn't argue with the Chief.

Jones took the envelope and stuffed it in his coat. He expected it to contain two thousand pounds but wasn't going to count it in the park. Though he had many of the trappings of success, a new car, a four bedroom detached house and children who had been educated at private schools, working for the government did not pay well. He was putting these payments towards his retirement fund.

"Will that be all, now?" Jones asked, eager to get away.

Connor didn't bother replying. He simply turned his back and walked away. He realised why he hated Jones. It wasn't just that he was a Brit or his offensive sexual preferences. It was because he was a fucking tout.

He'd pulled the trigger and kneecapped a tout one time. Been glad to do it. It was the least the Judas deserved for running to the Brits with bits of information, for a miserable few quid. Jones was the lowest of the low in Connor's eyes. Touts ranked below even perverts.

Sam Murphy had never been in a betting shop in her life. Her image of them was of seedy places inhabited by a combination of weird old men and losers spending money they should be giving their wives, instead of frittering it away on the horses. Or at least that was how she thought it was back home.

However, she was surprised to find that Ashdown Racing was nothing like she'd imagined. It was a bright well lit room, with a large television screen in the middle of one wall and comfortable chairs for watching. There were other smaller screens spread around the shop and a long counter where you placed your bets. The walls were painted in pleasant pastels and there was almost a coffee shop feel to the place. Not the least bit dingy as she had imagined.

She'd recognized Ashdown from the newspaper pictures as soon as she entered. He was behind the counter with a young looking man and a middle aged woman. He was taking bets and sometimes handing out winnings, which he seemed to do with remarkable cheerfulness, considering it was presumably his money he was dishing out. She noticed that most people seemed to know each other and all of them knew Ashdown. As new people entered the shop they were going up to him and congratulating him. There was loads of hand shaking and pats on the back. It sickened her to see how everyone was treating the bastard like some kind of hero. Didn't they know he had almost killed her brother?

On initially entering, she'd glanced around and spotting newspapers on the wall that detailed the day's racing, had pretended to read them. She felt conspicuous as there was only one other woman in the shop, who was probably three times her age. From the moment she'd entered, she'd been getting a fair number of what she thought were appreciative stares, from various men of all ages. She assumed she wasn't the typical customer they expected to see in their shop.

She wasn't entirely sure what she would achieve by coming to Brighton but had felt a compelling need to do so. Now she was here, she was getting a real buzz from being in the same space as the man she hated. She'd heard her father say you must know your enemy. He had a saying to cover most situations. Well she knew her enemy and now all that remained was to decide on her revenge. She'd given it some thought on the way down from London. Her brother was going to spend a very long time in jail. The most fitting revenge would be to put Ashdown away for a similar time but the question was how to achieve that.

"Would you like a cup of coffee?"

Sam turned quickly on her heels, recognizing the voice instantly. She looked startled.

"It's on the house," Tom said, smiling. "I don't think I've seen you here before."

"Err, thanks," she said. "I don't mind if I do."

"You're not a reporter by any chance?"

"A reporter?" Sam queried.

"Only we've had a few of them in here today."

"No, I'm not a reporter. Why would you think I am?" Sam was suddenly very conscious of her Irish accent.

"Firstly, you've been in here ages and haven't placed a single bet. Secondly, you look out of place. I doubt you know a yankee from a trixie."

"I promise I'm not a reporter," Sam said with conviction and trying to tone down her accent.

Tom gave her a look that suggested he wasn't entirely convinced but she seemed harmless. "Fair enough then. How do you take your coffee?"

"Just black please."

Ashdown moved away to fetch coffee and Sam breathed deeply to get her pounding heart under control. It was the thought of coffee that prompted her idea for revenge. She knew that the drugs from South America were often shipped alongside coffee, as it made it impossible for the sniffer dogs to detect. It was a simple plan but she had been taught that simple plans were often the best. Eduardo Garcia was always chasing her. He wasn't exactly her type but he would be able to put her in touch with a supplier. Then all she had to do was plant the stuff on Ashdown and make a call to let the police know.

Ashdown reappeared with the coffee. "Thanks," she said. "By the way, why is all the racing from France?"

"English racing is all cancelled," he answered. "Because of the terrible weather." He made it seem an unnecessary explanation.

She could see that her lack of racing knowledge had once again pricked his curiosity. "I'm really not a reporter," she stressed. "But the truth is I just came in to get out the cold. I have a bit of time to kill. Hope you don't mind?" Then she added as an afterthought, "And I might have a small bet."

Tom laughed. "Feel free," he said. "Enjoy the coffee. And if anyone here tells you they have a certainty, ignore them. There's no such thing."

As he walked away she felt more relaxed. She even recognized the tiniest self-questioning of whether she was right to want revenge on Ashdown. He'd seemed friendly enough – quite human even for a moment.

Then she remembered the troubles at home and who was responsible. It was the Brits fault. Everything was their fault. If it wasn't for them her father wouldn't have spent half her childhood in jail and her brother wouldn't be facing the rest of his life behind bars.

No, she decided, there was no room for compassion towards Brits in her heart. She'd save her sympathy for all those fine young men, many not much older than herself, who had selflessly given their lives for freedom. She wouldn't betray their memory. She knew who her enemy was and she'd confronted him and now she had a chance for revenge.

Geoffrey Miller had arranged to meet Tony Simpson for lunch. Simpson was an old friend, dating back to when they both worked for Special Branch and spent time together in Northern Ireland. At some point thereafter Simpson's specialist knowledge of Irish affairs had earned him an invitation to join MI5. It had been part of a drive to cement greater cooperation between the different forces combating terrorism. It wasn't a move Miller would have contemplated making but Simpson was always one of the first people Miller would choose to consult, when he needed a different and unofficial perspective on Irish puzzles.

Simpson enjoyed good food immensely and fine wine even more. A rotund jovial man of only about five feet six inches in height, a comparison with a barrel would not be inappropriate. He was bald on top but had bushy dark eyebrows and reminded Miller of a figure from the 'Guess Who' children's game he had played with his kids, when they were younger.

They had arranged to meet at a quiet little restaurant in the City, which they had used previously. Miller arrived to find Simpson already seated at a suitably private table in the corner. The place was never very busy at lunchtime. In Miller's opinion this was largely the result of a spectacularly expensive menu. The restaurant preferred to attract a select but appreciative clientele, rather than pure numbers. As Miller approached the table he could see a bottle of what was bound to be excellent wine chilling in the ice bucket.

"Good to see you again, Geoffrey," Simpson smiled, rising from his chair and shaking hands enthusiastically. "I took the liberty of ordering a wonderful Chablis they serve. I'm sure you'll like it."

Miller barely had time to sit before his glass was filled.

"May you have many more occasions to pick my brain," Simpson toasted. They brought their glasses together with a clink and Miller tasted the wine. Simpson was observing him, waiting for his judgement.

"An excellent choice Tony, as usual. Please just tell me it's under fifty quid a bottle." Miller enjoyed a glass of wine but had few pretensions to being a connoisseur. He usually paid about ten pounds at his local off license for what he considered a decent red wine, which was his preference. He suspected Simpson's upper class background meant he paid a lot more for something, he would describe as decent.

"I could tell you it was under fifty quid Geoffrey but then I would be lying," Simpson replied with a smile. "It is however good value. I've paid a lot more for the same wine elsewhere."

"Oh well that's all right then," Miller acknowledged with a liberal sprinkling of sarcasm.

A waiter appeared to take their order before they could say anything further on the subject.

"I'll have avocado followed by medium rare sirloin," Miller requested without looking at the menu. It was the same he had ordered on his last visit.

The waiter turned towards Simpson.

"For me the shrimps in garlic, followed by rack of lamb."

"I'm afraid the lamb is for two," explained the waiter politely.

"Quite so. Perfect," Simpson answered, beaming without any sign of discomfort. "I'll take both portions."

The waiter retreated looking somewhat perplexed.

Miller laughed. "Has no one told you, too much red meat isn't good for you?"

"Live for today. That's my motto."

"With a waistline like yours I think you should be worrying more about tomorrow."

"What's wrong with my waistline?" Simpson questioned, sounding genuinely perplexed.

"It's not exactly a six pack."

"Why settle for a six pack when you can have a whole barrel?"

Miller laughed. He liked Simpson and knew that his size made him the person he was. He had also seen a picture of him in his youth when he would compete in international judo competitions and was nothing like the same size. He hadn't been skinny but neither had he been so rotund.

"Anyway," Simpson said. "Before we get stuck into the food why don't you tell me what's on your mind."

"Melanie Adams."

"Thought it might be. The world is well rid of that Maguire. A nasty piece of work. Don't know the Murphy boy. Used to know his father. Also an evil devil." Simpson shuddered at the thought of Murphy. "Have you met the son?"

"Not personally but my boys say he's a bit thick and it looks like it was all Maguire's idea. Seems Murphy looked up to Maguire and just did as he was told."

"So he's talking?"

"Not at first but I think it's fair to say we pointed out the foolishness of remaining quiet. He needs us otherwise he's a dead man. We have him for two murders so the only issue is whether he ever gets parole and what happens to him while he's inside. We lock him up with his old friends and he meets a sticky end."

"So you hope he can clear up some cold cases?"

"You know how it works. It's all extra pieces fitting in the jigsaw."

"Do you think they acted alone?" Simpson asked. "I mean, as you said, they aren't the brightest duo. How did they know where to find her for a start?"

"Don't laugh but Murphy says they found out on her website. There's a diary for her visit and under Saturday evening it says, Christmas shopping trip to Harrods."

Simpson looked appalled. "How long was it on the web site?"

"Not sure but Murphy says Maguire told him Saturday afternoon they were doing a job. Didn't say who or what it was."

"Would probably only have cost them a few quid to check with someone working at Harrods what time she was expected."

"We are interviewing all the staff and checking the CCTV in case they were ever inside the store," Miller confirmed. "We might get lucky." Miller didn't sound like he believed that.

"So why are you buying me this exquisite meal?"

"Murphy also says that just prior to Maguire telling him about the job he'd been out to meet someone. Doesn't have a clue who it was but thinks it was someone important."

"So someone else is pulling the strings," Simpson mused.

"Looks that way. As you said, they're not the brightest duo so I think it's probably safe to say this other person planned the operation. He obviously has enough brains to want to keep in the background but relying on them two makes you question just how smart he really is."

"Any other leads?" Simpson asked.

"Not yet. Can your mob shed any light?"

"No but the boss is obviously pushing all the buttons... Do you think this third man could be running another team or teams?"

"That's the worry. Murphy doesn't seem to know."

"You know this isn't really my area anymore," Simpson explained. "Hasn't been for quite some time."

"I know but most of those sharp youngsters you work with, wouldn't be able to tell you the difference between a Catholic and a Protestant. They probably were still in nappies when we were in the thick of it."

"True," Simpson agreed.

"I thought Tony you might be able to keep your ear to the ground and act as an unofficial liaison between our two organisations. We need to cooperate better on this than we usually do." Miller regularly became exasperated with the infighting between the different departments fighting terrorism. "I'll also meet with your boss and suggest it formally but I thought I would run the idea by you first."

Simpson raised his glass in a toast. "Happy to help where I can. Officially or otherwise."

"Thanks Tony. You getting on any better with him?"

"Don't ask. I still can't abide the man. Coldest fish I've ever known and I'm used to swimming in the artic."

Miller had listened during their last lunch to Simpson's tirade against his new boss. Simpson had even mentioned, he was considering taking early retirement, in order to travel the world, sampling the culinary delights everywhere he went.

"Perhaps you could set up a meeting for me," Miller asked. "We can play, give away as little as possible without being accused of being uncooperative. I always enjoy that game."

Simpson laughed. "I'm afraid my money's on him to win that one. I'll call you and arrange something for the next couple of days. Now let's enjoy lunch."

Connor had heard back from the Chief. Make it look like an accident if possible. If not, get the bastard anyway you can. A fucking accident, Connor thought. He's taking the piss. Anyway, the message confirmed what he wanted to hear. The weapon and approach he had in mind was sanctioned. He had little chance of hitting Murphy on the drive to or from court. He would be out of sight, in the back of a speeding van, and he was only going to get one shot.

His best chance to get at Murphy would be as he actually arrived or left the court building, when he would no doubt have to slow down and a man with the right weapon could target him and his vehicle, without too much collateral damage. Even then it would be difficult and the security would be very tight. Connor was a positive person by nature but he wasn't confident he was going to pull this job off and he had decided a long time ago, he was no martyr to the cause. He wanted to have a better than even chance of pulling it off or he wouldn't attempt it.

The second part of the Chief's message had been interesting. Murphy's sister was in England and her father was worried she might try something against the man who had foiled the kidnap attempt. The Chief owed Murphy and didn't hold what his son had done against him. Neither did he want to see the woes of the father compounded by losing both his son and daughter. She was also a valuable asset to the organization. The Chief wanted Connor to look out for her. If that meant disposing of Ashdown, that was okay. Just get Sam Murphy safely out of harm's way and back to her father.

It was this that had prompted Connor to make the trip to Brighton. He had been writing out a dog bet when he spotted the girl enter the shop. His suspicions were quickly aroused, as he noticed how she continually focused on the man behind the counter, who he knew was Ashdown. After a while, Ashdown offered her coffee and Connor was close enough to detect the Belfast accent when she replied. She wasn't an exact match for the description he'd been given but she was the right age and shape. Hair colour was easily changed.

He didn't expect her to do anything stupid in the shop, so returned to his car to wait for her to leave. When she did, he noticed she had a smirk on her face. Not a bad looking lass, he thought to himself, as he watched her get in a silver Ford Fiesta. A hire car presumably, as it was very new.

She was a bit more of a looker than his usual partners and quite a bit younger. He could do with a screw. Hadn't had one for a couple of weeks and then he'd had to pay for it. He liked the simplicity of paying for what he wanted. He wasn't averse to a freebie but couldn't be buggered with all the talking women expected beforehand. And the money you spent buying them food and drinks would pay for whatever you wanted from a pro, who knew what she was doing. If he wanted sex he wanted it. And looking at the Murphy girl quite turned him on. Perhaps she'd be appreciative if he helped her get rid of Ashdown.

What was the damn girl doing though? She was just sitting in her car. Connor guessed she was waiting for Ashdown and hoped she wasn't planning anything daft like running him down with her car. There would be little he could do to stop her, if that was her intention.

After waiting an hour, Ashdown emerged from the shop, pulled down some metal shutters, locked them and walked a few yards down the road to where his car was parked. As he drove away, Connor was pleased the girl simply pulled out behind him and Connor in turn followed a couple of cars further back.

The procession drove ten minutes out of town, climbing a particularly steep road that emerged next to the racecourse. They turned left onto what seemed quite a major road and after half a mile, a sign indicated they were entering the village of Woodingdean. Shortly after passing a large cemetery on the right, Ashdown turned left into a cul-de-sac. The Murphy girl followed but Connor was worried a third car might be too noticeable and drove a few yards past the entrance to the road and parked on the side of the main road. He was out of his car quickly and walked back in time to see, Ashdown had turned into the driveway of a detached chalet bungalow, about halfway up the cul-de-sac, which Connor assumed was Ashdown's home.

The girl seemed content she had established where he lived because she had turned around at the end of the road and was now driving back down past where Ashdown had stopped. Connor returned to his car, noticing the great views down to the sea in the distance and eased back out into the traffic as she drove past.

He was glad she hadn't tried to run Ashdown down or anything so stupid. But the very fact she had been in Ashdown's shop and followed him home, meant she was planning something, as the Chief had suspected. She had the potential to be a very loose cannon. Connor amused himself by imagining how he might spend a couple of hours with her, as he followed her out of town towards the motorway.

CHAPTER FIVE

Tom awoke in his own bed. He had set the first alarm by his bed for 7.00am. He instinctively hit the snooze button and almost simultaneously heard the alarm in the bathroom ring. Damn his efficiency, he thought. He dragged himself out of bed and headed for the bathroom. While he showered, he contemplated a day without seeing Melanie. Absurd as the thought was, he knew his feelings for her were growing every day. His rational side said he should enjoy her company while he can but not expect more. Some other part of him though wanted to find a reason to call her today, just so he could hear her voice.

He emerged from the shower a confused man. He had to think of his feelings in terms of an infatuation that wouldn't last. After all, the odds of him ever having a real relationship with Melanie Adams, were at least a thousand to one against.

The negatives were easy to identify. He sought some positives. He liked Americans. Always had done. Las Vegas was the holy grail of the poker player and he had twice managed to qualify for the greatest poker show on earth, the world series of poker championships.

Okay their sense of geography was poor and they could distort history rather in their blockbuster movies but they were outgoing and generally fun. If at times it came across as superficial so what? Better an attempt at friendliness, even if a contrived "have a nice day," rather than the cold and unwelcoming nature of the English.

Was he being a bit harsh on his fellow countrymen? Probably, especially as they weren't responsible for the inclement weather that drove them all indoors but nonetheless he did find their propensity to stand in queues and say nothing to those next to them, a quite alarming trait.

Anyway, what was important was that Melanie had already said she liked the English. Although slightly strangely it seemed the accent more than anything else that was the attraction. One point scored in his favour.

Next positive, Melanie said she didn't like relationships with film stars. That made two points scored. He was never going to be a film star.

Okay not exactly an exclusive club so far but thirdly and perhaps most importantly they had discovered they both shared a passion for Monty Python. Perhaps not the soundest basis for a relationship but it did signify she had a quirky sense of humour, which he had already grown to like. Melanie hadn't heard of Fawlty Towers and he made a mental note to get her the complete box set of episodes of his favourite comedy series, as a going away present.

Tom dried and moving to his bedside table checked the time. It was ten past seven and he had to be at the television studio in Southampton for nine o'clock. As the drive was at least ninety minutes, he needed to pull his finger out and get going. Still he wasn't being actually interviewed until after ten, so that left some room for manoeuvre.

The phone call late the previous afternoon had come as something of a surprise. He had just finished chatting to that very attractive Irish girl, when the call came through asking him to appear on the regional magazine show, which followed on from the news. He was informed he was a major local celebrity and they wanted to interview him about how he saved Melanie Adams life. He recognized that the use of words like hero in the same sentence as his name massaged his ego as never before.

He wasn't averse to the thought of appearing on television. As Clifford Maxwell had said, "the more publicity the better. Make the most of your fifteen minutes of fame." Clifford had even suggested that the next step would be to appear on some reality celebrity show.

Although the idea of being a celebrity was slightly absurd, Tom was more than happy with the idea of being paid to spend time in the jungle or on a tropical desert island, with some of the beauties he knew generally took part in such shows. He had however made it clear to Clifford that he had no wish to be locked up in a house with anyone.

Breakfast was some orange juice and toast, his staple morning diet during the week. He turned on the radio and listened to the morning show on Heart FM while he ate. He liked their mixture of music and humorous chat. He was feeling quite pleased with himself as he sat glancing at the Racing Post, which was delivered to his door early every morning.

He'd spent a couple of hours the previous evening playing poker on the Internet. His newfound wealth enabled him to play with a sense of financial confidence rather than his normal desperation to win. As a result he actually found himself enjoying playing, a feeling he hadn't experienced for a long time. Playing in a relaxed manner, he ended the evening three hundred pounds richer.

Now if he could just achieve that every day he would have an annual tax free income of about one hundred thousand pounds. Maybe, he thought, but there had been too many new dawns over the years for him to get very quickly carried away with one evening's success. He turned the pages of the paper quicker than usual, just stopping to read a couple of articles with predictions for the big Christmas races. He finished his breakfast and checked his watch. Time to be going.

Tom had dressed in a navy blazer and grey trousers that conveyed a smart but casual appearance. He had considered putting on his lucky suit but decided it was unnecessary as the interview should be straightforward.

There was a bounce to his step as he headed for his car. As he sat behind the wheel of his ten year old BWM he realised he could buy a new one if he wanted. He would have to make some further plans for the money from the paper. A holiday somewhere exotic would be high on the agenda.

Maybe Melanie would like to come away with him. Maybe he could visit her in the States and combine it with once again playing poker in Vegas. Now that would be interesting. Maybe she would introduce him to all her film star friends. He laughed out loud. Sure and maybe he would never gamble again! Too many maybes for one morning but life just keeps getting better, he thought to himself.

Sam had checked out of her hotel and retraced her steps to Brighton. She found a small and cheap hotel close to the seafront. It was more of a guest house actually than a hotel. She saw little point in being in London if Ashdown was in Brighton.

She had seen her brother's solicitor and he wanted his client to plead guilty to murder and attempted kidnapping in return for a life sentence with the chance of parole after twenty years. She knew there was no option, as pleading not guilty would be considered an expensive waste of the court's time and he would spend far longer in prison. Even though he hadn't pulled the trigger, he was equally as guilty in the law's eyes. In Sam's eyes though only one man was guilty.

She had made the call to Eduardo who had been very happy to hear from her. They had met probably a dozen times over the previous two years. Mostly she was taking messages between home and Eduardo. He was a good looking man in a tanned South American kind of way. Sam thought he was originally Colombian but he lived in Spain and travelled on a Spanish passport. He was about ten or possibly fifteen years older than her but he looked after himself and sleeping with him would be no hardship.

In fact the more she thought about the idea, the more it appealed. Eduardo was a wealthy and powerful man. He was used to getting what he wanted but had always treated her properly. They had enjoyed several dinners together in fine restaurants in Madrid and he had always behaved like a gentleman. He'd certainly been a lot less pushy than most of the men back home and he'd understood what No meant. Even so she'd always flirted a little and held out the promise that one day he might have a chance.

She had learned at a quite young age that boys and then men wanted her. She could use a smile to encourage and get what she wanted. She could deal with a man's bad mood by offering him sex. She could celebrate with a man by having sex. She knew she could often attract a man just by saying No to him. Men always wanted what they couldn't have. Once they had it, she had also learned that their interest could quickly diminish. She had used this knowledge to her advantage for several years and used it now with Eduardo.

She had spoken in riddles to avoid eavesdroppers but he understood what she needed was the name of someone in England, preferably London, who could supply her with a sufficient stash of cocaine for a very large party. She hadn't mentioned to Eduardo the specifics relating to Ashdown and how she planned to use the drugs. He knew from previous meetings, she wasn't much of a user but he didn't pry. When she explained she had no current access to funds to pay for the drugs, he had been very obliging. Her explanation that it would be considered a personal favour and she would repay him, left him in no doubt he would get the shag he had been after for so long.

He was at home in Spain when she called and announced he needed to make a business trip to England anyway and would take the next day's plane. He was obviously not planning to wait long for his repayment. She told him she was staying in Brighton but he decided to take a room at a central London hotel, as he would have a little business to attend to while in town. Sam assumed that meant getting his hands on the coke. Sam gave him her mobile number and told him to call her, as soon as he was settled into his hotel. She imagined they would then go together to collect the drugs. Sam thought it a more than reasonable trade.

After agreeing all the details to meet, Sam had an inspired thought and suggested that after her current business was finished she was thinking of spending a few days in Paris. It wasn't particularly subtle but Eduardo had immediately mentioned how much he enjoyed the George V in Paris and would free his calendar for a whole week, if she would like his company.

Sam knew the hotel well by reputation from her time as a student in Paris but had slept in cheap hostels and never been inside its doors. They'd walk pass on the Champs-Elysees and try to spot celebrities coming or going. She promised herself that one day she would return and stay there. The chance to see Paris with Eduardo, opened up all sorts of exciting opportunities. She had no doubt he would take her to expensive restaurants and nightclubs.

It would also give her a chance to practice her rusty French. She used her Spanish regularly but had spoken very little French since university. So she told Eduardo she would love to spend time in Paris with him but it should remain their secret. He understood that she would not want her family to know of their plans. As she finished the call she suddenly remembered how she had changed her appearance. She hoped Eduardo liked a brunette as much as blondes.

Sam knew it would be unwise to return to Ashdown's betting shop and it was too cold to be wandering the streets, so settled down to an evening in front of the television in her hotel room. When the local news followed the main evening news she was shocked to see Ashdown being interviewed.

A few minutes later she heard a knock on her door and got up to answer, expecting it to be the landlady who had been overly chatty when she arrived. She didn't recognise the man standing in front of her but immediately didn't like the look of him.

"Hello Samantha," Connor said with a glint in his eye. "How you doing?" He brushed past her as he entered the room without waiting for an invitation.

"Who the fuck are you?" Sam challenged. His accent had already told her he was bad news.

"I'm a friend of your father's. I'm here to see you come to no harm"

Sam was still standing by the door of her room. She had no intention of closing the door with this bastard now inside the room.

"I don't need babysitting, so why don't you piss off back where you came from."

"Now, now. That's no way to talk to a friend. Especially as I'm here to help."

"I don't need your help. And if you don't get out my room, I'm going to start screaming."

"Look, you aint going to get anywhere with Ashdown by yourself. If you wanna hurt him I'll help you. But you have to do as I say. Your Dad and the Chief are worried about you."

The reference to the Chief decided her to shut the door. That and the thought she recognized the intruder in her room but wasn't certain. "What's your name?" she asked.

"Connor. Brendan Connor." He smiled a knowing smile.

She knew him all right. Or at least knew of him. She'd seen him around a couple of times but never properly met him. Everyone back home though knew his reputation for violence. He was a man you didn't want to cross.

She sat in the only chair and he perched opposite on the edge of the bed. She didn't need or want his help. Especially not now Eduardo was on his way. She had to tread carefully though. She couldn't let on about Eduardo and neither did she want to wind Connor up.

"If you really want to help, then kill Ashdown for me," she said matter of factly.

"If I do will you promise to go straight back home?"

Sam was shocked Connor sounded serious. She hadn't really meant what she said. She was just testing him.

"Tonight," she added, knowing Eduardo was arriving tomorrow and wanting to get well away from Connor before then.

"You don't waste time," Connor replied. He was warming to the idea of disposing of Ashdown. He certainly had no problem in principle with getting rid of a bloody Brit. The Chief had said it was okay. And the sooner he did it the quicker the Murphy girl could go home. Not too quickly though. Face to face he liked what he saw. He wasn't going to be able to do anything about her brother for a while and once he did, she wouldn't come within a mile of him so best act now.

"Okay," he agreed. "If you promise me you go home to your father tomorrow, I'll take care of Ashdown tonight."

"I promise," she lied.

Miller was struggling to establish whom Maguire had met with prior to attacking Melanie Adams. He believed Murphy when he said he didn't know who it was. He wasn't the brightest guy and it was obvious Maguire was the leader. Miller was thinking that possibly Maguire had a mission being coordinated by the unidentified stranger but had impulsively decided that Melanie Adams was too easy and potentially rewarding a target to miss. Or maybe there was no other mission. Perhaps they were a new republican group that wanted funds to kick start a new campaign of violence.

There were no real firm clues and even Simpson's insights had been less useful than usual. What he had confirmed was that there was currently a lot of infighting between different factions of the IRA. Some of the diehards still saw disarming as a form of betrayal and were joining the likes of the Real IRA. Others seemed willing to go along with the idea at least for the time being. The likes of Maguire were more and more branching off into crime, which was hardly surprising, as they didn't possess the skills for anything else.

Simpson had promised to check his sources to try and establish whether Maguire and Murphy were part of any entirely new breakaway organization. Simpson's boss had agreed to him acting as liaison and described him as the obvious choice, given his experience.

While Miller agreed that was the case, he was sure that the man thought he would be getting one way feedback of information. Miller was happy to be working with Simpson again. He liked and trusted him. He expected him to play fair in his liaison role, whatever his boss thought.

Forensic reports had provided nothing of use, so for the time being the focus was on extracting everything possible from Murphy. Miller didn't believe it was likely any new break off group from the IRA was loose in London, intent on causing further trouble but it was his job to be vigilant. Murphy naively seemed to believe he was still a member of the IRA and just following orders passed down through Maguire.

They believed they had dragged as much as possible out of Murphy regarding the kidnap attempt and now he was being debriefed from the very beginning of his first steps in the IRA. Miller was interested in some specific information but the proper way to do this was to start at the beginning and not rush it. They also had to be sure that what they learned was reliable. They didn't want Murphy using this as an opportunity to resolve any personal grudges. There had been no amazing revelations yet but Miller was expecting better to come, the further forward they came in time.

The interviewing was mainly being carried out by Bob Thomas and Miller trusted Bob one hundred per cent. He had thirty years' experience, including time in Northern Ireland, in the early nineties, when times were really difficult. If there was something to be learned Bob, would get to the bottom of it. He was a blunt man brought up on a rough estate in South East London. Miller found him intimidating and was sure anyone he interviewed felt the same.

Miller always remembered one time, when he had described a very rough estate in Belfast, riddled with violence, as very similar to where he was brought up. Miller wondered what that childhood had been like. Very different he suspected to his own middle class upbringing.

Once Bob was finished with Murphy, Miller would have a further meeting with him, to see if he could find out something about Brian

Potter's death. He was too young to have been personally involved but his father was high on the list of suspects. Miller was hoping his son may have overheard some useful snippet of information. Maybe even something he didn't realize was significant. Often in policing, it was a case of putting together the tiniest scraps of information that led to solving cases.

Miller decided it might be worth meeting personally with Ashdown. He didn't believe it very likely he'd learn anything new but he liked to hear things first hand. Reports were all very well but you couldn't beat hearing it directly from the horse's mouth. It was as much how someone said something as what they said. He would set up a meeting for the next day. If necessary he could travel down to Brighton.

Any reason to get out the office was always welcome nowadays and a visit to Brighton would bring back mixed memories. He remembered the late nights and extra shifts that had followed the bombing of the Grand Hotel in Brighton in 1984. The IRA had tried to kill Margaret Thatcher while the Conservative Party Conference was taking place. She had narrowly survived but five people were killed and many injured.

It took them a year to track down and arrest Patrick Magee the bomber. Of course Magee had been released in 1999 as part of the Good Friday Agreement, which granted early release to paramilitary prisoners. Miller had understood the need for a radical gesture, to help win the support of the wider community for the agreement, but even so it troubled him that someone who killed five people should be released so early. That was the problem with Ireland. Everything about it was complex and confused. Nothing was straight forward and to a man of simple ideals, it caused chaos with his value system.

Miller had watched and admired Thatcher's speech at the conference the next day. He fully supported her assertion that all attempts to destroy democracy by terrorism will fail. Sadly though he had learned that many people can suffer before terrorists learn that, in the words of Abraham Lincoln, the ballot is stronger than the bullet!

Jones was parked about fifty yards along and across the road from his target's Georgian style town house, waiting for him to leave for his regular Wednesday night assignation. On three occasions in the last month Jones had surveyed the house to verify the information he had obtained was correct and each time the target had kept to the same timetable.

It was early evening and cold enough to freeze hell over but Jones was happy that he was not only finally going to get rid of the bloody man but thanks to his blackmailers they had provided the perfect cover for a scapegoat. This would be a good night's work.

His anger at the men in Dublin was replaced by smug satisfaction. There was a worry he should have to be personally carrying out the job, as it had been a long time since his days as an operative but necessity dictated he act. The target was part of a plot against the service that had been hatched in Whitehall, by politicians who didn't have a clue about security. He had given a lifetime to the country's security and wasn't going to let some fools temporarily elected to office, simply because of the incompetence of the previous government, destroy his service. They would be out of office again at the next election and with them would go the foolhardy vision of a single security service. Tonight would lend extra credence to the view that there was a new breakaway faction of the IRA, responsible not only for the attack on Melanie Adams but also tonight's events. Maguire's death and the subsequent meeting with the Irishman had indeed been quite fortunate.

It was a well-lit road and Jones had a clear view of the house, which backed onto an exclusive area of Regent's Park. Although he knew where his target would be headed and could have lain in wait there for him, he preferred to check there was no last minute change of plan that sent him elsewhere. A sudden desire to eat out or go to the theatre was unlikely but Jones always allowed for the unexpected. It was one of the factors that made him so good at his work. It was also true to say that he was meticulous in his work because the result of getting it wrong was inevitably very bad for his health and could even be terminal.

Jones had an unobstructed view of the entire road and had easily spotted the two policemen assigned as the target's protection. They were sitting in an unmarked car immediately in front of the house and Jones knew they would be armed. It wasn't the front door though that held his attention. From where he was parked, he could observe the road that ran along the side of the house. A door in the garden wall opened and the familiar figure hurriedly emerged and climbed in an inconspicuous Ford car. He turned on the engine and quickly pulled away and headed down the side road, in the opposite direction to his two police protectors, still parked out front none the wiser.

Jones followed in his Saab at a discreet distance, ensuring the target was indeed headed in the expected direction. He found it amusing that someone should choose to elude his protection, in order to gratify his lust for a girl half his age.

Jones understood that people in power no longer felt they could trust the police, servants or anybody not to sell the story of an indiscretion to the highest bidder. Even so, Jones found it hard to fathom why in the first place a man in such a position, with a wife and family, should want to risk everything for some momentary pleasure. Even as the thought occurred, he winced at the obvious similarity to his own situation. What he had originally paid for his pleasures was minor compared to the subsequent blackmail. They were both driven by their sexual desires. For the moment he was grateful that his target's weakness for young flesh afforded an easy opportunity for the job in hand.

By the time he'd followed the Ford down Park Lane and turned right towards Knightsbridge, Jones was feeling fairly confident there was to be no change from the usual routine. Sure enough, the target turned into Cadogan Gardens and Jones hung back, not wanting to arouse suspicion and now knowing for certain where they were headed.

Jones found a convenient place to park, a short way from the tiny mews where his target rented the small pied-a-terre, he kept especially for these occasions. By the time Jones walked to the entrance to the mews, there was no sign of anyone but he could see the red Ford as expected, parked outside number five.

The need to move quickly had limited his options when planning how to carry out his plan. He could not afford to lift the bonnet of the car and risk being spotted, so he had settled for a remote controlled device.

He checked nobody was present in the poorly lit mews and placing his bag on the ground, he bent down to tie his shoe lace. He took one more look around, then took the bomb from his bag and swiftly attached it, by its magnet, to the underside of the car on the driver's side.

He was back up on his feet in less than ten seconds. He picked up the empty bag and glanced around one final time as he hurried from the mews, checking as best he could that no one had been observing his actions from their window.

Jones had to wait an hour and a half, before he noticed the front door of number five open about a foot. He didn't want to run his engine and risk attracting attention, so had become progressively colder as he sat waiting. The target's head finally appeared and glanced up and down the mews, presumably to check it was clear. Jones had managed to repark his Saab directly opposite the entrance to the mews and it was from there he was able to watch the undignified haste, employed by his target, to reach his car. There was no sign of the girl he had been visiting. No farewell kiss on the doorstep or wave to an upstairs window.

Jones was faintly amused that the man went to such lengths to protect his reputation, while being so lapse about his personal security. He was worried about photographers not bombers. Jones didn't dwell long on the thought. Once the man was behind the wheel of the Ford, Jones shattered the calm of the mews by turning the car into a blazing yellow and orange inferno, which hurtled jagged pieces of metal and splinters of glass, to all corners of the mews. He didn't hang around to check what he knew to be inevitable. The distinguished career of Lord Bancroft had been brought to a premature end.

Tom was at Brighton station at five to seven. He had left his car at home and taken a ten minute bus ride into town, planning to get a taxi home. There had been no heating on the bus and he was again very grateful for his new coat and the scarf he was wearing.

The gritters were out again and the forecast was the cold weather was here to stay. There had been a brief flurry of snow earlier but it wasn't yet settling. At least not in Brighton. The news was showing deep snow in the north of the country. The odds in his shop on snow on Christmas day, were the shortest he could ever remember them being. Even so he had a spring in his step and was in a good mood as he walked from the bus stop to the station.

Colin's train was on time and as he emerged from the ticket barrier he gave a broad smile when he recognized Tom. In fact Colin was unusually ebullient in his greeting. As Tom prepared to shake Colin's hand, he found himself instead being enveloped in little short of a bear hug.

Tom assessed that his brother was at least thirty pounds heavier and being a couple of inches shorter, it was evident he spent more time at a desk than in the gym. He had the same blue eyes and brown hair as Tom, though it was worn shorter and not yet showing any signs of greying. Tom doubted anyone would easily identify them as brothers from their looks. He being tall and slim. Colin shorter and stockier.

There was a sincerity in Colin's, "it's good to see you" that took Tom by surprise. He wasn't used to such overt expressions of emotion from Colin. Indeed, Tom had sometimes wondered whether Colin felt any emotion at all or was just the result of some complex computer program.

"That's a hell of a shiner you have," Colin laughed.

Tom touched the bridge of his nose. He knew the bruises had turned a bright blue and yellow and were quite a souvenir. "Looks worse than it feels luckily," was a response he was getting used to giving.

Tom had given a lot of thought to where to eat. He had finally decided on Brighton's best known fish restaurant because he remembered Colin had quite often ordered fish in the past, when they went out. It didn't have any Michelin stars and the décor was a bit dated but it used fresh fish and was always reliable. Tom would have preferred Thai but he knew Colin wasn't a fan of spicy food. He thought that might again be the influence of Liz. He was sure she would consider eating Thai as somehow debauched. It was a short ten minute walk to the restaurant and they agreed to save all storytelling until they were seated comfortably out the cold.

They shared a bottle of dry white wine while considering the menu and it was evident to Tom that his brother was up for a good night out. Probably because he wasn't often allowed off the leash for a night on the town, Tom thought.

He would have liked to have eavesdropped when Colin announced to Liz that his worthless gambler of a brother had saved Melanie Adams's life and they were going out to celebrate. By now she must have read the newspapers and seen the news on television so would have to accept for fact it was true and he was not so useless after all.

Tom ordered six Lindisfarne Oysters to start, followed by Sea Bass and on his recommendation, Colin followed suit. Tom explained that the Lindisfarne oyster farm lies on the site of the oyster beds established in 1381 by the monks of Lindisfarne priory, so they would be eating a bit of history. Colin was impressed by Tom's history lesson until he admitted he was reading it from the menu.

They finished their second bottle of wine half way through the main course and so ordered a third. The wine seemed to loosen Colin's normally rather conservative manner and he was genuinely enthralled to hear Tom recount, in great detail, the events of the past few days. Tom noticed that every time he mentioned Melanie's name, his brother seemed to be extra interested. Colin admitted to being a fan of her films. He seemed able to conceive that Tom had acted bravely in rescuing Melanie but he was overcome by the notion that Tom was now on first name terms with her and they had actually sat and eaten dinner and breakfast together. Tom assured him he was not inventing anything and then had what he considered to be a brilliant idea.

"I'll tell you what," Tom said. "Why don't I call her and you can say hello."

"You are joking?"

Tom reached into his pocket for his phone and found the number she had given him to her private mobile. He watched Colin observe in a state of shock, mixed with disbelieving, as he pressed the call button. He was showing off a bit but what the hell. He didn't often get to impress his younger brother. And it gave Tom the perfect excuse just to hear Melanie's voice.

"Hi Melanie. Hope I'm not disturbing you?" Tom hoped he wasn't slurring his words.

"Of course not. How are you?" She sounded genuinely pleased to hear from him. "I thought you were having dinner with your brother tonight."

"Actually I am." Tom looked across at Colin who was looking very sheepish. "He's quite a fan of yours so I thought it would be nice if you could just say hello to him. I'll put him on."

Tom thrust the phone at his brother. "Melanie wants to say hello."

Colin took the phone like it was a hot coal. He slowly put it up to his ear and said a weak, "Hello."

Tom watched as Colin muttered how much he liked her films. He seemed a bit lost for words and after a minute said how nice it was to speak to her and goodbye. He handed the phone back to Tom who spent a couple of minutes asking about her day and reminded her about his racing invitation, before wishing her a good night.

"I just spoke to Melanie Adams," Colin said, when Tom ended the call. "I can't believe it."

Tom was smiling. He understood how his brother felt. Just a few days earlier he would have thought the idea equally absurd.

Tom eventually managed to change the subject from Melanie and they spoke of their childhoods and their parents. Tom realised that they were discussing subjects they had never previously done. Conversation over most of their occasional dinners was very shallow, never exploring emotions or the past. He wasn't sure why that was the case but in one evening he felt closer to his brother than ever before.

By the time they staggered from the restaurant, Colin was in no fit state to put on a train, if indeed there was still one running. For his own part, Tom found the freezing night air helped make him quickly feel more sober. He suspected Colin rarely drank as much as he had this evening and the effect was quite funny.

He found Liz's number and called to let her know Colin had decided to stay over, as he was a bit the worse for wear. She did not receive this news well and demanded to speak with Colin, who was standing there waving his hands dismissively to suggest he did not want to talk to her. He also seemed to have a fit of the giggles like a naughty schoolboy.

Tom explained to Liz in the least slurred voice he could manage that Colin was in the Gents and he would give him the message to call but in all honesty Colin was looking very tired and quite likely to fall asleep in the taxi, on the way home. Tom tried to tell Liz not to worry because he would be sure to get Colin safely to bed but her final words were that he should tell Colin to phone or else! Exactly what the "or else" would be, Tom wasn't at all sure but was certain it would be horribly unpleasant.

Tom decided further conversation was pointless and said a cheerful goodnight and ended the call. He could imagine Liz seething at the other end of the phone. She already viewed him as the devil incarnate and wouldn't forget this in a hurry. How Colin lived with her was completely beyond Tom's comprehension. Then again he knew from personal experience that ninety per cent of couples seemed an unlikely match.

There was a taxi rank right outside the restaurant and the driver of the first in line looked less than keen given the state of his passengers. Tom's assurance Colin wouldn't be sick in the car, barely seemed to dispel the driver's fears but Tom guessed it was a quiet night for business, so they eventually made it into the back seat. Tom wound down the window and within seconds Colin was asleep, his head falling against Tom's shoulder.

Tom felt quite brotherly for the first time in a very long time. He struggled getting Colin out of the car and half carried him to the front door of the house. Tom propped his brother against the wall and fumbled in his pocket for his keys. Colin started to slide down the wall and Tom grabbed him under his arms while holding the door open with his foot. Somehow Tom managed to get Colin inside and support him as they climbed the stairs to his bedroom.

"Sorry," Colin apologized for the umpteenth time, as Tom laid him down on the bed.

"Don't worry about it. Sleep it off and I'll see you in the morning."

Tom closed the bedroom door on an already snoring Colin. Over dinner while drinking the second bottle of wine and knowing they would inevitably have more before the end of the evening, Tom had checked with Colin whether he had to get into the office early in the morning. Fortunately, given the state Colin was in, he had confirmed he was working from home the next day and wouldn't need to be up early for a change.

Back downstairs, Tom was not yet ready for bed. A few drinks usually led to him feeling like a visit to the Casino down at the nearby Marina. He could see no harm in going out for a couple of hours. There was no chance of Colin waking but in case he did Tom went back up stairs and turned on the landing light, so he would easily find the bathroom. Tom prayed Colin would at least make it to the bathroom if he felt sick in the night.

Tom called a taxi and not much more than twenty minutes later was seated at a table playing Blackjack. Tom liked casinos. Gambling at home was sometimes more convenient but nothing can beat the atmosphere of a casino. He was a regular visitor and greeted warmly by all the staff. He always felt at home in a Casino. It was like being part of a brotherhood of gamblers and the Casino was where they came together to meet.

He would play without any stress and enjoy himself for a couple of hours. Maybe when Colin left in the morning, he would slip a business card or something inside Colin's jacket that suggested he'd visited the den of iniquity with Tom. Or even better would be a card from one of the town's lap dancing clubs that he occasionally visited. That would really make Liz mad and Tom was quite sure she was the sort of woman who would go through Colin's pockets, when he returned home. Better not, he thought. Colin doesn't deserve that and I'm growing to quite like having a brother.

Connor had left the girl in her hotel room and gone out for a couple of drinks. He'd invited her along but she'd refused. She was treating him like a bad smell and getting right up his nose. He'd told her he was staying with her until he saw her back on a plane to Belfast. That meant he was spending the night in her room. She'd told him in no uncertain terms not to get any ideas. He pointed out he would be working half the night doing her a favour and she should watch her lip, or he might just bundle her straight back home.

When he returned to the room, she was lying stretched out on the bed watching television. At least she hadn't done a bunk the first moment she was able. She was obviously serious about getting Ashdown. He had thought about taking her with him later but on balance decided it was better to leave her in the room, while he was working. He tried being nice but the bitch wasn't interested. She wasn't going to open her legs for him no matter what he did to Ashdown. He felt tempted to take her anyway but she would probably go running to the Chief or her father and that could lead to real trouble.

He took a shower and when he returned to the bedroom with just a towel wrapped around his waist she again ignored his attempts at friendly conversation. He had a couple of hours to kill before he planned to visit Ashdown's home. He knew how he would like to fill the time. He went to lie on the bed beside her but soon as she realized his intention, she shot up from the bed like a scalded cat.

"What you think you're doing, "she snapped. "I told you, no funny business."

"I was just getting comfortable to watch some telly."

"Well get fucking comfortable with some clothes on."

The towel wasn't tied very securely around his waist. He got up from the bed and intentionally let it fall as he crossed the room towards the bathroom. He met her eyes with a smile but she immediately averted his gaze and turned her back on him.

Connor dressed and when he returned to the room, found Sam had moved a chair to in front of the television, where she was now sitting. He hadn't really wanted to watch television, just to lie next to her and the small room was now getting claustrophobic with her playing the ice maiden.

He fancied another drink but there was no mini bar, so decided to go down to the small hotel bar. No point in asking the girl if she wanted to come. He wouldn't normally drink much before a job. After a job that was different. He'd have to get a bottle of scotch from the bar to take back up his room, so he could have a drink after his work was done. He'd had two pints earlier in the evening and reckoned a couple of whiskies now wouldn't hurt. Anyway, he needed warming up. The bloody girl had made the room seem almost as cold as outside with her frigidness.

The Prime Minister, flanked by the Home Secretary, walked out of number ten to confront the press. Despite the late hour, the media was out in force and the bright lights of television crews, from several continents, illuminated the darkness, creating an unreal atmosphere.

As the PM arrived at the lectern, set up in front of the ranks of assembled press, he was met with an expectant silence, similar to that a famous conductor receives when he walks to his podium. He had a short and hurriedly prepared statement to read but first he spoke with emotion of how personally sad and shocked he was, by the news of the death of Lord Bancroft. The lies rolled easily off his tongue.

The statement was unimaginative and factual, reporting the explosion and confirming what everybody already knew, namely that the cause had been a bomb. The PM's voice managed to quiver with false anger, as he promised that those responsible would be found and brought to justice, although no one had yet claimed credit for the atrocity. He also stressed that these terrorist actions would not be allowed to thwart the aims of the government, to fight terrorism wherever in the world it was found.

Finally, he paid a brief tribute to Bancroft's contribution to government and especially his time as Minister for Northern Ireland. A barrage of questions from journalists was met with nothing more than an announcement that he was unable to take any questions. Even so, one female journalist, in receipt of an anonymous telephone call, did shout out and ask what was Bancroft doing at the place of the explosion? The PM simply ignored the question and withdrew back into number ten.

"What was he doing there?" the Home Secretary asked, once back inside.

"Seems he was up to his old tricks. He was having a bloody affair with a girl thirty years younger." The PM managed to sound incredulous. "God knows what women ever saw in him!"

"The press will have a field day," the Home Secretary remarked thoughtfully.

"Just promise me you never follow in his footsteps." The PM replied.

The Home Secretary looked aghast at the idea. He was a happy family man. "His poor wife..."

"She should have left him after the first time," the PM interjected. Then, realising the lack of sympathy he'd displayed, added rather tritely, "It's always the innocent who suffer."

In truth the PM was angered more by the fact he would have to change his plans. Bancroft had been pushing to bring together the various security and intelligence services under one umbrella and had been earmarked to be head of the new organization. It was an idea that appealed to the PM. He wanted some control of the spooks who seemed to think they were a law unto themselves. Now he would be back at square one, as there were few viable candidates for such a role.

"There'll be a large cry of bring back hanging," the Home Secretary observed. "Something like this almost makes me in favour."

"I've a better idea. Let's hope the SAS find those responsible." Seeing the uncertain look on his Home Secretary's face the PM added, "I'm only joking, Phillip."

"Of course, Prime Minister," the Home Secretary acknowledged but didn't sound entirely convinced.

"Is there any link between this and the attempt to kidnap Melanie Adams?" the PM asked.

"Well there is the Irish connection but with no one claiming any responsibility who knows. It could be a new cell operating over here."

The PM was already on the back foot with the economy but at least he could argue that was a global problem. Now he was going to be facing difficult questions about law and order. He couldn't believe his bad luck. The opposition would no doubt have a field day, blaming the recent budget cutbacks as undermining security operations but they would have an even better day when they learned, as they undoubtedly would, that Bancroft was having a further affair. The PM's credibility would be questioned for bringing him back into government, after the first time his affair had been plastered all over the front of newspapers.

"I need some concrete information," the PM demanded. "And quickly. We can't return to the old days of bombs going off all over the place. This could really hurt us in the polls."

CHAPTER SIX

Tom knew there was a problem, as soon as the taxi turned into his road. A handful of people were gathered on the pavement and a couple of uniformed policemen were keeping them back from the house. He felt an instant panic brought on by the fear of the unknown. He was sure something terrible had occurred but what? The taxi slowed to a halt.

"This yours?" the driver asked concerned.

Tom handed him a ten pound note and didn't wait for the change that was due. As he hurried from the car, heads were turned in his direction and knowing whispers exchanged. Tom knew most of them but he headed straight for the nearest policeman and introduced himself, enquiring what had happened.

"Could you come with me please, Sir," the policeman instructed politely and turned towards the house.

"What's happened?" Tom repeated as he followed. "Where's my brother?"

The policeman looked long in the tooth to still be a constable and he obviously knew his place in the hierarchy. It wasn't his job to deliver bad news and Tom realised he wasn't going to prise anything from him.

"They'll be able to answer all your questions inside, Sir," the policeman smiled, patiently.

Tom imagined several different scenarios all equally disturbing as he followed the policeman through his front door. He knew with certainty that only a very serious incident would attract so many police and he offered up a silent prayer nothing had happened to Colin.

"Just wait here a moment, Sir," the policeman instructed, once inside.

Tom felt strange standing in his own hallway, watching strangers hurrying about his home. The lack of any sign of his brother was a worry. Where was Colin? He hadn't been outside. Why hadn't he come to meet him?

Two men appeared from the direction of his lounge. "I'm Chief Inspector Parkin," the older of the two men announced and shook Tom by the hand. He was about fifty years of age wearing a nondescript grey suit that didn't quite fit around his large belly. He was bald, unshaven and Tom guessed had been called from his bed in the middle of this night. There was a look of recognition in his eyes. It was a reaction Tom had come to expect over the last couple of days.

"This is Sergeant Grant." Parkin waved a hand in the general direction of the second man. He was much younger, probably no more than thirty, with a slim build and he stood with his hands nonchalantly in his pockets.

"Can you please tell me what's going on?" Tom asked. "And where's my brother?"

"I'm afraid there's been a serious incident. Your brother has been taken to hospital, along with Mr Harding."

Tom was confused. The questions all flowed at once. "What kind of incident? How bad is Colin hurt? And why is John Harding involved?"

"Best as we can work it out, it seems Mr Harding spotted someone sneaking around the back of your house. We learned that from his wife. He called the police and then rather foolishly came across here to see if you needed help. His wife says he brought his baseball bat with him."

Tom listened in silent shock. John Harding lived directly across the road and ran the local neighbourhood watch scheme. Tom remembered ignoring him just the other day when he was getting in his car and said he was in too much of a hurry to speak. He felt bad about that now.

John was a decent man of about sixty five who had once been in the army and retired a few years earlier. He carried out his neighbourhood watch duties with diligence and enthusiasm. On more than one occasion he'd spotted Tom had left his car lights on and come across to tell him, saving him having to wake to a flat battery in the morning. He was also the man you could turn to when you wanted someone to keep an eye on the house while you were on holiday.

Chief Inspector Parkin continued, "When we arrived we found Mr Harding lying on the kitchen floor. He'd been shot twice. We found another man, whom I now assume is your brother at the top of the stairs. He too had been shot. This is pure conjecture but it's possible Mr Harding disturbed the intruder, probably thinking him a common thief, and was shot. The commotion brought your brother out of his bed and he was shot before the man made his getaway."

Tom gasped at the news his brother had been shot. He wasn't sure he wanted to know the answer to his next question. "Chief Inspector, how is Colin?"

"Your brother is seriously ill but alive. The bullet appears to have entered his chest but I can't tell you any more than that. Mr Harding I'm afraid, died in the ambulance on the way to hospital."

Tom was dazed and bewildered by the news. Before last Friday he'd never seen or known anyone shot. Now in the course of a very short space of time there seemed to be shootings and bodies all around him.

"Why?" was all Tom could think to ask.

"It's too early to speculate but in view of your recent involvement in a shooting in London, I think we have to consider they may be linked."

Tom's shoulders slumped and he put his hand to the wall to steady himself. "Are you saying the gunman was after me?"

"It's a strong possibility. Unless you can offer some other explanation?" Parkin replied.

Tom knew the Chief Inspector was correct in his assumption. Even if Colin had enemies, which Tom was sure he didn't, they wouldn't have attacked him in Tom's house. He seemed to have become a magnet for trouble.

"I guess they must have been after me," Tom agreed. "Nothing else makes any sense. Was it some sort of revenge attack for what I did in London?"

"It's too early to say for certain but that would be my first thought. By the way, might I ask where you've been tonight?"

"I've been at the Casino at the Marina." It was a simple statement of fact but led Tom to feel a huge surge of guilt that he'd been playing poker while his brother was shot. Had the gunman confused Colin for himself? If he'd stayed at home John Harding might also not be dead.

"What time did you go out?" Parkin probed gently.

"Colin and I went out for a meal earlier. I brought him back home a bit the worse for wear and put him to bed about eleven. Then I went out to the Casino."

Tom noticed the second policeman had removed his hands from his pockets and was writing his answers in a note book.

"If you'll excuse me now Chief Inspector I need to get down the hospital to check on my brother."

"Of course, Sir. I'll have one of my officers take you. We can speak again tomorrow."

A policeman in plain clothes suddenly hurried up to Parkin and whispered in his ear.

Parkin turned back to Tom. "Sergeant Grant will organise your lift for you. We've had an anonymous tip off that just might lead us to the gunman." Without further explanation Parkin turned and was gone.

Sam waited in the room unable to sleep and wanting to know how Connor had got on. It was just past two thirty in the morning and she had resigned herself to the thought of spending the rest of an uncomfortable night, once he did return, getting a little sleep on the bathroom floor. She didn't trust that pig Connor to behave and at least the bathroom had a door she could lock.

Right now though she was watching a boring film on television while her mind travelled to the idea of Paris with Eduardo. She would make the most of the chance to spend a week in a five star hotel at someone else's expense. And she was sure he would take her shopping when she pointed out she had nothing suitable to wear to a smart restaurant. She'd buy a beautiful dress and some nice shoes and enjoy some five star luxury. And then she would drink champagne and go to bed with Eduardo.

She wondered what he would be like as a lover. Would he be kinky and demanding? It was a thought that sent a tingle through her body and her hand slid down between her thighs. She stroked herself with her fingers on top of her jeans and then undid the zip. She slid two fingers inside her panties and felt the moisture that signalled her desire. She laughed and forced herself to stop. She didn't want Connor coming back and finding her in the midst of playing with herself. It would be like rocket fuel to his libido. She fastened her jeans and lay back with her hands behind her head.

The anticipation of Eduardo was sufficient excitement for now. She didn't doubt for a second that he would give her what she wanted. Maybe after their time in Paris he would even invite her to go back to Spain with him and just maybe she would accept. After all, Belfast only offered the likes of Connor.

Sam heard the key turn in the lock and knew Connor was back. She jumped up from the bed excited by the anticipation of his news and stood facing him as he entered. He ignored her and went straight for the bottle of whisky he'd left on the table.

"So...?" she asked impatiently.

Connor took a large swig from the bottle and wiped his sleeve across his lips before responding.

"Ashdown's history."

He took another large swig of whisky. He wasn't going to tell the bitch it hadn't gone entirely according to plan. Anyway, at least he had got Ashdown. Who the fuck the other bloke was who attacked him with the baseball bat, he didn't know or really care.

"How?" Sam asked simply.

"Don't fucking matter how."

Sam didn't like Connor but she was pleased with the news. With Ashdown out the way she would have to apologise to Eduardo for him wasting his trip and promise to make it up to him. She smiled at the thought of what that would entail. She would be able to lose Connor the next morning at the airport if not before. Then it would be straight to London to see Eduardo.

"Fancy a bit of that, do you?" Connor leered, interrupting her thoughts.

Sam followed his gaze to the television screen. A naked bum was moving up and down at a rapid rate that was causing the young woman underneath on the ground, to make loud appreciative noises. Connor's gaze was now fixed firmly on the screen and the late night movie that was playing.

Sam hoped he wasn't going to become a nuisance. She tried ignoring him.

"I forgot. I'm not good enough for you," Connor sneered.

"Piss off," she said, as she made to head for the security of the bathroom.

He lunged for her and grabbed her arm, pulling her down beside him on the bed. She twisted and lashed out with her feet and hands but he covered her with his much larger body, making it impossible for her to escape.

"The more you fight, the more I like it," Connor warned.

He had hold of her wrists and there was no way she could escape, so she gave up struggling and lay limp under his weight. She could smell the whisky on his breath as he leaned close to kiss her. She turned her head to the side trying to avoid his lips, then suddenly relaxed and turned back, smiling encouragingly. For a second he thought he'd won, then she spat venomously straight into his face. His jaw fell open, then he composed himself and didn't even bother wiping away the spittle running down his cheek. He smiled and she knew then that she was in deep trouble. He hit her with an open palm hard across her face.

"You'll regret that, bitch. I was just going to play with you a bit but not now. Not after that."

She thought about screaming but knew it wasn't an option. She'd brought this on herself and was just going to have to get through it. He wouldn't enjoy it. She wouldn't fight him. She'd just lie and do nothing like a statue. She closed her eyes to avoid looking at him and felt his hand crushing her left breast. The other hand was already roughly pulling open the buttons on her jeans.

Her own hands were now free but she was resigned to the inevitable. There was no point in fighting and provoking him further. He pushed his hand up under her T-shirt and freed one breast. His lips covered her nipple and she hated the way it responded of its own accord by becoming hard and erect.

She was just grateful he wasn't trying to kiss her on the lips anymore. If he put his fucking tongue in her mouth, she was going to bite it off. He had his hand between her thighs and her dryness made her cry out when he tried to thrust two fingers inside her.

"Wait," she pleaded. "Not like this. You're hurting. You can have me properly if you take it slowly."

He looked into her eyes. "No games," he said hoarsely. "Or I swear I'll kill you."

"Take my trousers off," she said quietly. She'd never felt so degraded in her life but her only thought was of the revenge she'd extract. For now she had to get through this with the minimum damage. She doubted it would take long for him to finish. In five minutes it will all be over. Then she would make him pay for a very long time, for his few minutes of pleasure.

He climbed off the bed and standing at her feet pulled her jeans down off her ankles. She pushed her knickers halfway down her legs and he finished the job. She didn't bother removing her top.

He was already erect and to Sam he looked absurd standing there, still wearing his shirt and socks but she didn't feel like laughing.

"On your hands and knees," he commanded. He undid his shirt buttons and removed it while leering at her.

So you like it doggy style Sam thought. That suits me. I won't have to look at your bastard leering face. She did as instructed but he didn't move behind her as she had expected. Instead he moved in front of her. The truth dawned on her what he wanted. She wasn't as tough as she liked to pretend. She couldn't go through with this. Anything was suddenly preferable.

"Please don't," she begged. "I can't..." Her voice tailed off. She could see the anger in his face.

She sat back on her hips before turning away to try and clamber from the bed. He grabbed for her hips and pulled her back toward him. She tried to break his grip but he was too strong and she heard him utter a sound between laughter and a snort of derision.

She fought to control her fear and distaste for him. She knew the more she resisted he was likely to enjoy forcing her and the end result would in any case be the same. Anyway, she'd lost the strength to continue fighting. She just wanted this over. She felt her arse being raised off the bed and realised he did after all intend to take her doggy style, while he remained standing at the end of the bed. She could cope with that. It was impersonal. It was what she had been ready to accept originally. She fought unsuccessfully to stem the tears and assumed the position he wanted. She felt his hand on her breasts again and then it was stroking her face. Suddenly his hand covered her mouth and she felt at the same instant the pressure from the arm around her middle, pulling her back onto him.

"This will teach you not to fuck with me," he whispered, leaning forward against her ear.

For a second she was filled with panic he intended to try and fuck her in the arse. It was something she had only experienced a couple of times but it was sufficient experience to understand the potential it offered him to hurt her.

She relaxed a fraction when she realized it wasn't his intention but she still didn't want him and her body didn't want him. He took several stabs before he pushed his way into her. Her dryness made it hurt like hell. After the initial shock, followed wave upon wave of further pain and indignation as he cruelly and relentlessly assaulted her body. She emitted muffled sobs and grunts each time he buried himself to the hilt inside her. When finally he'd finished he withdrew and she sank to the bed.

"Like that, did you?" he said grinning.

She rolled onto her side, tucked into a foetal position and cried like she'd never cried before in her life.

After a couple of minutes, somewhere in a corner of her mind she registered the sound of running water. It was a bath filling up. She opened her eyes and saw with great clarity what she must do. She heard the taps turned off, followed by the sound of a large body entering the bath. She forced herself to get up off the bed, although her legs almost buckled under her when she tried to stand.

She moved weakly to the cupboard and took out her small suitcase. She quickly threw her few clothes inside. Feeling nauseous she sat herself down once more on the edge of the bed. She took a few large breaths. She could hear Connor splashing around in the bath. She dressed in the clothes he'd made her remove.

She was feeling stronger. A wry smile crossed her lips. It was over. Practically speaking it hadn't been a much different physical experience to some others in her past. Fortunately on this occasion, he was as crap and quick as other men she had known. But she had offered those other men her body. This evil bastard was going to pay for taking her uninvited.

"We'll have some more in the morning," he shouted from the bath.

"Fuck off," she answered, just so he knew she was still there.

"Thanks but I've done enough fucking for a while," he laughed at his own joke.

After a moment's silence she moved quietly to the door. She was out the room and hurrying down the wooden stairs half expecting him to give chase. But she heard no sound of Connor behind her. He was both arrogant and stupid. Had he really expected her to stay in the room to be abused again, whenever he felt like it?

As she reached her car, she remembered he would be naked when he came out the bathroom and that would give her a few extra minutes to escape, while he dressed. She drove away uncertain which direction to head and then settled for the one route she knew, which was towards the centre of town. There wasn't much traffic and she felt conspicuous. She didn't fancy being stopped by the police, even though she hadn't been drinking or directly committed any crime.

She drove for ten minutes to put distance between herself and Connor, then turned into a side street with cars parked down each side. She found what she wanted halfway along the street and spotted a small parking space just a few feet further up the road. She hurried to the telephone box, wishing she had worn more than the flimsy jacket that did little to keep out the cold weather. The door was heavy and stuck but she forced it open with her shoulder. The stench of urine was foul and she was careful where she stood. She gingerly lifted the receiver with little expectation of it working but at least with this small matter, luck was on her side tonight. She dialled 999.

Tom arrived at the hospital and introduced himself at the Accident and Emergency department. He was asked to take a seat and sat alone away from the handful of others that were waiting their turn for treatment to a variety of injuries. He stared at the large Christmas tree stood in one corner, which seemed an inappropriate reminder of what should be a season of celebration. Not many visitors to an Accident and Emergency department had much cause for rejoicing.

Tom had been a patient in this very department a couple of times in the distant past. Both times as a result of running injuries. An ankle with badly torn ligaments had needed bandaging and a cut lip had needed a couple of stitches. Nothing serious, certainly nothing to compare with being shot but he'd been well treated.

It was a teaching hospital with a good reputation but how many gunshot wounds would they see in a year? Would they have anyone with the experience needed to save Colin's life? He knew he must call Liz and let her know what had happened but first he wanted to establish Colin's condition. He would have liked to accept the policeman's offer to call her but it wouldn't have been right, just personally easier. She was family after all and deserved to hear from him not a stranger. It was going to be bad enough having to wake her in the middle of the night to tell her Colin had been shot but he was desperately hoping he was also going to be able to tell her not to worry and that her husband would live. Whatever he said though she was going to suffer a terrible shock.

Unfortunately, Janet Harding already had to face up to the rest of her life without her husband. Why had John been so reckless as to interfere? Why hadn't he just waited for the police to arrive and do their job? Then again, hadn't he been guilty of exactly the same foolish behaviour when he went to Melanie's aid. He'd probably saved her life and maybe John had saved Colin's.

Tom knew he didn't just want Colin to survive because he felt like he'd only just found his brother. The truth was he didn't fancy spending the rest of his life blaming himself for his brother's death. He should have known better. Life always had a habit of kicking you back down just when things seemed on an upward path.

After ten minutes of recriminating with himself, he returned to the reception desk to remind them he was still waiting to hear news. The nurse gave him a sour look and informed him someone would be there as soon as possible. Then she quickly went back to the papers on her desk, signalling their conversation was over. What did as soon as possible mean? It was a meaningless answer. It could be minutes or hours. He stood for a few seconds hoping his presence might elicit further information from the nurse but she didn't even bother looking up.

He went back to his seat and decided to give them a further ten minutes and then he would simply have to call Liz. She would never forgive him if she found out he hadn't bothered calling immediately even if his intentions were sound. Then again she was never going to forgive him either way.

He picked up an old magazine from the table in front of him and leafed through a few pages without really focusing on the contents. His mind was jumping all over the place but his thoughts were all linked by what had happened to his brother. He glanced around and noticed the sign on the wall forbidding the use of mobile phones. He was going to get cold when it came to making the call.

Tom was getting restless in his chair and repeatedly looking at his watch. It had been nearly fifteen minutes since his last confrontation with the nurse. He had been more firm in his request for information but had met the same brick wall response. He noticed a rather distinguished looking man walk up to nurse no information, exchange a few words and then she pointed in Tom's direction.

"Mr Ashdown?" the man asked as he came near. He was in his early fifties and the stethoscope around his neck identified him as a doctor. Now he was closer Tom could see the dark bags under his eyes that spoke of too many long hours. The fact he was wearing a suit rather than a gown suggested he would be a consultant.

"I'm John Seymour," the man said. Tom jumped to his feet and shook the outstretched hand. "I'm about to operate on your brother."

"How is he?"

"I'm afraid it's too early to say. He's lost a lot of blood but the x-rays show the bullet has missed his heart. We've spent the last half an hour stabilizing him. Until I open him up I can't see the full extent of the damage. Does he have any medical history I should be aware of?"

Tom looked at him blankly.

"Is he allergic to anything?" Seymour prompted.

"No nothing as far as I know. I don't remember him ever being in hospital before."

"Good. I'll come back soon as I've finished operating." He turned to leave.

"What are his chances?" Tom persisted.

The consultant turned back and looked Tom straight in the eye. "As I said, until I open him up I can't be sure of anything. His vital signs are very weak but he has a fighting chance. I can't say better than that. Now I must be going."

Tom breathed a sigh of relief. They didn't sound like the best odds but what was a fighting chance. Was it thirty percent; forty percent? The doctor would surely have erred on the side of caution not wanting to build his hopes too high in case it all went pear shaped. At least Colin was alive and there was real hope. He had to trust in the doctors.

Tom glanced around and located a coffee machine. He helped himself to a disgusting tasting very sweet cappuccino and went outside to telephone Liz. He shivered from the change of temperature. He wished it could be Melanie he was calling but she would undoubtedly be asleep and it didn't seem fair to wake her. He really wanted to talk to her right now and hear what he knew for certain would be a supportive voice. He was equally as certain as he pressed the buttons for Liz's number that she would blame him for Colin's situation and perhaps fairly so. At least he could confirm Colin was alive and in good hands. It was going to be a long night.

Miller was woken from his bed by the call to inform him firstly of the shootings in Brighton and then of the anonymous tip off that had led them to a hotel room but no killer. He had only had a couple of hours sleep, as the earlier murder of Lord Bancroft had led to a large number of politicians running around like headless chickens, demanding answers without even yet really knowing the questions.

Miller was confused as he wiped the sleep from his eyes. He had a sudden spate of terrorist murders to contend with and he wasn't entirely sure if they were linked or not. There were superficial reasons to connect the shootings, namely the Irish link they shared but he was still far from certain that was the only significant factor at play.

He recalled the line from Goldfinger; Once is happenstance, Twice is coincidence, Three times is enemy action. Was there a bigger picture he couldn't see? The IRA was extremely unlikely to be responsible for Bancroft's death, given the current political climate and Sinn Fein's increased respectability. In the past all former Ministers for Northern Ireland would have been considered fair game for the rest of their lives but not any longer.

Since the IRA had decommissioned their weapons, and Sinn Fein shared government, the outlook for long-term peace in Ireland had never been more optimistic, despite the recent increase in violence from dissident groups. The optimism came more from the reactions of all politicians condemning the violence than actually solving the crimes. Sinn Fein had stood side by side with the Chief Constable and Unionists to demand an end to sectarian murders and attacks on the British army.

If the Irish link was important, as realistically it surely had to be, then it probably meant it was a renegade faction operating independently but so far no one had claimed responsibility, which was highly unusual. There was little point in carrying out these acts of violence to highlight a cause but then not linking the act to the cause. Miller preferred to know who he was dealing with. Then he could react and plan accordingly. An unknown enemy willing to create mayhem was very scary.

The security services were being of no help. Their focus on Irish terrorism was a fraction of what it had once been. Simpson was probably telling the truth when he said they had no leads. The proverbial was going to hit the fan if they didn't all come up with some answers fairly soon. And why this unknown enemy would choose to go after Ashdown was still a mystery. It seemed almost an act of personal revenge but Maguire was dead and Murphy locked up.

There were still more questions than answers but he suspected this probably wouldn't be the end of the trouble and that meant he better get used to not having much sleep. He would stop by the office for the latest news and then he really would have to head to Brighton and meet Ashdown. It had gone from an excuse to get out the office to essential. He'd also get the team to run a full background check on Ashdown. He seemed genuine enough but nothing could be left to chance.

It was about two hours after Tom phoned Liz that she came hurrying into the hospital. She spotted Tom and came towards him with an expression that to Tom defined the saying 'if looks could kill.' Tom had no doubt she was capable of doing him harm, should she have a weapon to hand.

"What have you done to my Colin?" she demanded. "Where are the police? Why haven't they arrested you?"

Sergeant Grant had made a visit to the hospital about an hour earlier and informed Tom he would be close at hand, as he was keen to question Colin as soon as he was awake. However, having spoken to the nurse on reception he had not been seen since. Tom assumed she had informed him there was little likelihood of questioning Colin any time in the near future.

Tom was keen not to fan the flames of Liz's anger further so he ignored her questions. "There's no news I'm afraid," he said gently. "The doctor is still operating."

She fell into the chair beside Tom's. She was a robust woman but she looked as if she was struggling to hold onto her emotions. The dam burst and she started to cry. She was not a woman Tom imagined who cried very often.

"What am I going to do if he doesn't recover?" she asked after a minute, without looking at Tom. She was dabbing at her eyes and nose with a handkerchief.

"Let's be positive," Tom replied, though he had been asking himself the very same question. By nature he was ever the optimist but that was being sorely tested and he wasn't truly convinced Colin would survive.

"It's all your fault," Liz said with renewed strength. "I always knew you'd lead him into trouble."

Tom had led one or two astray over the years but never his brother. There wasn't much point in putting up a defence. Liz had her mind made up and she wasn't someone he would ever be able to go to for a character reference. She had labelled him a long time ago as trouble and she was probably correct, whatever the rights and wrongs of her current assertion, he was responsible for Colin ending up in this hospital.

"Would you like some coffee?" he asked eager to get away. "They have a machine."

"White no sugar, please," she responded neutrally.

Tom ambled to the machine, wondering just how long he could stretch out the getting coffee experience. He cursed when he realised he didn't have sufficient coins for two cups. He would have to go without.

He returned with the coffee and as she took it she pleaded, "Can't we ask someone what's going on?"

"I'll check to see if there's any news," he responded but as he turned to confront the nurse once more, he spotted the Consultant heading down the corridor in his direction.

Tom was keen to have a first word out of earshot of Liz and hurried toward Seymour. As he came close, Tom tried to determine whether the news would be positive from looking at the Doctor's face but he was giving no clues.

The doctor came straight to the point. "Your brother's in intensive care. The operation went well but he is still critical."

Tom felt hugely relieved the first words out the Doctor's mouth hadn't been to announce Colin's death. "Thank you," he said with a broad smile. He felt like the condemned man given a last minute stay of execution.

The Doctor seemed less excited by the news he'd imparted. "His condition is still very serious," he stressed. "The next forty eight hours are the most important."

"Can we see him?"

"I'll send a nurse to collect you in a few minutes. He's unconscious so you won't be able to communicate with him. Now if you'll forgive me I have to rush."

"One last question. Do I need to pay for anything to improve his chances?" Tom realised it was tactless the moment the words left his lips.

The Consultant didn't look pleased by the question. "I can assure you he is already getting the very best of care available," he responded testily. "Your prayers might be more useful than your money."

Then the Doctor turned on his heels and was on his way. Off to save someone else's life no doubt, Tom thought. He watched John Seymour's departing back with admiration. It was a name he knew he'd never forget. He turned and could see Liz staring at him with a look of expectation in her eyes. Tom gave her his best reassuring smile and immediately saw her relax a little.

Sam booked into the hotel close to Heathrow Airport at 5.00am. Airport hotels were used to people coming and going at all hours and the reception showed no sign of surprise at her early, unplanned arrival. She had obtained a small pack of essentials from reception, which included a toothbrush and toothpaste, as she had left her wash bag and cosmetics in the hotel bathroom in Brighton.

She went straight up to her room and soaked for a long time in a very hot bath. She hated Connor for what he'd done but recognised that in some ways she'd escaped lightly from him. He was a sick bastard and there was no knowing what he might have done, if she'd stuck around any longer.

She was thankful she had turned up for her three monthly contraceptive injection just a couple of weeks earlier and so didn't have to worry about the possibility of being pregnant. The pig hadn't even bothered to check whether she was taking contraception. She hoped he didn't have any nasty diseases. She would have to get a checkup as soon as possible. Anyway, Connor was history. She didn't know if the police had found him still in the room back in Brighton but even if not they had his name and he wouldn't find it easy to evade them. She managed a small smile at the thought of Connor in the bath when the police charged into the room. At least he had served a purpose in getting rid of Ashdown.

She'd paid a high price for her revenge but with hindsight maybe it was worth it. If he'd asked her up front for a quick shag in return for killing Ashdown, she might well have agreed. After all she was basically bartering sex for Eduardo's assistance. And it wasn't the first time in her life she wanted to forget a sexual experience. There had been a couple of drunken occasions where she regretted who she woke up with the next day. This was different though and she wouldn't easily forget Connor. In fact she didn't want to forget him and when she returned to Belfast, she would seek him out and make him pay. For now she would look forward to seeing Eduardo and some pampering in Paris.

As she came out the bathroom she heard mention of Ashdown's name on the television. She hurried to turn up the volume and heard the reporter say he was in hospital in a critical state. Though immediately disappointed he wasn't dead, she was pleased to hear he still might not live. Her emotions changed rapidly though when she realised that it was his brother who had been shot and a neighbour had been killed. That fool Connor had managed to shoot two people but neither of them was the bloody intended target.

She slunk on the bed uncertain what to do next. There was no mention of Connor so she had to assume he'd not still been sat in the bath when the police arrived. It was ironic she decided but actually perhaps Connor's incompetence had worked out for the best. Her brother was suffering in jail and now Ashdown's brother was also suffering. Ashdown would have to live with the knowledge he was responsible for his brother's being shot. Maybe this was a more potent revenge even than actually killing him. Her spirits lifted.

Eduardo's plane was due to arrive in two hours. That still gave her plenty of time for a bit of shopping. There were some nice shops at the airport. She intended to look and smell her best for him. It would take him about another hour to clear customs and she would surprise him by waiting for him at arrivals. She wondered if he would recognize her. She had been a blonde the last time they met. Hopefully that hadn't been all that attracted him.

Then she could take a taxi with him to his hotel. She had returned the hire car at the airport, as the police would now be looking for her. At the very least the hotel in Brighton would have given a description of her and the car to the police and she didn't fancy driving around in it any longer. She now realised she had acted too hastily when she sent the police hurrying to her hotel room. In her desire to get back at Connor she'd overlooked the fact that the room also pointed straight to her. There had even been a video camera over the front door, which if working must have captured images of her and Connor. There would also be fingerprints but fortunately she had no criminal record. All in all it was a mess but she knew she would be safe once she was with Eduardo and out of the country.

Connor knew he'd been lucky to escape the police. Laying in his bath in the hotel room, he'd heard just the sound of the television and wasn't surprised when Sam, I'm too fucking good for you, Murphy ignored his request to get him a scotch. She was probably sleeping or had just returned to being a cold bitch. He'd finished his leisurely bath, wrapped the towel around his waist and returned to the hotel bedroom to discover the bloody girl missing. He'd dressed quickly and gone looking for her.

After a fruitless look in the local streets, which even in the early hours of the morning were still relatively busy with late night clubbers finding their way home, he returned after half an hour to see the arrival of armed police sealing off the road and entering the hotel. Glad he wasn't alone on the streets, he walked for five minutes and then asked the first couple of guys he came across if there was somewhere he could still get a drink. They directed him to a bar just a couple of streets away, which they said they regularly frequented and would be open all night.

When Connor arrived, he wasn't entirely shocked to find it was a gay bar. He needed to be inside both to avoid the police and to keep out the cold, so wasn't going to go looking for anything else. The bar wasn't terribly busy and he bought a pint of the Black Stuff with a whisky chaser before seating himself at a small table where he could keep an eye on the entrance to the bar. The only half decent thing about the Brits was their pubs all sold Guinness. The lighting was subdued and a George Michael song was playing in the background. A couple of men were shuffling around an improvised dance floor near to their table. He didn't get how a man could dance with a man. Men were great for having a few drinks with and many things but he found the thought of sex with a man as disgusting. They were mostly ugly, hairy, dirty sods who farted too often. How could you ever fancy one of them!

His demeanour didn't invite company but still a couple of men approached him individually to start conversations, which were abruptly met with a succinct "piss off". One persevered by ridiculously asking if he wanted to go round the back with him. Was the idiot deaf? Connor pointed out the only reason he would go around the back with the man would be to beat the crap out of him and he shuffled away. Being alone Connor realized he probably would be mistaken for someone looking for some late night action. He needed to be more careful if anyone else approached. He couldn't afford to get in a fight and have the bloody police arrive.

As he sipped his drink he cursed the day he'd ever set eyes on the Murphy girl. She'd brought him nothing but trouble. What the hell was he going to tell the Chief? Certainly not the truth. He wouldn't approve of him putting a mission at risk for a shag. Then again she wouldn't be the Chief's favourite person either. He could tell the Chief it was her who had ratted him out to the cops. That would seal her fate. Even if she felt she had a good reason, the Chief would never forgive her for calling the cops. Anything she said would be tainted by that action. Whatever lies she tried to construct, Connor would just have to say she was lying and had it in for him. Connor had done a lot of good work over the years. The Chief would surely believe him before her and even if he did suspect something was not quite right, Connor knew he was too useful an asset to be disposed of lightly. If it came down to it the Chief would simply measure his value against hers and there could surely only be one winner.

His mind went back to how he was going to get out of Brighton. It was risky to take the train but he had little choice as his car was in the hotel car park and now no doubt being crawled over by the cops. He checked his phone and found the first train to Victoria went at 5.10am. Only just over an hour away. That was good news. He would have to tread carefully in case the cops were watching the station. Though they might not react that fast. He'd buy a ticket from one of the automatic ticket machines.

He drank the remainder of his pint slowly. After a while he looked at his watch again. He didn't want to be hanging around the station too long, so time for one more scotch then he would be on his way. He would spend the journey mulling over what he'd do to Sam Murphy, if he ever came across her again.

He approached the bar and ordered his drink. Two men were chatting at the bar and looked up as he came near. He could see their reflection in the large glass mirror behind the bar.

"Let me get that for you," one of them offered.

Connor was about to object when he had a second thought and decided to accept. "Don't mind if you do," he said pleasantly. "The name's Brendan. Can I join you?"

"Please do," the man who had offered to buy the drink said. "I'm Ian and this is Simon."

Connor noticed they both had tattoos all the way up their arms. Their hair was cut very short and they were both thickset. They looked like they both worked out regularly at the gym, probably lifting weights.

"You Irish?" Simon asked.

"As Irish as they come," Connor answered, adding an additional lilt to his normal accent. "Where you guys from?"

Ian answered, "We live in Haywards Heath. That's about twenty minutes from here."

"You two brothers by any chance?" Connor asked. He thought they looked very alike.

That elicited a laugh from both of them.

"Definitely not," Simon answered. "We've been married for a couple of years."

Connor thought the idea of two guys being married fucking weird. It wouldn't happen back home. He forced a smile.

"Haven't seen you in here before," Ian stated.

"It's my first time," Connor replied. "It's a bit quiet isn't it?"

Simon responded, "A combination of the weather and being early in the week. The place is packed out at the weekend."

"Actually we need to be going quite soon," Ian said. "We have a train to catch."

"Is that the five ten? Only I'm getting that as well."

"It is," Ian confirmed. "Haywards Heath is the second stop. Perhaps you'd like to come back to our place for a drink?"

Connor couldn't believe his luck. He had accepted the offer of a drink because he remembered the cops would be looking for a man on his own. He needed some company and it looked like he'd just found it. He would change his mind about going for the drink when they arrived at Haywards Heath station. He would feign tiredness or some other excuse. Connor lifted his whisky to his mouth and downed it in one.

"I'd love to come for a drink. I'll just visit the bog and then I'll be with you," Connor said. Then he added with a grin, "We can have a bit of a party."

Ian and Simon both smiled at Connor's last remark. Connor smiled too at the thought of how disappointed they would be when they didn't get their threesome.

Jones was shocked to hear about the shootings at Ashdown's home. He didn't like being kept in the dark. He should have been told. He had no moral problem with trying to kill Ashdown. Any sense of morality he might have once possessed, had long since been replaced by the overriding need for self-survival. He was pretty certain Connor was responsible and decidedly angry his own plans had been put in jeopardy. Connor was a necessary evil but also a liability the longer he was roaming the streets. Unfortunately, this morning's early raid on the hotel where he'd been staying, had revealed the bird had flown the nest. That was not part of the plan. He was supposed to stay holed up in the hotel waiting to hear from Jones. In an ideal world he would then have been shot resisting arrest but in any event there was a trail that clearly laid the blame for Bancroft's death at Connor's feet.

It had been an uncomfortable couple of hours at the office wondering what the hell had happened to Connor, before the news came through that an anonymous tip off was naming Connor responsible for the events in Brighton. Although unplanned, this would seal Connor's fate. Every police force in the country would shortly be looking for him and there would be no hiding place. Fortunately the timing of Bancroft's demise was such that it appeared Connor had murdered him and then after gone directly to Brighton intent on also killing Ashdown.

Jones did wonder who was responsible for the phone call. He assumed it was the woman that the hotel had reported was staying in the room, where they were supposed to find Connor. Perhaps they had had some falling out. Anyway, he wasn't concerned with solving unnecessary puzzles. He was just grateful how things had turned out well in the end. The arrival of Connor had handed him the perfect way to solve the problem of Bancroft. Jones had removed Bancroft and planned Connor should take the blame. Now Connor was branded guilty of two murders, it could hardly have worked out any better.

Jones had not wanted to hand Connor details of the route by which they would be taking Murphy to Court but he had had little choice. It had been that way for a long time. He despised himself almost as much as the likes of Connor and his Chief, for passing across secrets but he had a family and couldn't bear the shame of the truth coming out. He was enduring a life sentence and he could see no way of getting remission on his sentence. He knew he would end his own life though before ending up in a real prison.

He had grown to hate Ireland and especially Belfast. It was a city torn in two and madmen roamed the streets carrying out terrible atrocities in the name of religion. He had been caught up in the worst of it many years earlier, when he was much younger and had allowed his desires to get the better of him. The Irish were to blame for all his troubles then and still today.

He thought of himself as a fundamentally decent man but he knew, if judged by his peers, his actions sometimes said something different. He hoped that by removing Connor he would avoid the information he had passed ever being used. He did have some misgivings that with Connor not yet apprehended he might still make an attempt on Murphy but it seemed unlikely. Connor's face had been released to the press and was already appearing on every television news broadcast. If he hadn't previously known he was being hunted, he did now, and undoubtedly the rat would be buried in some sewer planning the fastest way out of the country.

Jones felt able to relax a little. If they could find Connor quickly that would be an end to it. Connor must be the Chief's best man. There wouldn't be time to send someone else. Fortunately Jones also believed Connor was unlikely to ever be taken alive. If he had read him correctly, he would rather die in a shootout than surrender. At least Jones was hoping that was the case. And if he was wrong and Connor was taken, he was confident he would never disclose Jones existence. On the one hand he was old school who wouldn't dream of being disloyal to the Chief but more importantly, he would keep quiet and hope Jones could use his position of influence to help him escape. That would prove to be a false hope.

For once Jones had done as he was instructed and been well paid for it but his conscience may not have to suffer the burden of being at least indirectly responsible for further terrible deeds. In fact, he could be instrumental in removing a nasty piece of work in Connor from the streets. With a bit of luck it would all be over by the weekend and he would still be able to have an uninterrupted dinner party. Tonight's bottle of wine was going to taste even better than usual.

Tom was unpacking his suitcase in his new hotel room when Melanie called. There had been nothing more he could do at the hospital and he'd returned home hoping for a shower and change of clothes. The policeman standing outside his front door had at first refused him entry, on the basis the house was now a crime scene but a call was made to Chief Inspector Parkin and he had been allowed to pack one suitcase of clothes and toiletries, all the time accompanied by a watchful officer.

Tom was actually pleased to move a few hundred yards down the road to the cheap hotel, which he occasionally frequented for a beer. The house was full of unpleasant memories of the previous night's events and Tom didn't want to stay inside too long. In fact he'd already decided he would have to move house. He didn't fancy coming home every day to a place which would now always generate bad memories. As he went upstairs, he'd had to navigate past two forensic policemen on their hands and knees, combing the floor for clues. Where his brother had lain was now an outline on the floor and he guessed the kitchen would have a similar one for John Harding but he didn't plan to check.

Melanie had heard about the shootings on the morning news and had chastised Tom for not calling her earlier. She had arranged for a taxi to take her directly to Brighton and after obtaining the address where he was staying, promised to be with him within a couple of hours. Tom felt enormously relieved that she was on her way. He desperately wanted to see her and have her close to him.

He was worried it might be dangerous for her but she'd laughed off as ridiculous his suggestion that what she should do, was to take the first plane back to the States. He hadn't really said it from the heart though he hoped he sounded as if he meant it. The last thing he really wanted was for her to leave. If she did, he doubted he would ever see her again. Why would he? He had little to offer her except the risk of being killed. Yet right now he wanted her around him more than ever. With Colin in hospital he needed her support and strength. His was fast draining away.

Then he realized that Melanie Adams was about to visit him and would see his small house and how he lived his normal life. She lives in Malibu on the beach! He actually smiled. The comparison with Brighton was so ridiculous. Surely she would beat an early retreat to home once she saw how and where he lived.

Liz had remained behind at the hospital and promised to call if there was any change in Colin's condition. Tom found just being at the hospital depressing. The whitewashed walls were drab and in need of a new coat of paint. In places the paint was actually peeling and everywhere there were the definite signs of under investment and cut backs within the NHS. Little was out of place but there was no colour, no vibrancy and in need of something to lift his spirits, instead he found himself getting depressed not just by his brother's condition but also by the surroundings.

Showered and shaved he'd returned to his home and crossed the road to see if he could do anything for Janet Harding. She had her sister with her who made tea, while Tom struggled to find the words to express his sorrow. She was remarkably resilient and quick to insist that Tom wasn't to feel in anyway guilty for what happened. As she put it, "it was that damn fool of a husband's decision not to wait for the police to arrive." Then she added proudly, "and I wouldn't have had him any other way."

Tom drank his tea and reported that Colin was still critical but had a fighting chance. He accepted the offer of a chocolate digestive biscuit, which he dipped in his tea surreptitiously.

"I don't know what the world's coming to," Janet said solemnly. "What with my John and Lord Bancroft killed in one night."

Tom hadn't listened to any news since returning from the hospital. He immediately made the Irish connection but was unsure what this news meant. For a moment he regretted ever having gone to Melanie's aid but he dismissed that thought as pointless hindsight. It also wasn't true. He was glad he had been able to help her and not just because it turned out she was a beautiful and famous film star. He had done something decent in his life and managed to help another human being. He would always feel good about that. Maybe the deaths were linked but maybe they weren't. It was for the authorities to determine.

Janet recalled how she and John had met and after about an hour Tom explained he had to leave, as Melanie was due. This news caused several minutes excitement on the part of both Janet and her sister, who seemed almost disbelieving she would shortly be just along the road from them. He made a mental note to have them meet but didn't make any promises, as he didn't feel it fair to commit Melanie in her absence.

Back at the hotel again Tom sat in the lounge, which had a view of the hotel reception and through the windows he would also be able to see a taxi arrive. There was a television and he turned on the twenty-four hour news channel to learn more about Bancroft's death. He was still watching when he heard a car draw up outside. He watched through the window as Melanie stepped onto the pavement and cast her eyes about, before starting up the short path to the hotel's front door. He moved quickly to greet her on the doorstep and without words he took her in his arms and held her close for a few seconds.

She broke the embrace and looked up into his face, "Are you okay?" she asked concerned. "I seem to be always asking you that."

"I'm fine. Just a bit shell shocked." He led her into the hotel. "Let's go up to my room," he suggested. "We'll have more privacy." He was pleased the reception was almost deserted and nobody took any notice of the two of them, as they climbed the one flight of stairs to his room. He noticed Melanie was wearing a simple black dress under her coat and was sure she had done so out of respect for what had transpired.

Tom opened his room with the heavy key, which pointed to the old-fashioned nature of the hotel. No electronic key cards or modern furnishings were in evidence. He stood back to allow Melanie to enter first.

He took her coat and asked, "Would you like a coffee or tea?"

"I'm okay, thanks."

He realized she probably thought he was going to have to call room service. He doubted her hotels came equipped with kettles in the room. "I have everything we need to make tea," he said pointing at the kettle. "I'm going to have a cup."

Melanie smiled. "Someone once told me that the English see tea as the answer to any problem. I'll have a cup of Earl Grey if there is any please."

Tom searched the selection of tea bags and proudly held aloft one marked Earl Grey before depositing it in a cup. "It was good of you to come," he said while waiting for the kettle to boil.

"I'm so sorry about your brother," Melanie apologised, as she sat on the edge of the bed. "I seem to have brought you nothing but trouble."

"It's not your fault," Tom stressed. "You're not the one running around trying to kidnap and shoot people."

She didn't look convinced. "How is Colin?" she asked.

"There's no real change but I'm sure he'll pull through." Tom was feeling more optimistic with each passing hour he didn't hear any bad news.

"But what if he doesn't? You'll never forgive me. I'll never forgive myself."

"Enough," Tom demanded. "We can't blame ourselves for what's happened to Colin." Or at least you can't he was thinking. Then more gently he added, "I thought I'd pop by the hospital later. Do you want to come?"

"I'd like to."

"Good. We can't sit around moping. There's just someone nearby I want you to say hello to on the way out. If you're up to it?"

Sam met Eduardo at arrivals in terminal five of Heathrow. Although she hadn't seen him for three months he hadn't changed. There was the same dark hair and complexion plus the moustache and pearly white teeth. He wasn't very tall and she always thought he looked the typical image of a Mexican bandit and had told him so once, which caused him to rebuke her for calling him Mexican, though he didn't seem bothered about being called a bandit!

She had filled her time waiting for him by shopping. Eduardo was an elegant man with sophisticated tastes. He was always smartly dressed and she wanted to be sure she looked the part when she inevitably undressed for him. She greeted him with a kiss to both cheeks. He smiled and enthused about how good it was to see her and how great her new hair style looked. He had an infectious good humour that immediately made her happy to be in his company. He also treated her with a respect you didn't often get back home. He held open the door of their taxi for her and was attentive to her every word as if he really was interested in what she had to say, not just desperate to get in her knickers.

The taxi took them to the exclusive hotel in Mayfair where he'd made a reservation. It was impossible to talk openly in the back of a taxi, so they had settled for trivial conversation about nothing important. He had promised his business would not take long and then they would head for Paris. She hoped the weather would improve.

All the time in the taxi, Sam felt Eduardo's eyes on her, not in a creepy way but with an appreciative intensity. The hotel was opulent from the moment you walked through its front doors, which were opened by a very smartly attired doorman who smiled and wished them a good morning. The reception floor was covered in marble and Sam relaxed and felt safely shut away from the danger of Connor. Even Paris could wait. She could happily spend many days in this palace.

Once in Eduardo's hotel room, Sam felt able to relax for the first time in what seemed ages. Eduardo ordered coffee and sandwiches from room service and left Sam looking at a newspaper while he took a shower. She had half expected him to suggest her joining him but was pleased he wasn't rushing her. She liked the feeling of being pursued a little not just taken for granted. Of course, if he had asked she would have gladly joined him and there was no question of her being coy. She imagined Eduardo was a man who liked to take time and enjoy his pleasures. That was fine by her. She'd had enough quickies to last a life time.

Miller was looking at the first results of the background checks on Ashdown, which weren't revealing very much he didn't already know. No convictions for anything other than speeding and a drink driving in his twenties. Father was in the army and interestingly had done two tours of duty in Northern Ireland during the troubles. No information about whether Ashdown had been with him but it was highly unlikely. Anyway he would only have been a child then and no one in their right mind doing a six month tour of duty, took their families with them to Ireland. It was far too dangerous. It was though a tenuous connection with Ireland. He couldn't completely ignore it.

Ashdown's business was going through a tough period and he appeared to have multiple mortgages. He could certainly do with an injection of cash though that wasn't unique in the current economic climate. Miller wasn't seeing anything truly suspicious but he would order further checks. They needed to dig deeper. Although it took a huge stretch of the imagination to think Ashdown might have arranged the attempt to kidnap Melanie Adams and then saved her. Perhaps he'd had a change of heart when he saw how Maguire and Murphy were treating her and intervened. Miller liked a good mystery but he did feel this was probably beyond anyone's imagination.

His phone rang and he listened intently for several minutes before thanking the caller for the news. So Connor was no longer in Brighton. He'd been on the early train to London. Why hadn't the local police covered the station? Perhaps they did and he slipped by somehow. His caller had revealed that someone called Simon Sharpe had telephoned 999 to say that he and his friend had met Connor in a bar in Brighton and travelled with him as far as Haywards Heath, where they lived and had left the train. They had recognized his photo on the news and called in as good citizens. Miller was grateful for their call. It meant they could concentrate their resources back on London, rather than Brighton. As long as they were telling the truth. A local Chief Inspector by the name of Parkin was on his way to interview them. He should be able to tell if they were concocting any form of smoke screen to help hide Connor's true location.

In truth Miller doubted they would learn anything from Parkin's meeting but he was an optimist by nature. The glass was always half full not half empty. It was probable that Connor had simply used the Sharpe guy and his friend to help avoid detection at Brighton station. The police would have been looking for one man not three. Clever of him. Miller wondered when they were ever going to get a break in this case.

When Melanie had asked if there was a good hotel close by where she could stay, Tom had suggested the Hilton on the seafront. She announced she would take up residence immediately and called the hotel to check they had a suite available. She then sent to London for her things. He very much liked the idea of her being so close to home and he certainly wasn't going to ask Melanie to stay at his hotel. He had started to harbour some real hope that she might actually be interested in seeing him longer term but as a betting man wasn't getting too carried away. The odds were still stacked heavily against that happening.

They had visited the hospital and found Liz at Colin's bed side. She announced that there was no change in his condition, which Tom had learned to treat as positive news. The Doctor had been clear that every hour that passed without problem increased Colin's chances of survival. Tom observed Colin was connected to a machine showing his heart beating regularly and a drip feeding into his arm. To Tom's untrained eye Colin looked like he was just enjoying a deep and peaceful sleep. Tom went to the side of the bed and delivered a silent message encouraging him to keep fighting and get well soon.

Liz accepted Melanie's suggestion she should take a break and go for some coffee. Tom noticed that unlike almost everyone else over the last few days, Liz didn't seem at all overawed by Melanie's presence. What did surprise Tom was that Melanie said she was going with Liz and that Tom could keep an eye on Colin. Tom was once again impressed how easily Melanie could relate to people despite her superstar status. She knew Liz didn't really like him and was taking her off for what would undoubtedly be some words of encouragement and a female shoulder to cry on, if required.

They had gone from the hospital straight back to the Hilton where Melanie suggested ordering some lunch from room service and Tom was looking at the menu when he felt his mobile vibrate. It was a withheld number which made him wonder if perhaps it was news from the hospital.

"Tom Ashdown," he answered.

"Hello Mister Ashdown, this is Commander Miller at the Met. I'm in charge of anti-terrorist operations. I'm sorry to trouble you but I was wondering if I could meet with you?"

"Is it important? Only I wasn't really planning on being in London again at the moment. I'd like to stay close to my brother."

"I quite understand. I was thinking of paying you a visit down there. Would later this afternoon be possible?"

"I'm just about to have a late lunch here at the Hilton with Melanie Adams so basically any time after three would be okay."

Tom detected the slight pause while Miller digested the information that Melanie Adams was in Brighton with him. "Well if I leave now I should be there about three thirty," he said pleasantly. "Do you have a room at the hotel where we can meet privately?"

"Melanie does and I'm sure she would also like to find out what's happening. She's in the Seafront suite, so give us a call when you are near."

"Good, I'll see you later then."

As Tom turned back to Melanie he could see an expectant look on her face. "That was a Commander Miller," he explained. "He's in charge of anti-terrorism and he wants to meet us. He'll be here about three thirty so that just gives us time for some food."

Melanie gave him a slightly quizzical look. "Are you really desperate for food only I had a better idea for how to spend the time?"

CHAPTER SEVEN

Connor had reported in to a Chief apoplectic with anger. He'd been economical with the truth and mentioned nothing of the detail of what transpired in the small hotel room in Brighton. He painted a picture of a Sam Murphy obviously distraught with the arrest of her brother, running amok and shooting Ashdown's brother and killing a neighbour. He didn't know how she had managed to get herself a weapon. Perhaps from one of her father's family in England he had suggested. Then when he had approached her, she had done a runner and tipped off the police to his whereabouts.

She was out of control and in his opinion a danger to everyone in the organization. She knew too much and was unstable. It was his recommendation she be removed permanently. The Chief asked whether there was any way she could have been involved with the death of Bancroft, which had thrown Connor because he'd never considered the possibility. He'd answered that he didn't know but it was possible given her state of mind. That had sealed the girl's fate. The order was given. Connor should act with all haste to take her out.

At the same time, Connor had been reminded he still needed to focus on getting rid of her brother. Connor had the details of the route Murphy would be taking to Court that afternoon. He didn't normally argue with the Chief but did point out his fingerprints had been all over the hotel room in Brighton and by now the police would have put his name to those prints, that was if the bloody bitch hadn't actually named him in the call she must have made.

He didn't fancy his chances of pulling this off and coming out in one piece but knew better than to argue with the Chief. Ultimately even he was expendable. An asset to be used at the Chief's beck and call. He also knew though that he would be well rewarded if he could make the hit. The Chief had also uncomplicated matters by giving him free reign to use any means necessary to remove Murphy. Some collateral damage would be acceptable after all.

Connor had checked out the Court the previous day straight after he'd been given details of the route. To his mind there was too high a probability of a last minute change in the route they would take so he would be better positioned close to the Court itself. He knew the time Murphy was to appear in Court, so he reckoned his best chance lay in hitting the van as it slowed to enter the rear entrance of the Court, when it could be doing no more than 30mph. He had identified the best point from which to launch his attack. Now all he needed to do was collect the weapon from a flat in Finchley and try to stay out of reach of the cops for a few more hours.

Even by the measurement of recent days it had been quite exceptional. Tom felt a bit like he had taken a massive cocktail of potent and very illegal drugs. There had been the highs of hearing Colin was going to live and the almost unbelievable experience of making love to Melanie. The low was the meeting with Miller, which had left him with the distinct feeling that the police half expected further attacks on his life, although the only motive for such action seemed to be some form of revenge for his interfering in the attempt to kidnap Melanie.

Miller had admitted they were hunting someone they suspected was responsible for the current mayhem without naming him. He seemed confident now they knew who they were chasing and that the net would quickly close. However, in the meantime he did advise that Tom kept a low profile and was alert to possible danger.

Miller had enquired about Melanie's plans and raised an eyebrow at her response that she intended to stay around Brighton with Tom. Tom was of the opinion that Miller's perfectly sensible suggestion she might be better heading back to the States, was born of the desire not to have her added to the casualty list. No policeman would want the terrible publicity that would follow if anything now happened to Melanie Adams in England, when she could have gone back to the States, after the first attempt on her life. It wouldn't matter it was her choice to remain. Miller made it obvious he did not approve of her intending to spend time so close to a terrorist target. He didn't ask or receive Tom's opinion. What he said made perfect sense.

Tom had naively pointed out that if they knew who was responsible and he was on the run, then surely it was very unlikely there would be any further attempts on his life. Miller had agreed with the logic but stressed that the man they were chasing was very dangerous and might even have some form of personal agenda, which went beyond logic although they weren't aware of anything.

Another possibility was that he had been contracted to do the job and already paid, which would make him see it through regardless. Please don't relax, Miller had stressed, realising he wasn't going to be able to convince Melanie to take a plane home. Try not to go out too much before we apprehend this man. You should be quite safe in the hotel and it shouldn't be for too long.

Tom was suitably worried although far more for Melanie than himself. He would be quite happy for her to adhere to Miller's request to stay in the hotel, especially after their recent lovemaking. He could happily spend all day in bed with her. As he showed Miller to the door he was caught off guard by Miller's turning and asking him if he had ever been to Ireland. He had replied in the negative.

Currently though, Miller's words of warning were a long way from Tom's mind as Melanie had asked him not to return home but spend the rest of the day and night with her. Contemplating spending a whole night with her, he recalled the afternoon. He had been a little overawed at first when she had suggested she had a better way of spending the time waiting for Miller to arrive rather than eating. He had a momentary panic. After all, she was one of the world's sexiest women and he was definitely no Brad Pitt.

Melanie had kissed him passionately and led the way slowly as if understanding his slight unease and soon he was simply responding to her caresses and touch. An initially slow magical exploration of each other's bodies had quickly developed into an urgent and hungry desire, driven by the need to celebrate a snatched moment of normality in the midst of two lives turned upside down.

The only problem Tom realized after, was that he was hurtling into a relationship, which was almost certain to end in his getting badly hurt. His feelings for Melanie were growing stronger by the hour and he had no doubt that sanity would at some point return to her life and then it would only be a matter of time before she crushed his heart.

Tom was worried about Melanie's safety but she had waved away his support for Miller's suggestion she would be better off back home and it was evident he wasn't going to be able to change her mind. Therefore he intended to stay as close to her as possible. Melanie had never been to Brighton and she wanted to get out and visit, not stay holed up in the hotel, despite Miller's warning. Tom agreed to show her some of the sights, such as the Pavilion and the temporary outdoor ice rink. He was a reasonable skater and as she said she wasn't very good, he would enjoy helping her round the rink.

He suggested that afterwards she must allow him to take her to dinner at one of his favourite Thai restaurants, in the centre of town. He didn't say it but he was looking forward to being able to pay for dinner, as he was becoming uncomfortable with Melanie always paying for everything. She had readily agreed to his suggestion of Thai, which was also one of her favourites but pointed out that she hadn't been to the gym for almost a week and desperately needed some exercise.

Despite the bad weather, she intended going next morning for a run, a regular habit back home it turned out, but her suggestion he should accompany her was met with very little enthusiasm. He had offered to help exercise her all night if it would avoid having to go for a run. She had smiled and emphasized it would really have to be all night in that case.

When she appeared in the hotel reception ready for her sightseeing expedition, Tom barely recognized her. The long coat, hat, scarf and gloves left little in the way of distinguishing features on view. The cold weather would make it easy for her to move around town without attracting her normal level of attention.

She had expressed an interest in seeing his betting shop and he probably would pay a quick visit just to give his regulars something to talk about for years to come. But first it would be the Pavilion and a slice of culture. Then perhaps a walk on the pier. He doubted they had a pier in Malibu!

In the end Sam had taken the initiative and when Eduardo came out the shower wearing just a towel wrapped around his waist, she was waiting for him wearing the expensive underwear she had bought at Heathrow, while waiting for his plane to arrive. That and her best smile caused a noticeable movement under the towel.

She had knelt before him, removed the towel and been pleased with what she found. He was larger than average and as always it pleased her to see the effect she could have on a man. She teased him slowly with flicks of her tongue and was pleased he made no attempt to force the pace. So many younger men she had experienced would just thrust themselves into her mouth, desperate for a climax instead of savouring every moment. Eduardo lived up to her expectations and after her second orgasm she lay in his arms truly satisfied and deep in thought.

"What are you thinking about," Eduardo asked in an accent that revealed his South American roots. "Was everything okay?"

"God no," she replied. "That wasn't okay, that was fantastic."

She had been a little worried that after her experience with Connor she might find it difficult to respond to Eduardo's touch but that hadn't been the case. She had reasoned with herself beforehand it was like riding a bike. Even if you fell off and hurt yourself, the quicker you got back on the better. She wasn't going to let one bad experience ruin her life. The sex with Eduardo had been as good as with Danny the night before she came to England and he had raised the bar very high.

Eduardo smiled broadly. "I thought it was great too, especially for our first time."

"First and second time," Sam laughed. "I can't believe I kept turning you down all this time!"

"It was worth waiting for. Now tell me what you have been up to since we spoke on the phone."

Sam recounted the events of the last twenty four hours but hesitated when she reached the point in the story where she was raped by Connor. She was worried he would see her differently, somehow spoiled and dirty. However, she also knew that it was the surest way to gain his help.

Eduardo listened without interruption to her concise description of Connor's assault. His eyes fixed on her and he spoke in measured tones. "I know this man, Connor. I have met him a few times. He is well regarded by the Chief. My business interests do not allow me to be seen to interfere with this matter."

Sam could not hide her disappointment. It was not the reaction she had hoped for.

"Let me ask you an important question," he continued. "Why am I here? Are you just using me? Will you be finishing with me the minute I have served your purpose?"

Sam was shocked by the questions. She wasn't sure how to answer and now was beginning to regret ever arranging to meet Eduardo.

"Be honest," he prompted. "I don't entirely mind being used. Indeed please feel free to do so again tonight. However, I need you to be honest with me. Is this just a few days together in return for my helping you?"

Sam shifted nervously in her chair. "I will be honest," she said softly. "I needed your help and I know you have always liked me so yes I suppose that is perhaps a form of using you. But I don't think you're an eejit, quite the opposite. I have always liked you too but thought you were only interested in the obvious." She looked up into his eyes but couldn't determine what he was thinking. "I haven't put a time limit on this. Maybe it will be days, maybe it will be weeks or if you want, even longer. I don't know."

Eduardo was thoughtful for a few seconds. He stroked his chin and looked directly into her eyes. Then he smiled. "I believe you," he said. "Please understand that in my position I just have to know you are being honest with me at all times. I will not be made a fool of but you are right I have always liked you, so I would take this time with you even if it is only a few days. Although I do hope it will be longer."

Sam relaxed a little. His words encouraged her. She smiled. "There are no conditions to my being with you," she said. "I understand you can't do anything about Connor but that doesn't matter."

"You misunderstand, Sam. I said I could not be seen to interfere. From the first moment you told me what he did to you, he was a dead man. He is a pig and I will see he is spit roasted over a very hot fire. I just wanted to be clear about why we are here together in this hotel room."

Sam gave a huge smile. She jumped up out the chair and threw her arms around him. She snogged him full and deep on the lips. "Gracias," she said simply when they came up for air. They had an agreement that despite her language skills, she generally wouldn't speak Spanish with Eduardo, as he liked to practice his English.

"My pleasure."

"Actually there is one condition about my staying with you," Sam said teasingly. "You must keep making love to me the way you did earlier."

"Well I am not sure about that," he replied with a mischievous smile. "I had a few rather different ways I wanted to try out."

Connor was positioned on the flat roof of a small row of shops opposite the back of the court. He had worn two jumpers and a thick coat, to keep out the inevitable cold that would assault him, while he laid in wait. He had woollen gloves to protect his hands, with the ends of the fingers cut out so he could grip properly.

He had a clear sight of the busy road and the imposing double gates, which formed the rear entrance. He heard them approaching before he saw them. Two police motorbike outriders with sirens blaring, blocked the crossroads fifty yards up the road, so that the convoy would have an uninterrupted path through the traffic lights. Then he saw the van and two accompanying police cars, followed finally by two further police on bikes.

Connor raised the weapon to his shoulder in anticipation of the van's imminent arrival at the rear gates. The convoy slowed and the gates began to open. He knew he would only get the one shot. He also knew how valuable the RPG rocket launcher was. They had very few weapons of this magnitude still available after the decommissioning in 2005. It would be bad enough missing the target but especially so as he would be leaving the almost irreplaceable weapon behind.

He hadn't used one for a few years but they were simple enough to operate. He just had to point and fire. The van was the normal type regularly used to transport prisoners to court. There was no special armour to protect it from the rocket shell Connor launched in the direction of the van's rear doors. Any armour would in fact have been worthless anyway as the RPG was designed as an anti-tank weapon. It pierced the rear doors and exploded in a fireball, engulfing anyone inside the rear of the van and throwing the heavy van ten feet in the air.

The blast from the explosion threw two of the policemen from their bikes and the escort cars screeched to a halt, trying to avoid the wreckage of the van. The police car immediately behind the van had braked and swerved so hard the driver lost control for a few seconds and it skidded into the oncoming line of traffic. This led in turn to further cars breaking and swerving. There were at least two further impacts. Pedestrians were running from the scene of the devastation, worried both about further explosions and the mayhem of the skidding cars.

Connor didn't intend to hang around. He was confident his objective was achieved. Jones had come through with the correct information about the time and place. The Chief had come through with an appropriate weapon and he had done the job. It was a good result. Connor left the weapon on the roof with a touch of regret. It was extremely valuable to the organization but he had no choice. It was much too bulky to take with him.

In the confusion he was quickly down the fire escape and calmly walking away from the explosion, keen not to attract attention. He didn't look back. Fortunately the weather allowed him to wear his ski jacket with its hood up which revealed very little of his face. He was confident it would be virtually impossible to identify him from the photo that had been on television.

Five minutes later he was on the underground and looking forward to a very large whisky or two. He had finished what he came to London to do and now he could finally get the hell out of the bloody place. There would be a holiday to look forward to and a decent deposit in his bank account that would pay for a lot of booze and a lot of women.

CHAPTER EIGHT

Miller was convinced the attack on Murphy had required inside help. The route, timings and choice of court had been a closely guarded secret, which also meant that it was likely the source was someone deep inside one of the services and quite possibly was also senior. It was true the number of courts likely to be used was probably only a handful but he didn't believe for a minute that someone had been positioned at every one, armed with a rocket launcher.

He was shocked that those responsible had access to an RPG. It wasn't a weapon that you could just buy on the streets. He remembered the days in Ireland when RPG attacks on the troops armoured carriers were quite a regular occurrence. Had the IRA been responsible for this attack? It appeared the objective of the attack could only be to silence Murphy and the IRA were the ones to profit most from his death. He had a load more information in his head, which with his death was going to remain secret. Miller was disappointed he hadn't yet raised the subject of Brian Potter with him. As always with that case, it was one dead end after another.

Three police officers in the van had been killed in the explosion and the rising body count was not acceptable. About now, wives, parents and sadly also children were having to come to terms with a future life without a loved one. Members of the public had suffered a mixture of broken bones and other injuries. By sheer luck none of them life threatening, so it was a small mercy the body count would not rise any further.

The press was in a feeding frenzy desperate for developments and arrests. For a shambolic government in the last throes of its tenure this was a final straw. But Miller was far more driven by the thought of the loss of innocent life and families affected, than the threats being hurled at him by politicians increasingly concerned for their future careers.

Unfortunately, even a closely guarded secret such as Murphy's route and the Court was known to at least a dozen people including three on his own staff. He was willing to discount all of them so he was left with nine suspects.

As he stared at the list he noticed both the name of Simpson and his obnoxious boss. He took off his glasses and rubbed the bridge of his nose. It was difficult to imagine any of the names on the list had intentionally let slip the details. It could just have been a casual conversation between one of the names on the list and someone they trusted. It shouldn't happen but it easily could happen and was how so many secrets had been let slip over the years. Twelve names on a list could easily mean twice as many actually knowing. The driver and escorts had only been informed of the route at the last moment and been given no opportunity to contact anyone. Neither had they known who they were transporting until the very last second.

He decided lunch with Simpson, who was another name he felt he could quickly strike form the list of suspects, was once again necessary. Only this time it would have to be over a take away coffee, not an expensive meal. He called and arranged to meet by the river. Simpson had pointed out it was freezing cold outside but Miller had not listened. As he replaced the receiver Miller smiled at the thought of Simpson's lack of excitement at the choice of meeting place for lunch. Even in the midst of a national crisis Simpson's priorities never changed. Food first and everything else second.

Miller had telephoned Tom and let him know about the attack on the van and the death of Murphy. Despite the initial shock both he and Melanie had agreed they would lose no sleep over Murphy's death. What did concern them was the evidence this presented of further carnage on London's streets.

Tom returned to the task of trying to convince Melanie she should be on the next plane back to the States. Neither London nor Brighton seemed safe places to remain any longer than absolutely necessary. This time he uttered the words with conviction from his heart. He didn't want her to come to any harm and the best way of ensuring that was if she went back home. He was carrying enough guilt around thinking of what had happened to Colin.

When she asked him, he admitted it was the last thing he really wanted but it was the only sensible course of action. She considered it carefully and agreed to leave but on the condition he went with her. She had said it mischievously with a smile, knowing he had a business and a brother who needed him. She explained she was not easily intimidated and had no intention of running away. Much like when you came to my aid she had said, again with that small smile. Tom admired her ability to construct a convincing argument. So deep down he was happy that at least for the foreseeable future it seemed Melanie intended to stay in England. He just prayed that she would not be in any further danger.

Colin had been very sleepy and weak but at times conscious when they visited him that morning. He had a room to himself because of the seriousness of his injuries. Nurses came and went very regularly, checking the various machines to which he was connected and updating the notes at the bottom of his bed.

Colin's eyes appeared to light up in recognition when he noticed Melanie was with Tom. He had blinked and Tom felt sure his brother was making sure Melanie was indeed in his hospital room and he wasn't dreaming. He managed a whispered rather hoarse hello but that was it as far as conversation. Although he was definitely on the road to recovery, he would be spending several further weeks in hospital and there was still no definite prognosis about any long term physical injuries. He had not yet been well enough to ask what he remembered of the actual shooting and not been told of John's role in probably saving his life, while forfeiting his own.

Liz had been surprisingly welcoming, especially given she couldn't have had much sleep, having been parked permanently and dutifully at Colin's bedside since first arriving at the hospital. She revealed they were moving Colin next day to a London hospital, more experienced with trauma such as he had experienced, which would also make it easier for her to visit. Tom put her friendliness down to this news and the presence of Melanie and suspected had she not been there he wouldn't have been made so welcome. They all agreed that if the doctors considered it safe to move Colin then he must indeed be improving.

Sam was stretched out on the large hotel bed with Eduardo when she heard the newsflash. She sat bolt upright, focusing on the screen and pictures of a wrecked and smouldering van. She covered her face with her hand and let out an exclamation that quickly turned to an anguished cry. Eduardo took a few seconds longer to understand the reason. Then he wrapped his arms around her shoulders and pulled her reassuringly into his large chest. He held her close for a minute then she pulled away and looked up into his eyes.

"I bet it was that bastard Connor," she said with venom.

"Might well have been," Eduardo soothed, stroking her hair. "But don't worry about him. I promised he would be dead and I am a man of my word."

"He was a good brother. Why did Connor do that? He wouldn't have talked. Christ we are all meant to be on the same side." The words came with a rush. "I should call home, speak to Ma and Da."

"Of course but not from here," Eduardo suggested.

"I want to pull the trigger," she suddenly threw out. "I want to look him in the eyes just before I squeeze the trigger."

"It may not have been Connor," Eduardo responded, hastily retreating on his earlier encouragement it had possibly been him. "For all we know he could have already skipped the country. I would have in his place."

Sam didn't look convinced. "I'm sure it's him and I'm going to make him regret what he did to both of us."

Sam's reaction worried Eduardo. He understood some of how she was feeling but had learned that personal feelings clouded judgment and where such serious matters were concerned, it would be vital to keep a clear and unemotional focus. That Sam could act on impulse and be very emotional was beyond doubt. She had wanted drugs to implicate Ashdown but then on impulse had asked Connor to kill Ashdown instead. The result had been bad for her. Eduardo liked Sam and wanted to help her. They had agreed that her original plan for the drugs and his reason for being in England was no longer a good idea. It seemed Connor would now replace Ashdown as the focus of her hate.

"I have an idea," he said. "I am going to take you to dinner and over a nice Rioja we will drink to your brother and then I will explain why I am going to call the Chief."

Miller purchased two large coffees and joined Simpson on a bench by the river. After brief pleasantries Miller jumped to the reason he had asked to meet. "Is it just me or are you boys also wondering how the hell they managed to hit Murphy? The Court and timings were a closely guarded secret."

"We're actively looking for scapegoats to blame! I assume you are running checks on everybody in the know? Someone must have tipped them off."

"What about your end. There are a few names on the list that I can't check."

"Not likely to be one of us," Simpson answered dismissively. "Most likely someone in the prison."

"Nobody inside the prison knew the full details, only the time he was being collected. The officers accompanying Murphy were only briefed ten minutes before they left."

"Where are you going with this?" Simpson enquired. "It could be anyone directly or indirectly giving the location away. Maybe someone has a bug in their office they don't know about. It's hardly a first."

"True, but we're missing something here." Miller took a sip of his coffee and looked out across the river. "It doesn't make sense. We have a sudden rush of Irish associated murders and attempted kidnaps but who is behind it?"

"My guess would be the Real IRA. They recruited Murphy and Maguire and let them loose on London."

"But if Bancroft was their target why were they also trying to kidnap Melanie Adams? It doesn't make sense. And why haven't they claimed responsibility at least for the murder of Bancroft? They might not want to admit to trying to kidnap Melanie Adams but Bancroft is an entirely different matter. They would claim he is a legitimate target and want the kudos for his death. It just doesn't make sense."

"Perhaps they don't want to claim credit for Bancroft because they know they will automatically get the unwanted credit for Adams and the attempt on Ashdown."

"I'm convinced we are missing something important," Miller stressed.

"Perhaps there are two cells working independently," Simpson suggested. We know about Murphy and Maguire but the second cell target Bancroft. And maybe then are ordered to take out Murphy to stop him talking."

Miller didn't look convinced. "It doesn't fit. We have two very different types of action and frankly different levels of professionalism. I can see the Real IRA or for that matter Continuity wanting to kill Bancroft but kidnap Melanie Adams…" Miller shook his head as his words trailed away in thought.

"Well Bancroft will be no great loss," Simpson said after a moment of reflection. "Jones couldn't abide the man and though it grieves me to say it, for once I have to say I tend to agree with him."

Miller raised his eyebrows in question. "What did Jones have against Bancroft?"

"He was behind the combined service idea," Simpson explained. "With him earmarked as its first leader. Worse thing for this country's security that could ever happen if it came to pass."

Miller was surprised by the intensity of Simpson's feelings. He'd thought Simpson beyond caring about such matters. Miller had forgotten Bancroft's role in leading the government's push for a single security service. He'd met Bancroft a few times but wasn't directly impacted by his political manoeuvrings and had enough interfering politicians of his own to worry about, without widening the group to peripheral figures like Bancroft.

"Jones doesn't share your views either," Simpson continued. "He's got everyone focused on finding this Connor chap. Thinks he is the sole missing piece in our jigsaw."

"Finding him would certainly be a good start," Miller concurred. "One thing's for sure though, Connor didn't get the intel on Murphy without help. There must be at least one other involved and I intend to find out who was responsible for the deaths of three good police officers today."

"We've been to too many funerals over the years," Simpson said.

"One last request, Tony. Can you run one of your special background checks on Tom Ashdown?"

"Ashdown!" Simpson replied shocked. "Surely you don't think he's involved somehow?"

"Not really but I just want to be sure. My nose is twitching a bit. He's been at the centre of everything that's happened. Just being thorough."

"Okay but he saved Melanie Adams and his brother was almost killed. I think you must be barking up the wrong tree if you suspect him of any involvement."

Miller thanked Simpson for his help and as he walked back to his office he pondered once again what could be the missing piece in his jigsaw.

Eduardo had put a call in to the Chief on the pretext of being concerned about recent events and the possible impact the terrible publicity could have for their business dealings. He didn't want extra attention being focused on the Chief's business and contacts. The Chief was very understanding but quick to stress that his men were not involved. It was rogue factions outside his control. Eduardo knew the Chief was at least partially withholding the truth. Connor had been in London even if he wasn't now and he was the Chief's man.

"What about this man Connor who is all over the news? I have met him before. He is one of your men," Eduardo stated firmly.

"Connor is tidying up the mess."

"I do understand," Eduardo sympathized. "But frankly when I see his face on the news he is now very much at the heart of this mess. What if the police capture him as surely they must do…? He even knows my name. This puts at risk all our very profitable business together… I am in London at the moment and if there is anything I can do to help bring these events to a speedy conclusion…?" He let the offer hang in the air.

There was a thoughtful silence at the other end of the phone. "There is possibly one thing you could help with," the Chief finally responded.

Eduardo had gone fishing, dangled the bait and had a great bite. As he recounted his call to a scarcely believing Sam, they had then fallen into bed in a frenzy of further love making. She was intent on thanking him for what he had done and knew only one way to do that. Actually she again found more than one way.

It was late afternoon when they lay in bed planning the details.

Eduardo wasn't entirely happy at Sam's insistence that she must be there at the end. He would have preferred her out of harm's way but more than that, was concerned her emotional involvement might lead to irrational behaviour and complications. He knew though he would never be able to dissuade her from joining him so would just have to be doubly careful in his planning.

The Chief had asked him to do a spot of tidying up and he knew that not only would doing this favour earn him the Chief's gratitude, something well worth having, but also Sam would be eternally grateful, for letting her be part of removing the pig Connor from the Earth.

The Chief had provided details of the safe house where Connor was laying low. He was expecting to be contacted and as he had met Eduardo a couple of times would be only mildly surprised by him being the contact. He was awaiting a change of identity and the delivery of a new passport. Eduardo would be the courier but the Chief had decided that Connor had become dispensable. Murphy was out the picture and it was best to tidy up all loose ends, which now included Connor. Eduardo had agreed to act as the cleaner and was amazed at how easy it had now become to honour his promise to Sam. If only all business and pleasure could flow so smoothly.

CHAPTER NINE

Eduardo and Sam took a taxi to an address provided by The Chief. Sam stayed in the taxi while Eduardo went in and came out a couple of minutes later holding a brown envelope. He also had a weapon hidden in the rear waistband of his trousers. They then had the taxi take them nearby the second address in Finchley provided by the Chief, where Connor was laying low. They found a coffee shop where Eduardo left Sam while he went and scouted the property. Returning twenty minutes later he purchased a double espresso and joined her at the discrete table in the corner. He emptied two bags of sugar into his coffee before he spoke.

He huddled forward so he couldn't be overheard. "This won't be easy," he started. "Are you sure you need to be part of this? Can't I just call you to join me once I have dealt with him?"

Her look was enough to answer his question.

"Okay. It is a small house with a front door on the street. There is no way to approach the house unseen. I will secure him and then call for you to join me. You can then deliver the coup de grace."

"He's a Muppet but dangerous," Sam warned. "Take care."

"A Muppet?" Eduardo frowned. "You mean like Kermit the frog?"

"I mean he's a fool but he's known as a hard man so please be careful."

"I like that you want me to take care," Eduardo said appreciatively. "I assure you Sam I share your concern for my health and will take great care. Please also do not act impetuously. I too care for you. Now I shall have one more coffee and then be on my way."

Sam screwed up her face. "I don't know how you can put so much sugar in such a small drink. It must taste like treacle. And it's very bad for your health," she admonished him.

Eduardo pushed his chair back and stood. "I can see I have a lot to teach you," he smiled.

Miller was dwelling on the contents of the report on his desk from an old Special Branch colleague in Ireland. As a result of the upsurge in violence on the mainland, he had asked Special Branch to rattle cages and push all their informants to discover who the hell was responsible. It was being put about on the streets of Belfast that Connor had gone missing and was suspected of joining the Real IRA. The suggestion was that he could be responsible for taking Maguire and Murphy across the sea and causing the recent troubles. It made some sense to Miller. Connor could be the man Murphy had mentioned Maguire meeting. After the demise of his team, Connor had then killed Bancroft by himself before going after Tom Ashdown for some sort of revenge. And had Connor been behind the attack on Murphy? Perhaps removing someone he rightly didn't trust.

His thoughts were interrupted by his mobile ringing. He recognized the voice at the end of the line asking him if he could please call back urgently when he was free to speak. Miller realized that it wasn't a discussion to be had in the office. He left his office and walked towards Victoria until he found a phone box, which afforded him privacy and some protection from the cold. He dialled the number back on his mobile. He listened intently to his old friend from Special Branch in Ireland, his excitement steadily growing.

They had arrested a senior member of the IRA, carelessly caught with a large stash of cocaine in the boot of his car. Just what he was doing transporting drugs so openly was still a complete mystery. He had been spotted with a broken rear light and if he had pulled over, the police officer would have politely pointed out the fact and continued on his way. Instead the man had accelerated away with the police car in hot pursuit. Driving an underpowered saloon he had not gone far when he was cornered by three police cars at a junction and forced to stop. The quantity of drugs was sufficient to have him put away for many years and having been to jail before he wasn't keen to return.

The man had tried bartering for his freedom with snippets of information but the local police weren't interested. Then he asked to see a senior member of Special Branch because he had something very important he wanted to trade for his freedom. The piece of information in question was that the IRA had a highly placed informant in MI5. In fact the suggestion was that the informant was so senior he could access and pass on absolutely anything demanded of him. If such an informant did exist, then it would explain how the killer found out details of the route for transporting Murphy to Court. It also meant that the same person had the death of not only Murphy but also more importantly three police officers on his hands.

Miller's brain was racing as he listened, analysing what he was hearing. The informant was unlikely to be passing information for any ideological reason so they must be blackmailing him. Unless it was pure greed and he was being well paid. At the moment Special Branch had disclosed this information solely to Miller and currently only unofficially. They too knew that if someone senior in MI5 was indeed the IRA's contact, then it was vital they kept this information to the fewest people possible. However, they wouldn't be able to sit on the info for long.

Miller wasn't sure how the revelation about an MI5 informant, fitted with his analysis that the IRA wasn't responsible for the attacks on Bancroft or the actress. Perhaps the two weren't connected. Was this informant simply helping the IRA gain retribution against the renegades? Or was their some other agenda?

There was also the further very real possibility that the man they had arrested was playing Special Branch and intentionally pointing the finger of blame at an entirely innocent person, just in the hope of causing some disruption in the security services and securing his freedom. In fact, the more Miller considered the question, the more he thought that was the most likely answer. The fly in the ointment was that he was being left in no doubt by the man at the other end of the phone that he in particular and Special Branch in general, were convinced the information was authentic.

Unfortunately the IRA man wanted a high price for the name of the informant. He wanted to start a new life in Australia. The odd thing about the request was that despite having a large family he wanted the new life only for himself. He would be forever hunted if the deal was made and he thought he would have more chance of avoiding his past if he had only himself to worry about.

To Miller's way of thinking this made it more likely that his information was genuine because he was afraid of what the future would hold. Whether he cared for his family and didn't want to put them in danger or just wanted rid of them, Miller didn't really mind. He'd long since given up trying to second guess people's motives for their actions. This was an opportunity that didn't come along often. Even so, learning the informant's name was still going to cost a great deal of money to move this man halfway around the world with a new false identity. There would be other useful things the local Special Branch boys would learn but everything hinged on being able to offer the new identity. And they needed to act fast. The IRA knew the police had him and would become suspicious after seventy two hours if he disappeared. It was too much money for the local Special Branch boys to agree the deal. They needed Miller to pick up the tab.

Miller was desperate to find the name of the informant for more reasons than putting an end to the current troubles. If there was a senior informant today in MI5, then perhaps that same person could have been a less senior informant some years ago. Again he thought of the tortured body of Brian Potter. He needed to know the name.

He returned to his office, made a couple of phone calls and wrote the necessary emails. Then he called Ireland and informed them to agree to the man's terms. He just hoped it would be worthwhile. He didn't like rewarding a senior member of the IRA with a new life but he was pragmatic enough to do so for the bigger picture.

Later in the afternoon he picked up the phone and heard the name of the MI5 informant. He could hardly believe what he was hearing. The name provided after the agreement to a new life had been confirmed in writing was Jones. Miller only knew of one Jones and he was indeed very senior in MI5. He was Tony Simpson's boss.

The problem now was knowing how to proceed. How could he draw Jones out into the open? He didn't want to scare him and give him the chance to cover his tracks. And given his senior position, it was going to be very difficult to know just who could be trusted. It would be near enough impossible to prove anyway. He had friends in high places and was no fool. Even just trying to run any checks was almost impossible, without him getting to hear about it. Miller thought of running the news past Simpson but he doubted he would be able to offer any additional insight.

There were some things Miller could do and the first would be to investigate Jones' financial affairs. That he could do without setting off any alarm bells. If Jones was living above his means or could not explain specific deposits in his bank account, then Miller would have some ammunition to take this further. Even as he thought of it, he knew he had little chance of finding out anything so easily. If Jones was guilty, he would have squirrelled his payments somewhere in an account that would never be found. That would be true of anyone in MI5. Still he would run the checks as at least he would feel he was doing something. After all Jones had been on the very short list of people aware of the details surrounding Murphy's transfer to Court.

He would also ask around about Jones' sexual preferences. If Jones was being blackmailed, then it could possibly be linked to a mistress or perhaps even a man. Miller didn't know a lot about Jones' private life but did know he had a wife and children. He was in a job where scandal could quickly end a promising career. Whatever he found, it was doubtful anything would ever up in a court of law. What he needed was evidence that would satisfy Jones' Director not a Judge.

He didn't like Jones personally but he was shocked he might be the informant. He couldn't remember him ever being in Ireland though he still could easily have been there undercover. If he came up blank with Jones, he was going to have to go to him and discuss the information he had been passed. He didn't have much time. His friend in Ireland could only sit on the news for twenty four hours. Even doing that was putting at risk his career. Then Jones would hear via official routes soon after or probably far quicker through his own contacts.

Once the news was out in the open, Jones would simply deny everything and claim he was being framed. Miller had just authorized the huge expense of relocating someone to Australia and there were going to be repercussions if Jones was completely innocent. In fact, Miller might be taking that cruise with Mary sooner than expected. What didn't make sense to Miller was how Connor linked to Jones. Who exactly was pulling whose strings?

Eduardo approached the white door quickly and gave a short firm rap. There was no sound from within the house but he knew Connor would be observing him and determining whether it was safe to offer entry. After a minute, the answer came with the front door opening, although there was still no sign of Connor. Eduardo entered and found Connor, gun in hand, behind the door.

"Hello Connor." Eduardo gave what he hoped was his most friendly smile.

Connor didn't return the smile but waved him in the direction of the living room. "Sit," he instructed, beckoning to a couple of old and very worn sofas with especially frayed armrests.

Eduardo did as instructed, careful to keep his arms in the open and clearly visible to Connor. "The Chief asked me to come," Eduardo said, knowing he was stating the obvious. "I was in London anyway and happy to return a favour. I have a new passport for you." Eduardo reached slowly inside his inside jacket pocket and withdrew a brown envelope which he placed on the sofa. Eduardo had met Connor a few times and though they weren't, by any stretch of the imagination, friends, Eduardo was comfortable his relationship with the Chief, would ensure Connor would never suspect his real motives.

Connor tucked the gun in the back of the waistband of his trousers. He seemed to relax a little. "About bloody time... Want a drink?" he asked.

Eduardo had smelt the whisky on Connor's breath as soon as he entered the house. "Thanks," he said, accepting the offer. "By the way, the Chief says well done. You've earned a long holiday."

Connor moved to the adjoining kitchen and reached up to a cabinet for a glass. Eduardo could see a half empty bottle of whisky and a glass on the kitchen work surface. He poured two large measures into the tumblers. As he returned to the lounge Eduardo got up from the sofa and extended his left hand to take one of the glasses. At the same time his right hand came forward revealing the gun he had taken from the strap around his ankle. "Take a seat," Eduardo ordered.

Connor showed a hint of surprise then quickly took control of his emotions. Eduardo was sure he was assessing whether to take immediate action or do as he was instructed.

Eduardo backed a pace further away without having taken the whisky. "Take a seat," he repeated, waving his gun in the direction of the sofa. He waited for Connor to be seated before speaking again. "We need to have a chat but first please put down the glass, take out your weapon holding the barrel between two fingers and place it on the floor in front of you. Then just slide it carefully towards me with your foot." Eduardo tried to make it seem like an everyday request. He hadn't needed Sam's warning to understand that Connor was a very dangerous man. He knew Connor's role in the organization.

Despite being the one holding the gun, Eduardo was under no illusions that his own life was now in great danger. Any slip on his part that allowed Connor to gain control could only have an unpleasant end.

Connor did as instructed, having first placed the wine glass in his left hand on the floor. Eduardo picked up the weapon without ever taking his eyes from Connor and stood holding both guns pointed in Connor's direction.

Connor raised the glass in his right hand to his lips and took a large gulp of the whisky. "This was yours," he then said, recovering the second glass from the floor and offering it towards Eduardo.

"I don't think so," Eduardo replied with a wry smile. "You're welcome to it." He had no intention of getting so close to Connor, despite the strong attraction of the whisky. He took his mobile from his pocket and when it was answered said simply, "I am ready." He turned back to an inquisitive looking Connor. "I am a very good shot so please don't make any move that I might interpret as threatening while I welcome an old friend of yours."

Connor gave a small shrug of his shoulders but his face showed no emotion. Eduardo walked carefully backwards towards the front door, never taking his eyes from Connor. He opened the door a few inches and then stepped aside to allow Sam to enter the house. As she did so Eduardo studied Connor's face and spotted the brief look of surprise once again quickly replaced by a passive expression.

"You fucking bastard," Sam quickly spat out as she moved to the centre of the room. "Not feeling so fucking cocky now are you." It wasn't really a question, more a statement of fact.

"Nice to see you too," Connor replied flatly. He took another large drink of whisky.

Eduardo wanted to get the job done and be away as quickly as possible. He picked up a cushion from the sofa. "Sure you still want to do this," he asked Sam.

She made a point of looking at Connor as she answered in the affirmative, "looking forward to it."

"Use this then to muffle the noise," Eduardo urged Sam. He moved towards her and handed her both the gun he had taken from Connor and the cushion.

"She's never going to shoot me," Connor stated confidently.

"I wouldn't bet on it," Eduardo replied. "Not after what you did to her."

Sam took a couple of paces closer to Connor.

"She loved it," Connor sneered.

Eduardo could see sweat breaking out on Connor's forehead.

"Not as much as I'm going to love this," Sam said, raising the gun and placing the cushion in front of the barrel.

Eduardo knew what Connor was going to do before he even moved. "That's close enough," he warned. In the same instant that Sam ignored him and kept moving even closer, Connor raised the full whisky glass as if to take another drink but instead threw it at Sam, who by now was only a couple of feet away. Eduardo watched Sam shy away from the glass and its contents as Connor launched himself from the chair.

Eduardo wasn't certain but he thought he saw Sam smile, in the same instant in which he heard the muffled retort of the weapon. She had fired instinctively without great aim but had hit the onrushing body at short range. Connor staggered and then fell against her as she fired a second shot. He slid down the front of her body his hands trying to grasp her arms but failing.

Eduardo hurried to check the slumped body with his back propped up by the chair. He wasn't dead but blood was pouring from wounds in his chest and stomach. He tried to speak but blood spattered from his mouth and the words were quiet and incoherent.

Sam moved close enough so her face was right in front of him. She was smiling.

Eduardo found the smile disturbing. "Shall I finish him?" he enquired, not expecting for one moment Sam to agree.

"That's my pleasure," Sam responded quickly.

"Bitch," Connor managed to weakly spit out.

Sam hit him across the face with the gun handle, breaking his nose.

"We need to get out of here." Eduardo's voice was insistent. He made a mental note never to cross Sam.

Sam looked disappointed. "Pity," she said turning back to Connor. "I would have liked to stay and play some more." She raised the gun and cushion one last time. She placed the cushion covering the lower part of Connor's face but left his eyes uncovered. "You always did talk crap," she said, forcing the gun barrel towards his mouth but pointing upwards towards his brain. When satisfied she had the best position possible she smiled at Connor and pulled the trigger.

The Chief was at home pacing his front room waiting for some news. The whole world seemed to be going bloody mad. He was in danger of catching the disease. He had asked Eduardo to remove Connor, one of his best men and there were all too few good men he could call upon. He didn't understand what was going on in London but he knew there was a massive manhunt underway and Connor was the target. The bloody fool was running amok and everything he touched was a disaster, although he had at least removed the Murphy boy. Better to have him silenced rather than fall into the hands of the Brits. He was getting old and careless. Everyone eventually reached their sell by date. And he couldn't afford to upset Eduardo. But it still left a bad taste in the mouth. Connor had done good work in the past.

Right now the Chief had problems closer to home. He glanced anxiously at his watch. Almost four which meant he would receive the call any minute. He'd needed confirmation of what he was told a few hours earlier. It was too important not to be certain. He didn't rush to the phone when it rang. He didn't want to reveal the tension he was feeling to those listening in.

"Hello," he answered.

"It's Billy here. I'm afraid I have to cancel this evening's drink. Sorry but the little ones are sick."

"No problem Billy. We'll do it some other time soon. Give my best to the family. Hope they get better soon."

"Thanks. I'll call you soon. Bye"

He replaced the receiver. So Billy had to cancel the drink. They hadn't actually planned to have a drink but the message meant his worst fears had been confirmed. Fuck it was bad enough losing the drugs but now he knew they had a tout and not just any tout. Someone who knew virtually everything about every operation going back twenty years. The whole organization would have to take evasive action and bloody quickly. Some people were going to have to head south, at least for the time being. And Eduardo is worried about Connor. This could be far more serious.

In an ideal world he would simply have the bastard eliminated but that wouldn't be easy. He was a big prize and they would be doing everything in their power to keep him hidden away. His own informant had been part of the initial interview but once Special Branch was involved he was quickly out of the picture. He didn't know what his prisoner had to trade but knew who he was and had understood well enough it was something very big. That was when he had passed on the information via Billy. The Chief rubbed his eyes. He was tired. Tired of one fucking problem after another. He would call a meeting immediately. Then it hit him. Christ! He even knows about Jones.

The Chief stroked the stubble on his chin deep in thought. If Eduardo was questioning what was going on in London then so would others be. And now one of his key men had been arrested and was looking to turn informant. There would be those younger opportunists who might try to stir trouble, seeking to erode his power and authority. If he didn't seem in control of events then he would be having difficult questions to answer. The only thing he'd ever been afraid of was losing his power. It had taken a long time to acquire and he knew it could disappear very quickly. The future was looking very unsettled. He would do what he'd always done. He would squash any dissent before it could gather momentum. Cut it off at the roots.

He was going to start by having a word with Murphy. Make sure there wasn't a problem. He was a good man but if he was thinking about revenge for his son then he could cause trouble. He was a man you wouldn't want to meet on a dark night if he had it in for you. His specialty was giving a good beating. The Chief could take care of himself but he didn't fancy chancing his arm against Murphy. Of course, he hoped it would never come to that. The Chief would deny having any involvement in his son's death. He'd blame the bloody renegades he'd joined. Swear to find the bastards and make them pay. Murphy couldn't be certain what was true. And Connor wouldn't be around to put him straight. Murphy would want to believe the Chief. If he did suspect, he'd also know it would be healthier for him to keep his thoughts to himself. He had other family to think about, including his daughter. How the hell did he ever end up with both of his kids so out of control?

Eduardo was pleased to be safely back at the hotel. He hadn't entirely liked what he'd seen of Sam. He did though have a grudging admiration for her determination and ruthlessness. Although they were characteristics that would not be out of place in his business, he wasn't really very keen on finding them in a lover. He preferred to go to sleep next to someone of a less dangerous nature. And that she could be dangerous he had no doubt. When the time came to walk away, he wasn't quite sure how she would react.

Sam wasted no time in climbing on top of Eduardo. As soon as they came through the door she pushed him back on to the bed and started tearing at his belt buckle. Their sex was frantic and born of a hunger for each other's bodies that had to be urgently sated.

"I needed that," she smiled.

"I noticed!"

Eduardo smiled to himself at the thought Sam would have tried to rape him if he had said no to her advances. He lay quiet for a minute while his breathing returned to normal.

She propped herself on one elbow and looked at him while stroking the hair on his chest. "That was real good," she said.

"I thought so too." This woman beside him was far more complex than he had anticipated. Eduardo found that revelation both exciting and somewhat of a worry.

"Eduardo, I need to ask another favour." She continued lightly caressing his chest. "I want to kill Ashdown."

Eduardo jumped up quickly into a sitting position. "That is madness. We need to get well away from here."

Sam pouted. "I have a plan. And then I promise I will make it up to you."

Eduardo couldn't help but smile. He now knew this woman would do anything to revenge her brother and whatever he said would be irrelevant. He also knew how she would make it up to him. Better to help her and perhaps keep her out of trouble. Otherwise she would simply ignore him.

Tom had enjoyed his quietest day in almost a week. For once, there had been no one trying to kill him or his family and he had even shown his face in the shop, for a second consecutive day. Only a handful of people had been in the shop the previous evening when he arrived with Melanie but the news had spread of the famous guest. Young Ben had been particularly overawed and hardly said anything to Melanie but now was keen to speak about nothing else.

Tom detected a noticeable increase in customers despite the bad weather. It was a trend he was informed by Ben, which had been on a sharp upwards curve since details of his story appeared on the front page of the newspapers. Whether the new customers were actually spending money or just enjoying his free coffee, he wasn't certain. Tom dutifully spent an hour chatting to regulars and newcomers, handing out coffee, taking bets and accepting congratulations from everyone. Yes it was true Melanie Adams had been in the shop the previous night. He had to admit to once again quite enjoying his new found celebrity status.

Melanie had returned to London for a meeting with her Agent. Their early morning love making meant she was going to be late for that meeting and had left Tom feeling the luckiest man on the planet. They had had what was really their first serious discussion about the future. It was a subject he had always chosen to avoid but as she lay in his arms, she had said simply that despite the terrible events of the previous few days, she was so pleased she had met him. He had muttered something similar and then she had come right out and said it, "I don't want this to end. I don't want to live on a different continent to you."

He'd thought about this moment several times. What he was going to say when the subject arose. He had thought she would be announcing her return home to work and they would agree to stay in touch. Maybe even he would go out for a visit but this was quite different. Melanie was hinting at a future together. This wasn't in Tom's script but it was exciting. In the short term she had to return home for Carol's funeral but was suggesting he accompany her and stay for Christmas. The break would do him good. She could show him her home and life. For a moment he was carried away with the enthusiasm of the moment but he couldn't leave now, not while Colin was still in hospital. She had forgotten Colin for an instant and apologized profusely. Of course he couldn't leave. But when Colin improved then she expected Tom to pay a visit. He smiled and promised he would.

Tom dared to believe for the first time that they might actually have a future. Then in the same moment the voice in his head warned him not to get too carried away. He was punching well above his weight. He was sure nobody who knew him would understand how he was with Melanie Adams or more importantly why she was with him. Everywhere she went she turned heads. When he was with her Tom felt the proudest and luckiest man alive. He was concerned about the many practical details but she dismissed them with a wave of her hand.

One issue that particularly concerned Tom was finances. A subject that always seemed to follow him around. While most couples would worry about whether they had enough money to buy a house, Tom was more concerned they had too much money. Or at least a disproportionate balance between the two of them. Melanie was used to a certain lifestyle that he would never be able to afford to provide and he couldn't see himself living off her income. He didn't know the answer and guessed Melanie wouldn't even see it as a problem. She was like a tornado, entering his life and ripping everything apart. However, unlike the typical tornado this was a positive experience and he was happy to be carried along by its energy, taking him he wasn't entirely sure where but he had no inclination to escape its clutches.

Tom's home was still a mess, constantly invaded by numerous police forensics officers in white coats looking for clues. He stopped by the house to collect a few extra clothes and crossed the road to check how Janet was getting along. She had asked after Melanie and seemed amazingly resilient, given how recently she had lost her husband. She also gained comfort from the fact Colin was showing signs of improvement. She felt his survival would give some meaning to her husband's death. Tom considered he would always be in John's debt for saving Colin's life and he intended to help Janet in any way he could. He made sure she understood if she needed anything at all, she only had to ask.

Tom was crossing back over the road when Miller telephoned. He was intrigued by Miller's request for him to come immediately to London. As Melanie was already in London, Tom found it easy to agree despite only the briefest explanation from Miller. The details could wait until they met. He promised to be on the first possible train.

CHAPTER TEN

It was a couple of minutes past five when Tom arrived at the Kingston gate entrance to Richmond Park. He directed the taxi right at the mini roundabout and followed the road tracing the circumference of the park for about a mile, until making a left up the familiar hill to the car park closest to the appointed meeting place.

In his early twenties, after leaving university, he had rented his first flat in Kingston and for a few months even shared it with Rachel, a third year student studying art at Kingston University. They had been good times and the one summer they spent nearly every weekend with a rug and a bottle of wine in the park. She would sometimes produce a sketch of him and somewhere at home in a bottom draw, he still had a sketch she had signed and given to him for his birthday. When the course finished she had returned home to Bath and they had said goodbye without regrets. Six months later he had met Alex and rushed headlong into commitment and marriage.

Paying the fare Tom declined the driver's offer to return and pick him up later. If everything went according to plan, obtaining a lift home would be the least of his problems. He was pleased he had taken the time to purchase the new steel grey wool coat he was wearing. It had an inner lining which he zipped up to his chin and pulled the high collar around his neck. He had paid a price he wouldn't until recently have ever dreamed of paying for a coat and though he said so himself, he thought he looked smart and fashionable. It was something he would feel comfortable wearing out with Melanie. The old leather jacket had been consigned to the back of the wardrobe for the foreseeable future. The weather wasn't showing any sign of improving and he felt that without the new coat, he was as likely to freeze to death as meet his end any other way. Tom didn't know if the girl would actually come but she'd sent the invitation and he'd accepted. He just hoped he wouldn't be leaving the park in a horizontal position.

Miller had explained to Tom that it was a good location to meet. With it's wide open spaces, he felt there was little danger of any innocent bystanders being caught up in whatever might be about to unfold. It would also be impossible for someone to sneak up unawares. The girl had probably chosen it as their meeting place for the exact same reasons.

It was late afternoon and soon Darkness would start to fall. He stepped carefully on the slippery path as he began to walk down the gently sloping hill towards the ponds. He was particularly wary of patches of black ice. He knew he was being watched and didn't want to end up unceremoniously falling on his backside. He glanced around as he walked. The area to his left was lightly wooded and covered in fern. To his right there was only long grass.

He was shaking a little and it wasn't just from the cold. He felt he was entitled to behave nervously after everything that had happened. It shouldn't scare anyone away. There were a couple of joggers and a handful of other people taking a leisurely stroll, although what drove them to be out in this weather he had no idea. There was no sign of anyone he could immediately label as suspicious or dangerous.

Tom had agreed without too much pressure from Miller, to meet with the girl who was supposedly able to provide the whereabouts of Connor and had some other vital information she had to impart but wouldn't share on the telephone. Miller assumed she also would want something in return. He had explained to Tom that she didn't trust the police and wanted an intermediary. Someone she could trust. That someone was Tom.

She had informed Miller that Tom would recognize her because they had met previously in his betting shop. That had made Tom relax. He remembered the pleasant and attractive Irish girl who knew nothing about horse racing. He couldn't think of anyone less dangerous. What finally clinched the meeting for Tom was Miller reporting that the girl had sworn it was Connor who had attacked his brother and she too had reasons for hating him, so they both wanted to see him put away.

As Tom came close to the first pond, he could see no sign of the girl but he wasn't alarmed as they weren't actually due to meet for a further ten minutes. There were a number of other adults and even a couple of children walking back up towards the car park. A couple of dog owners were playing with their pets on the grassy bank at the water's edge. It was a favourite spot in summer for families to bring a picnic but in the current freezing temperatures nobody was thinking of picnics or swimming.

Tom had been a frequent visitor in that warm summer with Rachel, which now seemed a life time ago. Nothing though had really changed. One man was throwing a plastic ball into the icy pond for his black Labrador to retrieve. Surely worth reporting to the RSPCA as a case of animal cruelty. As the dog emerged from the water he shook his coat dry and soaked a nearby couple in the process. They took it with good humour but quickly moved out of reach of a repetition.

Tom stood with his hands in his pockets to wait for the girl with no name. He scanned the vicinity, trying to spot her approaching. There were several likely spots where a woman could use the trees and bushes for cover, perhaps even now observing him and checking it was safe to meet.

A Jumbo Jet flew low overhead on its final descent into nearby Heathrow airport, making him think of some of the many warm places he would rather be right now. But despite his fears he was hoping the evening wouldn't end in anti-climax. It may even add another chapter to the book that had been mentioned.

Tom spotted a large rotund man breathlessly walking towards him. Not a man who enjoyed walking or any other form of exercise, Tom thought. He was probably used to taking his car to visit his next door neighbour.

"Do you know what time the park closes?" the man stopped and asked Tom.

"About twenty minutes I think."

"Thanks, I'm on your side by the way." He smiled and continued walking back the way Tom had come.

Tom was surprised by the man's words and doubtful what help he could be. He knew Miller had promised to have a few men positioned to help if necessary and he begun to see if he could spot who they were.

He was grateful for the backup. It was some small comfort. The time passed slowly and he kept glancing at his watch. She was late. He shivered again. This time it was purely from the weather. His new coat was zipped up around his neck but still his ears were exposed and feeling the cold.

He decided he should walk back towards his car. Perhaps she had left something there for him or maybe it was her idea of a joke, to have them freezing half to death.

"He's heading back up the hill," Taylor said into the walkie-talkie.

He was positioned inside the ice-cream van at the top of the hill which at this time of year was in demand for its hot tea if not its ice cream. Taylor was Miller's right-hand man and had organized the support team. He was glad Miller had thought to arrange for Simpson to bring the walkie-talkies. Communication would have been impossible otherwise.

The ice cream van was conveniently placed for him to be able to monitor the whole of the car park and the path down to the ponds.

Luigi, the owner of the van had quickly agreed to the presence of his new assistant, not that he'd been given any choice in the matter. The car park was emptying fast and soon there would be no customers for teas or ice cream. As Taylor looked around he could detect nothing out of the ordinary.

"Everything's quiet," he reported.

Sam had also entered the park by the Kingston gate and keeping to the cover of the trees followed the wall of the park around in the direction of the ponds. She had to stop at one point to make preparations for her return. It was a distance of about three miles but she was supremely fit and anyway, having arrived early, she didn't have to hurry.

She took the circuitous route because she wanted to look for any signs that she might be walking into a trap. By the time she reached the ponds she was reasonably confident there would be no nasty surprises lying in wait on the return journey. Eduardo had suggested the meeting place and suggested the location to meet. It turned out he had used the park a couple of times for business transactions.

It was a further quarter of an hour before she identified Ashdown walking down the hill. She was surprised by the shape of the man who approached him but seemed just to ask a question. Certainly he was no danger. To say he was overweight would be putting it mildly. If he slipped and lost his footing he'd roll down the hill like a ball. This is going to be a piece of cake she thought to herself.

Miller was about one hundred and fifty yards parallel and to the left of Tom as he walked back up the hill. He was hidden from his view by a line of trees that marked the beginning of a wooded area. He and one of the men – Dave, who normally served as a bodyguard in the back-up car, were protecting the flanks against any attack from someone using the trees for cover. They had been particularly worried about the possible presence of a sniper and while Miller kept watch on the targets, Dave had free reign to search for potential trouble.

Miller's other backup – Pete, was sitting behind the wheel of his car in the car park. The final member of the team, his regular driver – Steve, was parked by the entrance of the park. All the men were connected by the walkie-talkies he had asked Simpson to bring.

"Anything your end, Pete?" Miller asked into his walkie-talkie.

"Car park's quiet."

"Anything, Steve?"

"Nothing much happening here."

Maybe this was going to be a waste of time.

"Someone with black dog starting to move up hill," Miller reported with little interest. "About thirty yards behind target. Could be a woman. Difficult to tell at this distance."

"I see him," Taylor responded. "Looks harmless." No killer was going to turn up with man's best friend for company. Tom was now only fifty yards away from the van.

"Land Rover with tinted windows has just entered park and is heading in your direction," Taylor heard Steve announce over his radio. "A bit late for a visit."

There was a few seconds silence then Pete advised, "I can see Land Rover. It's parking up now."

Taylor tensed. He was the nearest to go to Pete's aid if it was required.

"Don't panic, guys. Middle aged woman and small mongrel just got out the Land Rover. The mongrel looks like it's probably her husband."

Taylor smiled. He was beginning to get the feeling this was going to be a waste of time.

Miller's attention had been diverted by listening to the report of the Land Rover. He noticed, in the last few seconds the person walking the dog had cut in half the distance between himself and Tom. The stride was purposeful. Then again so was everybody's given the weather.

"Couple and two kids starting up hill," Miller reported.

He could see Dave emerge from the trees up ahead and begin to walk casually in the direction of the car park. He was aiming to reach the car park at about the same time as Tom. Simpson was walking back down the hill in Tom's direction.

"We have a jogger running up path from pond," Miller said suddenly. He sounded concerned for the first time. "Looks like a youngish woman. She's closing fast on target. Bob, keep an eye on her."

What the hell! Sam was getting close to her target when she saw a man in a suit wearing an open coat walking from the trees towards the car park. She became instantly concerned. Men in suits don't go for walks in the park after a day at the office. They go home and change first, especially when it's freezing cold. This man was probably still working and that spelled trouble.

She was near enough to shoot. She needed to make her mind up quickly. There might not be a second chance. She'd hope there was some explanation for the man's behaviour other than what she feared. She put her hand inside her jacket to the shoulder holster she was wearing.

Tom heard the approaching pounding feet of the jogger. He glanced nervously behind, drawn to the sound of the feet. The figure was wearing a balaclava and was barely distinguishable but he realized it was the shape of a woman advancing towards him. She seemed vaguely familiar.

He was trying to recollect the girl from the shop when the next second he felt Simpson's shoulder barging into him, sending him sprawling to the hard ground. He heard the muted crack of a silenced gun, saw Simpson fall to the ground. Not again he said to himself, as he looked up from where he lay to see a gun pointing at him. He rolled and rolled, fearing it was a waste of time and cursing the fact he'd been stupid enough to listen to Miller.

The black Labrador jumped on the man on the ground. He was barking like mad and generally having the time of his life. Humans weren't normally so obliging as to roll around playing on the ground.

"Simpson's been shot," Miller yelled into his radio as he ran. "It's the woman with the dog. Get her, Bob."

He saw Taylor dive out the front of the ice cream van. Miller still had at least one hundred yards to cover. Knew he'd never make it in time as he saw the woman level her gun on Tom. She hesitated for a second. The dog was in her way. It was only momentary and then Miller saw the dog go limp. He hadn't heard the shot but knew who the woman's next target would be. Miller lifted his gun to fire at least hoping to cause a distraction.

"Damn," he cursed. What's the bloody jogger doing? He watched as the jogger threw herself at the woman with the gun, not really believing what he was seeing. The two of them fell to the ground.

Miller could see Taylor sprinting towards the action. Just as well, because he was slowing down. He regretted the amount of time spent behind a desk in recent years.

"Shit!" The woman was bloody escaping down the hill.

"Boss, what the hell's going on?"

"Steve, get an ambulance and then call the cavalry. Our suspect is escaping down towards ponds. We are giving chase. Stay in your car and maintain your position for the moment."

You're mine, Sam was thinking, as she aimed at Tom rolling on the ground. She cursed the dog for being in her line of fire and shot it through the head. The dog had been Eduardo's idea. He had also provided the weapon.

She had been aware of the jogger but not unduly concerned by her close proximity. She knew instantly who was responsible, when the body crashed into her with such force, that it drove all the breath from her lungs even before she hit the hard ground. Her gun skidded away out of reach.

Her attacker had landed on top and her arms were flailing at her body and face in a frenzied attack. Sam parried the blows. Her left hand grabbed the jogger's collar while her right punched up into the solar plexus. The jogger gasped and Sam grasped a leg and threw her off and to the side. She leapt to her feet and started running back down the hill towards the pond. She barged the couple with their kids out of the way. As she ran she bent and took the second gun from its strapping against the bottom of her leg.

Tom felt the weight of the dead dog collapse on his body. Blood spluttered over him. He had rolled several yards from the killer and as he pushed the dog's body away he continued to roll and roll away from the direction of the gun.

He had expected to hear and feel the next bullet. Then he saw the jogger wrestling the assailant on the ground. It was a very brief image because then the killer was on her feet and running. He climbed unsteadily to his feet. He saw the weapon a few feet away.

As Taylor neared Simpson, lying prone on the ground, he saw Tom stoop to pick up the fallen gun and set off in pursuit of the attacker. The jogger had also regained her feet but was bent double, clutching her stomach and obviously winded. Taylor knelt over Simpson and was relieved to see his eyes flicker open.

"Help's on the way," he said, then sprung up and began to chase after Tom.

Taylor could see that the attacker was about a hundred yards ahead of Tom, who in turn was thirty yards in front of him. He'd not run far before he realised that both of them were rapidly drawing away and the attacker was steadily increasing the distance between herself and Tom. He was too old for this game and was starting to blow hard.

"She's getting away," he shouted into his radio. "I think she's heading towards Kingston gate. Steve, she's coming your way. Be careful though. She's fucking dangerous!"

Tom had slowed his pace to a steady trot. He knew he was losing ground but he didn't have the stamina to keep up his initial sprint. He glanced behind and could see, a long way back, Taylor suffering even worse.

Ten years earlier he'd run around the park a hundred times in training for the London marathon. If you kept close to the wall the circumference was nine miles. The direction they were headed, it had to be at least another mile to the road and just beyond lay another car park and Kingston gate. He hoped Miller and his men were organising a reception committee at the road.

As he ran he had only one thought. Please by some miracle let the man who had saved my life be alive. The overweight so and so had barged him clear and taken a bullet in the process. Never judge a man by the outside.

Tom controlled his breathing, forcing himself to take in and expel oxygen in a steady rhythmical fashion. He could feel the muscles in his legs tightening. He was now two hundred yards behind and the woman in front was showing no signs of flagging.

The terrain was hilly and Tom lost sight of her as she disappeared over the brow of a hill that led down to the road. He pushed himself for a final effort and accelerated a little.

Miller arrived at the spot where Simpson was lying at the same time as Pete who had rushed from the car park. He heard Taylor announce the man was getting away and ask Steve to intercept. He could see Simpson was going to live and decided he was needed elsewhere.

"Where are the car keys?" he asked urgently of Pete.

"In the ignition."

"Stay here and help," Miller commanded and then was off again, running towards the car park.

His personal backup car, of which Pete was one of two regular drivers, was a Volvo V70. Dave arrived seconds after Miller had already sat himself behind the wheel, pulled open the passenger door and flung himself into the seat.

"What kept you?" Miller asked as he accelerated away, the door not yet closed. He wasn't used to the Volvo and underestimated its power, accelerating too fast, and felt the wheels spin in the gravel. He eased his foot off the accelerator a little and then raced back down the unfinished road connecting the car park for the ponds with the main road, which ran on the inside and parallel to the outer wall of the park. He turned on his siren and lights and drove at a ridiculous speed towards the Kingston gate entrance.

Accelerating over the brow of a hill he noticed Dave give him a look that suggested less than total confidence in his driving. He prayed no deer would decide to take a leisurely stroll across the road. At the speed he was driving it would be like hitting a brick wall. As he finally came in sight of the park gates he could see his own car parked up ahead at the side of the road.

What the hell... The woman they were all chasing had run across the road immediately in front of the car he was driving. He slammed on the brakes and skidded violently onto the grass verge, throwing the rear of the car sideways. He was out and running in seconds, closely followed by Dave but the woman had a hell of a head start and was moving too bloody fast.

The area between the road and the wall, where the woman seemed to be heading, was wooded. Miller slowed slightly as he was unarmed and didn't want to be retired sooner than planned. The woman was getting herself cornered. He motioned with his arm for Dave to spread out to the left. He had his gun in his hand.

"Steve," he said into his radio.

"I see you, Boss. I'm coming," came the instant response.

"What about the cavalry?"

"On their way."

Miller had been following the woman as much by sound as sight. Suddenly it was quiet up ahead and he could see the wall. He stopped behind a solid oak tree listening for any sound of the woman.

Sam was smiling to herself. She was annoyed she'd once again missed Ashdown but she'd easily outrun her pursuers. At last her running ability had served a purpose. She had never been very excited by running around a track in circles at school but this was completely different. She loved the power in her legs working with purpose to put distance between herself and her pursuers. It was a complete adrenalin rush.

She knew they would expect her to head for the gate but after crossing the crest of the last hill before the road and out of sight of those chasing, she headed not for the gate but a point two hundred yards further up the road.

She heard the siren of the approaching police car and actually saw the look of horror on the face of the driver as she raced across the road. She heard the car skid to a halt behind her but didn't bother turning to look. She had only another hundred yards through the trees to safety.

As the wall loomed up in front she quickly obtained her bearings, found the tree she'd identified much earlier in the evening and made directly for it. She took only a few seconds to climb to the branch that hung over the top of the wall. She moved along the branch, hanging upside down on all fours, until she could sit on the top of the wall. She turned and fired a shot at someone she saw stick his face out from behind a tree, then suspended herself by her fingertips and dropped the few feet to the ground where she knew Eduardo would be waiting.

Miller drove Tom and Taylor back to the ponds car park. They had searched but found no sign of the woman. The consensus was that she had used the tree to escape over the wall into the new housing estate where probably she had a car waiting. Certainly, that was the general direction from which the shot had been fired at Miller. He hadn't heard the shot but heard the impact it made on the bark of the tree he was hiding behind.

From where they lost her to the busy A23 was only five minutes and it would have been easy for her to get away. They were organizing a house to house search of the housing estate but more in the hope someone had seen her, rather than thinking they would actually find her hiding in some garden bush.

Tom was surprised and relieved to learn Simpson had been wearing a bullet proof vest. When they arrived back at the car park, Pete was waiting to greet them with the news Simpson had been taken away by ambulance but was obviously going to live. The bullet had missed his vest and gone through his upper arm causing just a bit of superficial damage.

"How was the jogger?" Miller asked. "And who the hell was she?"

"I'm fine, thanks," came the response in a decidedly American accent.

Melanie had been bent over tying up her shoe lace and neither Miller nor Tom had spotted her. Now together they both turned in her direction in shock.

"What the hell were you thinking of!" Tom exclaimed. "Are you raving mad?" He recalled his telephone conversation with Melanie, telling her what he planned to do and her initial protestations. She had asked him specific questions about the location and time of the meeting and now he understood why. He was almost lost for words.

Miller was smiling, observing the interaction between Tom and Melanie. It was the second time he had seem them together and it was apparent to him they had a strong bond.

"Seems to me Miss Adams we all owe you a vote of thanks. Isn't that so Mr Ashdown?"

Tom mumbled agreement. Melanie had saved his life and he felt a fool for having shouted at her. He moved towards her and took her in his arms. He was oblivious of the faces staring at him as he bent to kiss her.

"Perhaps we should all say thanks like that," Taylor remarked when Tom had finished.

"Don't mind if you do," Melanie joked.

Tom laughed. "As they're all on duty perhaps I'd better act on their behalf," and he kissed her again, even more passionately than the first time.

CHAPTER ELEVEN

Miller accepted that tip offs were an essential part of policing. This though was taking the piss. An unknown female with an Irish accent had called to report the whereabouts of the body of a certain Brendan Connor. Miller knew who the bloody woman was. Didn't know her name but knew her work. And she was laughing at him. The caller had directed them to this address but she had also made a point of leaving the message, "better luck next time."

Miller surveyed the lounge where Connor was found and wondered if this was the end of the killing. Ashdown and Melanie Adams were going to organize permanent bodyguards, which she'd suggested, declining the offer of police protection. Given he had only been proposing a single officer for protection, she had felt the need for a much larger team. Miller was very happy to agree that his officers' time would be better spent finding the guilty rather than on protection duties.

It was a small terraced house with a musty smell that at first glance looked sparsely furnished. To Miller it looked like a safe house rather than somewhere someone lived permanently. It was probably the bolt hole where Connor had fled from Brighton. Miller smiled at how this young girl had managed to enter the house and kill a professional like Connor.

He certainly wouldn't bemoan Connor's passing. In other circumstances he would have raised a glass to the girl. Perhaps it was her very youth that had made him careless and allowed her to get so close. He did wonder if perhaps she had not acted alone. She had been alone though in the park.

What was her reason for killing Connor, he had no idea. Perhaps it was personal. He smiled at the thought Connor was an ex-boyfriend who had dumped her and this was her revenge. Not likely. He was a fair bit older and the girl in the park had been fit and attractive. Miller couldn't see her being attracted to Connor. But if she was the same woman who had phoned in revealing his whereabouts in Brighton, then she could have been working with him until they had a falling out. That was more likely.

He must have really upset her. There was one particular way that came to mind, he might have done so. They had been sharing a small hotel room. Miller could easily imagine Connor trying to force himself on her. That might have made her mad enough to want to get back at him.

There was one other personal involvement she could have had. Connor had almost certainly been responsible for the death of Murphy. Could she have been Murphy's girlfriend maybe? He put a call into the office. He needed to know if Murphy had a girlfriend. At the same time he was informed Simpson had come through with the full background check on Ashdown and it was waiting for him in the office. Since the events in Richmond Park, he had pretty much lost interest in Ashdown so felt in no rush to see the contents of the report.

Miller had an idea. He approached the Chief Inspector responsible for the investigation and confirmed he was indeed not joking, once he had explained what he wanted. Connor was no longer dead. The idea was full of holes but there was just the chance he could use a not dead Connor to get to the informant if he did exist. Miller made it clear to the Chief Inspector that he could forget about his pension if news of Connor's death leaked out.

It was a long shot because in all likelihood Jones or whoever the informant was, was working with the damn girl and already knew full well Connor was dead. Hell he might even have ordered it! But there was just a slim chance that the girl was working independently, for personal reasons and the informant may not be in the loop. Miller was still of the opinion that there were at least two teams playing in this game, so he had to play out the hand and see if his bluff would come good.

Sam knew full well what she was going to do. She just didn't know whether she should tell Eduardo anything and invite the inevitable argument. She reasoned that nobody in their right mind would go after Ashdown, after what had happened in the park. They would expect her to have flown the country and Ashdown to be out of danger. She was sure she had the advantage of surprise for one final attempt on Ashdown. She knew where he worked and was confident she could get close enough for a shot. The cold weather would provide the perfect excuse for covering her face under a scarf and hat. She wasn't going to just give up. She'd dealt with Connor and needed one last attempt at Ashdown.

Eduardo had gone out for a walk, saying he needed to stretch his legs and make a couple of phone calls. His business would not run itself. On his return he had suggested she accompany him while he ran one further errand, with the promise of dinner afterwards. She decided to hold off discussing what she wanted to do until dinner. Men always listened better over a meal with a drink in their hand.

Eduardo had driven the Mercedes he had hired to help Sam escape from Richmond Park for thirty minutes, when he pulled into the car park of a country park, which from the signs she'd been seeing was somewhere near Slough. He had driven straight to the park without needing his Sat Nav so it was obvious he had been there before.

She had also seen the signs for Heathrow airport, which was nearby and thought the close proximity was probably not a coincidence. There were just a handful of other cars parked. One man was holding open the boot of his car while a medium sized golden retriever jumped in the back. She was intrigued by who Eduardo was meeting but didn't ask. It was his business and he would tell her if he wanted her to know.

"We are early," Eduardo announced, glancing at his watch. "Let's take a walk."

Sam followed him down a well-trodden path. There seemed to be nobody around. Not really surprising given the weather. She zipped up the bright pink ski jacket she was wearing, removed the matching knitted gloves from her pockets, putting them on as she walked. The jacket, gloves and jeans she was wearing were all newly purchased that morning while Eduardo was out seeing to his business.

He moved slightly off the path into some bushes and trees. She was used to clandestine meetings in strange places and followed, intrigued to know where they were headed. She bumped into him as he stopped and suddenly turned towards her. He leaned into her and kissed her passionately on the lips. "We have some time to kill," he smiled. "We might as well enjoy ourselves."

Sam knew what he was suggesting and was very excited by the idea. She liked spontaneity. She glanced to either side but there was no one else visible in the vicinity. Anyway, she quite liked the idea there was the possibility of someone walking by and seeing what she was doing.

She was quickly on her knees tugging at the belt to his trousers. The floor felt cold and damp beneath her knees. She hoped he wouldn't find it too cold and change his mind once she exposed him to the elements. He immediately encouraged her and when she enveloped his half erect form in her mouth she felt him quickly become fully hard.

She was impressed the cold didn't affect him. He immediately started thrusting. It was different to before. He went deeper than usual and didn't stop even when she gagged a little.

"Don't stop," he demanded.

Sam had no intention of stopping. She offered her throat as best she could to his urgent and deep thrusts. Every few thrusts she had to draw back to stop herself gagging too much.

His hands held the back of her head, encouraging her to take him ever deeper. She was careful to maintain eye contact all the time. She wanted to please Eduardo. He had done so much for her.

His grunts and faster thrusts told her what to expect. When he exploded in her mouth she was careful to waste nothing and smiled broadly when she had finished swallowing.

"That was different," she said.

"I'm sorry," he replied, quickly tucking himself back in his trousers with one hand.

"Don't be silly. I loved it."

She was still on her knees as he moved behind her. He bent down and kissed her lightly on the neck. He pulled her head back and smiled. He slipped his hand inside his jacket. "I really am sorry," he repeated.

Sam didn't understand why he was saying he was sorry until she saw the knife in his hand. She still didn't really understand but without hesitation he swung the knife in an arc towards her throat. As she tried to move away she realized he still had a firm grip on the back of her hair and she was unable to avoid the blade slashing across her exposed throat. Her eyes pleaded with him for understanding. Her final thought was of her brother.

Miller telephoned Simpson and explained that Connor had been captured after a gunfight and wanted to do a deal. Connor knew of a high level IRA contact in the security services and was willing to trade the name and a description for a lighter sentence. Simpson was shocked he hadn't heard of Connor's arrest but Miller explained the general news blackout and specific intention not to let the security service know, so the IRA contact wasn't forewarned.

"He'll be in hospital for a few more days but he's fundamentally okay," Miller explained. "The doctors say we have to let him rest, so we are going to give him twenty four hours before we get into a serious negotiation with him."

Simpson asked the obvious question. "Who is the contact?"

"Don't have a clue," Miller replied. "But I believe Connor does probably have something worth trading."

"So why are you telling me?" Simpson asked.

"I just want you to pass on our call to Jones."

"You think it's him?" Simpson shot back quickly.

"I don't know. But Connor says he is very senior and they are blackmailing him."

"It could be any number of people then. Even me!"

Miller ignored Simpson's flippant remark. "Will you do it?"

"Where are you keeping him?"

Miller took that as a positive response. "He's in the Chelsea hospital. We've got him in a private room. He won't be fit enough to move for a couple of days but there's nothing much wrong with his brain or speech."

"Jones isn't going to take kindly to this. If he isn't the contact and I have to say it doesn't sound very bloody likely that he is, then he'll go ape shit at you trying to keep this from him. And even if it is him, I wouldn't want to be in your shoes."

"Will you just tell him, please? Leave me to worry about the consequences."

"OK. On your head be it."

Simpson hadn't bothered with any farewell pleasantries. Miller suddenly found himself holding a phone with nobody on the other end. He replaced the receiver confident that Simpson would play his part in the deception.

As the one call finished his phone rang again. He listened intently before thanking the caller for the update. So Murphy didn't have a girlfriend but he had a younger sister Samantha, who had flown into Heathrow the day after the capture of her brother. She fitted the age of the girl in Ashdown's betting shop and the park. That could explain a great deal. She would want Ashdown dead and Connor as well if he had been responsible for the rocket attack. Now they had a name they were making progress. They would find Samantha Murphy.

CHAPTER TWELVE

Tom and Melanie had gone back to the Imperial directly from Richmond Park. The first thing Tom had then done was to call the new hospital to ask after his brother. The news was positive. His brother had been moved to the London hospital without problem. There would be a long recuperation and some possible long term damage but for the first time the new Doctor had confirmed he was recovering well.

Allied to the safe return from the park, it was cause for a celebration and they ordered room service and a bottle of champagne. It would be a slightly muted celebration given recent events. The real celebration would have to wait for Colin's return home. Before that though, Colin was going to have another memorable visit to his bedside as Melanie was adamant she wanted to visit again, as soon as the doctors allowed. He had previously been very sleepy and drugged so Tom did wonder if he would just think of it subsequently as a dream. Tom was looking forward to seeing Colin in conversation with Melanie. His face was going to be a picture and the moment priceless.

Melanie had made a call to organize the protection they had discussed with Miller and two bodyguards were going to be with them from tomorrow morning. Tom thought it could be quite intrusive having two people follow them around everywhere but felt they had little choice. They wouldn't be armed though, so he hoped they weren't just recruiting two professional shields that would put themselves in the line of fire. Neither he nor Melanie wanted to be responsible for anyone else getting shot because of them.

Tom knew he had fallen in love with Melanie and was fairly sure she also had strong feelings for him. However, he was still unsure whether they could have a future together. There just seemed so many practical hurdles to overcome. Not forgetting also that they had come together when both in danger and the circumstances had almost certainly had a significant short term impact on their feelings. Was what they were feeling simply the result of the shared danger they had survived? How would their relationship stand up to real life? She would be away for months on end on film sets. What was he going to do? Follow her around like a lapdog. He didn't think it would be the recipe for a great relationship.

If he sold his betting shop and house it would just about pay off the outstanding loans and so he would be left with virtually nothing. He had a few pounds in the bank now but that wouldn't last very long. Not a great way to start a relationship with Melanie. And then there was another really big challenge he would face. Melanie was famous for her romantic roles in movies. Would the thought of her doing love scenes with other actors drive him wild with jealousy? Of course it would!

He sure was great at coming up with a long list of obstacles. He wasn't so good at finding answers. That was going to have to change if he was serious about the future. He couldn't expect Melanie to solve everything. As he turned once again to kiss her and explore her body he temporarily put all thoughts of the future to the back of his mind. For now the present was going to receive all his focus.

Miller was sure if it was Jones he would have to act fast. If it was someone else then he had to hope that, as they were supposed to be in a senior position, they would somehow find out from Jones. Connor could reveal the informant's identity at any time.

Miller couldn't leave Connor unprotected in his room. That would be too suspicious. There were two men maintaining guard on the door of the private room. One was Taylor who Miller trusted completely to stay alert to any sign of danger. Taylor knew what Jones looked like and was aware how potentially dangerous he could be. If Jones arrived, Taylor would let him in the room but would be ready to join Miller at a second's notice. Taylor was armed with a traditional pistol but the reliable Sergeant with him had a Tazer. Miller thought the Tazer may be more useful than a real weapon as he was keen to take Jones alive.

So how would Jones plan to get to Connor? It would be an official visit Miller decided. He would brazenly enter the room and probably plan to use an injection or look to interfere with the drip. Least that was how Miller would do it. So Miller planned to stay in the room and await a visit. The very arrival of Jones would confirm his guilt as far as Miller was concerned.

The medical staff had helped provide a realistic dummy that was bandaged and connected to a couple of monitors. The lighting in the room was turned down very low, which was to be expected as it was night time and at a glance, certainly from the door, it would appear Connor was in the hospital bed and still alive but sleeping.

Miller was sat in a chair at the back of the room where he wouldn't be seen at first by anyone entering the room. He wasn't armed but as he hadn't carried a weapon for years was happy to rely on support from the officers outside.

Taylor had rightly questioned whether they should simply refuse admission to everyone but Miller had said no to that suggestion. Taylor shared Miller's view that the very arrival of Jones would be sufficient evidence of his guilt. Not evidence to put in front of a court but enough for them to be certain. Miller was hoping for more though. He needed Jones to show his hand.

Now it was a case of waiting patiently and hoping that Jones would make an appearance. It was at times like this he missed smoking. Not that he would have been able to smoke in a hospital even if he hadn't given up twenty years ago. In his youth, cigarettes had helped him get through many a stakeout or long wait for news.

Eduardo had no regret for his actions. Not even for using her one last time. In fact that had been a necessary part of trying to make it look like a random sex attack, although ultimately they would discover who she was and no doubt put everything together. But that would take time. The Chief had wanted it this way. It could not lead back to him.

Eduardo had decided in the house, when he saw Sam kill Connor, that she was out of control and too dangerous. He knew then he couldn't trust her and their relationship had to end. And in his line of business, there really was only one way of ending a relationship.

When he called Belfast to report Connor's demise, he also mentioned Sam had been in contact. The fact she had his number wasn't questioned. They had worked together in the past enough times. He'd admitted he was a bit surprised to hear from her and she had asked to meet, saying she needed his help.

In life he always looked to maximize the results from every opportunity. Though Sam had become a personal problem, he had thought there might be some value to be earned from what he had to do. He found he wasn't alone in finding Sam to be trouble. He was economical with the truth but had agreed he would meet her and remove her, earning the promise of a very significant payback. He'd shown some reluctance at first suggestion he should kill her and that had led to an increased offer. It seemed there was a strong desire to never see her return to Belfast. The Chief was insistent her death could not appear to be part of the current troubles in Brighton and London. There must be no suggestion her death was linked to the organization or him personally.

Eduardo had decided he would waste no time in contriving a fancy way of making her disappear. Speed would be his ally. He would finish her, then head straight to Heathrow. He had remembered the country park, where he had previously met a couple of contacts and decided it would suit his plans perfectly. He had told Sam to pack her bag as they would be moving hotel to one in the Heathrow area. He had used the excuse he didn't like to spend too long in one place and anyway the new hotel was well positioned for when they flew to Paris.

She had complied happily and he had paid their bill with cash. If he was ever traced to the hotel, then the front desk would have a copy of his passport but he would be well gone by then. He went by many names and though he couldn't use this one again, it was of little consequence. He had no shortage of passports.

In the busy hotel he had kept a low profile since registering. He had wiped the room of fingerprints, even though he had never been arrested in any country and there was no record on file of his prints. They would have his DNA but again no match. It was all a little messy but he was content it was low risk.

For a while he had been very infatuated with Sam but now he would head back home and remember her fondly, until inevitably another girl would come along. He would ensure the next girl was simply a good cook and good in bed. A girl like from back home, not one of these Western Europeans he didn't really understand.

A woman back home knew her place. She didn't dictate to her man. She didn't cause him trouble. She was there to attend to his needs. Sam had been too independent. It had been like the most exciting roller coaster ride at the fairground but it was so scary, it would be a long time before he took the ride again.

Miller heard sounds outside the door and knew he was about to greet a visitor. His body tensed in the expectation and hope that it would be Jones about to walk through the door. He was disappointed when the rather more rotund shape of Simpson entered the room. He watched Simpson stare at who he assumed was Connor in the bed. Miller said nothing for a second. Simpson took a couple of paces towards the bed.

"Didn't expect to see you," Miller interrupted Simpson's approach to the bed.

Simpson whipped around, obviously shocked to hear Miller's voice. "God you surprised me," he stated, trying to regain his composure and wiping his brow with his hand. "Didn't see you there," he continued, forcing a smile.

"Sorry, didn't mean to make you jump like that. Rather hoped I would be seeing Jones, not you." Miller didn't hide the disappointment in his voice.

"Thought I'd check out if anything had happened. Had any other visitors?"

"Sadly no. Would have thought you'd seen enough of hospitals for a while." Simpson's left arm was supported in a sling. The result of the bullet he'd received in Richmond Park, which rather unfortunately for him had missed the bullet proof vest.

Simpson gently rubbed his arm. "True but my curiosity got the better of me. Has our bird been singing?"

Miller hesitated for just a second. He was about to share the truth with Simpson when he observed him once again wipe sweat from his brow. Some instinct made him keep up the pretence. "Not yet unfortunately. He spends all his time sleeping." Miller wondered if he was imagining a slight look of relief on Simpson's face.

"Listen, do you need a break?" Simpson offered. "Take a pee or get a coffee or something?"

Miller climbed out the comfortable armchair. "Good idea. Could do with both actually. I'll only be five minutes."

"No problem. I'll mind the fort in here while you're gone."

"Thanks." Miller was grateful for the chance to stretch his legs. He turned back as he reached the door to see Simpson settling into his recently vacated chair.

As Miller emerged from the room, Taylor and the Sergeant both looked up expectantly. "Be back in five. Bob, why don't you just keep Simpson company till I return. Sergeant, if by any chance Jones does arrive, simply don't let him in the room till I get back." In truth Miller now thought it very unlikely he would see Jones. As Taylor got up from his chair, Miller added, "No need to mention about Connor. Not even to Simpson."

Taylor shot him a quizzical look but said nothing.

Miller moved a few yards down the corridor where there was no chance of being overheard, took out his mobile phone and found the number he needed. It was getting late but he pressed the call button anyway. It took a few seconds before a grumpy voice answered at the other end, "To what do I owe this pleasure?"

Miller had been gone a good ten minutes before he returned to the room. Taylor and Simpson were engaged in a conversation about football.

"Sorry I was so long," he apologized. "Tony, do you mind looking after the fort a bit longer, only I need to borrow Bob. It will only take five minutes"

"No problem," Simpson confirmed.

Taylor followed Miller out the room. Miller ensured he pulled the door properly closed behind Taylor. "Bob, in one minute we are going back inside and I'm not sure what we will find but be aware I now believe that Simpson is the man we want, not Jones. Keep your weapon close to hand." Turning to the Sergeant he added, "Stay alert."

"Simpson? You sure boss?" Taylor seemed disbelieving.

"Afraid so, Bob. And remember he's dangerous. Let's go."

Taylor instinctively put his hand inside his jacket to feel his weapon. He was still holding it as he followed Miller back in the room. He carried a Glock 17 semi-automatic pistol which was both his weapon of choice and standard issue.

Miller threw the door open to find Simpson standing by the bedside. He was holding the bag hanging above the bed that fed a tube into the dummy's hand. Simpson wheeled around in shock. He was no longer wearing his sling. If Miller had had any remaining doubts they were removed by the look on Simpson's face. Taylor saw the same look and without hesitation drew his pistol from its shoulder holster.

Simpson realised he had been discovered and moved with a speed that defied his size. He grasped Taylor's extended arm holding the pistol, at the wrist, turned into him with a well-practiced judo move and threw him to the ground in one quick movement.

Miller tried to wrap his arms around Simpson's wide back to hold him but found himself on the receiving end of an elbow that connected with his nose and caused him to lose his grip. Simpson followed up by lashing out with his leg and sweeping Miller's legs away causing him to fall to the floor.

From his prone position, Miller saw Simpson pick up Taylor's fallen gun from the floor just as the door was thrown open. The bulky Sergeant appeared in the doorway holding his Taser weapon at the ready, trying to assess the scene and without hesitation, Simpson shot him with Taylor's pistol. The sound was deafening in the confined space. As the Sergeant crashed to the ground Simpson was already rushing from the room.

Tom and Melanie had spent an amazing twenty minutes with Colin. He was still very weak but able to communicate, though he spoke softly and slowly. It was the first time that Liz hadn't been at Colin's bedside. The nurse informed them she had gone home for a proper night's sleep and a change of clothes. Tom had been impressed by the devotion she had shown. There was no doubting she loved Colin. The thought made Tom happy for his brother. He hoped that one day Melanie might feel the same about him.

The nurse also warned them that Liz had told Colin about the death of John and how he had saved Colin's life. He had remembered the night's events and asked Liz about John, so she had answered truthfully. The nurse said she was pleased to see them arrive as it might lift his spirits.

Tom was sure that meeting Melanie had improved both his spirits and his recovery. She had held his hand on arrival and Tom was worried the heart monitor would set off some alarm. He smiled as he watched them chat. Yet again Melanie seemed completely at home speaking to Colin, despite he was obviously in awe of her.

She kept the conversation brief and promised to return again soon. She added, she expected to be seeing a lot more of him in the future as she was planning to see a lot more of his brother. Colin had glanced at Tom with a look of surprise at that comment and he had just smiled in response. Tom hardly said a word as he was sure Colin much preferred speaking with Melanie. He now believed there would be lots of future opportunities for them to speak as Colin was undoubtedly getting better. Whether Melanie would truly be around in the future was still very debatable so let Colin spend time chatting with her.

They kept the visit brief on the doctor's instructions. They had had to wait to see Colin while the doctor did some further checks and it was getting quite late by the time they left, promising to return again soon. Outside the room, Tom thanked her and once again listened to the response that it was she who owed him the thanks. All she had brought him and his family was trouble. Tom suggested they get a coffee from the machine they had passed earlier down the corridor.

As they rounded the corner arm in arm they walked into what seemed like a stampeding bull elephant such was the force with which they collided. The result was that all three of them were thrown to the floor.

"This is a hospital," Tom started to complain, when he realized he recognized who had charged into them. He also saw Simpson had a weapon in his hand. "What the hell's..." Tom didn't finish his sentence.

"Get up," Simpson ordered, climbing to his feet. All the time he was pointing the gun directly at Tom. At the same time Tom heard a commotion in the distance and the sound of running feet coming closer.

"Get up," Simpson repeated. He grabbed Melanie and hauled her to her feet. Tom reached out to intervene but Simpson kicked him hard in the midriff causing him to double up on the ground clutching at his stomach.

Miller and Taylor emerged into view and slowed to a halt as they appraised the situation. Simpson was using Melanie as a human shield. He was pointing Taylor's gun at Melanie's head. "Keep back," Simpson warned. "You know I won't hesitate to use this."

"OK Tony, take it easy," Miller implored. "You are just making matters worse."

Simpson let out a small sardonic laugh. "Couldn't really be much worse could it?"

Tom's pain in his stomach had been replaced by anger. "What the fuck is going on here?" he asked. No one seemed immediately inclined to answer. "He saved my life," Tom continued, looking at Miller, hoping it might prompt some explanation.

"Why did you save him?" Miller asked of Simpson.

"Believe it or not I abhor killing. Unfortunately sometimes it becomes necessary. On that occasion it wasn't necessary."

Simpson started backing down the corridor, keeping Melanie as a shield. Miller and Taylor both took a step forward as if to follow. Simpson fired a warning shot into the wall beside them. "Don't anyone move. I won't pretend I want to shoot you but in the interest of self-preservation, I will do so if necessary."

Miller and Taylor were both unarmed and made no further effort to move. Tom slowly got to his feet so as not to cause any alarm. A nurse appeared from a room behind Simpson, attracted by the commotion. Simpson glanced behind as he heard her exclamation and waved the gun in her direction.

"Get away," he screamed and she scurried away down the corridor.

"Give up, Tony," Miller begged. "We called it in already. This place will be swamped with armed officers within minutes."

"They better be careful then. Wouldn't be good to see someone as famous as this get harmed." He pushed the gun a little closer to Melanie's face.

"Why?" Miller asked, hoping to buy some time while the armed response team arrived.

"Had no choice, it was help them or go to prison for a very long time."

"What did they have over you?"

"Doesn't matter," Simpson said dismissively.

"Was it you?" Miller asked.

"What do you mean?"

"Was it you betrayed Brian Potter?"

Simpson went pale at the mention of a name from the past he had tried hard to forget. He said nothing but the silence told Miller what he wanted to know. Of all the times Simpson had been forced to provide information, it was the occasion he detested himself the most for. He had known Brian Potter personally. Been drinking with him and shared a joke. Simpson knew what they would do to him but had still told them how to find him.

"You bastard," Miller swore. "He didn't deserve to die like that. No man should."

"I agree but it was a very long time ago. Times were different then. Everyone on both sides has dark secrets we don't want to remember. Even you!" Simpson didn't really believe what he was saying. He just felt the need to defend himself.

"The difference is the rest of us didn't betray our friends," Miller snapped back.

Miller, Tony and Tom were creeping forwards but not seeking to close the gap on Simpson who was only succeeding in moving very slowly as Melanie was making his job harder by dragging her feet.

Simpson used his forearm to wipe the perspiration from his brow. "By the way, satisfy my curiosity," he asked. How did you get on to me?"

"The Godfather, Miller said simply." Seeing Simpson didn't understand he explained further. "There's a point where Marlon Brando warns his son that whoever comes to broker peace will betray them. No matter how much they trust the individual and it seems impossible he would betray them. I thought of that when you turned up at the hospital. Then I called Jones and he knew nothing about us holding Connor. Said you were retiring and taking a holiday. Very remiss of you not to bother informing him."

"I was going to tell him in the morning. After my visit here tonight."

"I'll give you another line from The Godfather. At one point in the film Don Corleone says 'revenge is a dish that tastes best when it is cold.' There is no escape for you now. Nowhere you can hide. I will hunt you down wherever you go and make you pay for what you did to Brian." Miller's tone was cold and carried absolute conviction.

"Good luck," Simpson retorted.

"You know that Connor is already dead?" Miller asked, feeling very pleased with himself.

"What do you mean?"

"That was just a dummy in the bed."

Simpson looked shocked by the revelation. "You always were a clever bastard."

"Satisfy my curiosity, Tony. Did you have someone in Ireland give us the lead that they had an informant called Jones?"

"A nice idea but no. Jones was always my cover name. Seemed a better idea than Smith at the time. I did smile when that idiot Jones became my boss."

Simpson was edging backwards along the corridor still keeping the gun to Melanie's head. "Keep your distance," he warned. "I won't hesitate to shoot her or you. Another death will make little difference now."

Tom looked at Miller for inspiration but just received a gentle nod as a warning to do nothing. He didn't like feeling powerless to help Melanie. He could see she was in pain as Simpson had his arm clamped tightly around her windpipe, as he dragged her back by the throat.

Simpson was now twenty meters away and about to round a curve in the corridor that would put him temporarily out of sight. Tom realized it would also afford an opportunity for them to close the gap without being seen. He was under no illusion that he could rush Simpson the way he had the two IRA kidnappers.

Tom hadn't heard of Brian Potter but he understood from what he'd heard that he had been betrayed by Simpson. Now this same Simpson was threatening all of them and in particular Melanie. Tom once again felt out of his depth and this time he needed the professionals to rescue Melanie but he wasn't confident they would be able to do so, without her being harmed.

It was the nightmare scenario he'd hoped to avoid, when she had refused to go back to the States. He'd let his own selfish motives get in the way of doing what was best for her. He should have driven her to the airport and made her get on a plane. It was what Miller had wanted to do. But no, he had been too worried if he did that he would never see her again. He had played his hand very wrongly.

Had Simpson also been responsible for the attack on Colin? Tom didn't pretend to fully understand what was going on here but there was a fair chance he was involved. Tom remembered the sense of optimism he was feeling when he left Colin's room just a short time earlier. Now here he was plummeting the depths again. This man had a lot to answer for. With hindsight though Tom could see he too had a lot to answer for. He prayed Melanie wasn't going to pay the price for his selfish stupidity.

Simpson had not prepared an elaborate backup plan but the years of experience had taught him to identify an additional escape route, in case of unforeseen trouble. As he rounded the bend in the corridor, he turned to his left and smashed the fire alarm he had noticed earlier. Next to it was an emergency exit and he pushed the bar on the door to open and was immediately met by a blast of icy cold air from outside. He had loosened his grip on Melanie in order to open the door and she was struggling to get free.

"If you want to live much longer, stop this," he threatened as he gripped her tightly and pushed the barrel of the gun to her ear. "I prefer to take you with me but if I have to leave you behind, you won't be breathing."

She stopped struggling and he managed to drag her outside as he slammed the door shut behind them.

Tom, Miller and Bob Taylor all moved forward in unison the moment they lost sight of Simpson. A careful approach turned into a run when they heard the alarm. Miller surveyed the corridor ahead and seeing no sign of Simpson guessed he had used the fire exit. He opened the door and peered out into the cold, cautiously. He realized the door emerged onto the edge of the hospital car park.

A bullet spat against the wall and he quickly drew back within the hospital. He had just had time to spot Simpson beside a car with an open door, pointing a gun in his direction. At the same time he was trying to push Melanie into the car.

Other doors along the corridor were opening and a mixture of nurses and patients were peering out trying to establish if the alarm was for real. "It's okay," Miller tried to assure everyone. "Please go back inside. I accidentally broke the alarm." He turned back to Taylor. "Bob, keep everyone away from the car park and let the boys know what's happened. I'm going after Simpson."

"I'm coming with you," Tom stated firmly.

Miller started to object but from the look on Tom's face knew he would be wasting his breadth, so settled for delivering some advice. "Okay but keep behind me and your head down."

Taylor moved a little way down the corridor and made a call on his mobile.

Miller opened the emergency exit door once more and glanced nervously to where he had last seen Simpson. Tom was right behind looking over his shoulder. Simpson was now inside his car and

Melanie could be seen seated beside him. She was staring in their direction with a look of horror on her face.

Miller shouted back to Taylor. "Bob, he's driving a white Audi and he's got Melanie Adams in the passenger seat so tell them to take care."

Without waiting for a response, Miller was off and running, quickly followed by Tom.

Simpson was pulling away at speed from the parking space he had occupied and never saw the car that was crawling along the lane looking for somewhere to park. Simpson's Audi barged the other car out of the way as their wings collided but the collision had slowed him.

Miller lunged for the door but the Audi accelerated and he was prone on the ground before he really knew what had happened. Swearing, he regained his feet and saw that Tom was chasing the car down the next parking lane.

The car couldn't accelerate to any truly great speed as the parking lanes were short and then required a hundred and eighty degree turn. By running directly across the lanes, Tom was quickly able to get ahead of the Audi and stood in the lane as the car approached. At the last second he realized it had been a stupid idea to stand in the middle of the lane, somehow expecting that Simpson would come to a halt, just because he was standing there. Simpson had already saved his life once but it was now evident he would happily run Tom down, if he stood in the way any longer. Tom threw himself to the side just in time.

He regained his feet and cut through two more lines of cars, to see the Audi once again heading directly towards him. He felt completely powerless to intervene as the Audi roared past and he saw the imploring face of Melanie at the window.

He watched as Simpson negotiated the last lane of cars and then was at the exit to the car park. Tom could hear the approaching sirens that confirmed the arrival of reinforcements but Simpson was accelerating towards the exit and safety.

He looked around and saw a man about to get into a silver BMW. Without thinking he rushed at the man and pushed him aside.

"I need your car," Tom screamed. He tore the key from his grasp as he pushed him aside. The man seemed too stunned to react and in the time it took him to regain his composure, Tom was already seated behind the wheel and accelerating away.

Miller joined the man a minute later and they both stared after the BMW, as it disappeared into the distance.

Simpson glanced in his mirror and could see the BMW giving chase. A police car with flashing lights and alarm ringing arrived at the car park entrance at the same moment he was about to exit. The police driver spotted the Audi and flung his car across the exit to try and block his escape. Simpson floored the accelerator and crashed into the rear of the police car and managed to keep going, as the police car was spun around by the crash, just leaving enough room for Simpson to continue.

The BMW followed him through the space and accelerated right up to his tail. Simpson kept his foot to the floor and overtook two cars before darting back into his lane, just before colliding with an oncoming white van. Simpson could see in his mirror that the BMW had not immediately followed but did so once the van was past.

Simpson was worried by the traffic coming to a halt up ahead for the red lights. He didn't want to come to a stop and give the girl a chance to escape. He pulled out to overtake the queuing cars and let out a small prayer nothing would come towards him as he threw the car around the front of the queue in a left turn. The BMW was still right behind him. He could also hear multiple police sirens in the distance, which seemed to be coming from all directions. He knew he had to ditch the car and quickly.

Tom had almost lost control when he followed Simpson through the red lights and turned sharply left in front of the queuing traffic. His rear wheels spinning on a patch of ice. He had followed close behind Simpson without really thinking further ahead. He now realized he couldn't do anything while Simpson had Melanie hostage.

He certainly couldn't ram the Audi which had been one of his first thoughts. In fact he was worried that just by following so close behind, he could be putting her life in greater danger. On the other hand though, he couldn't just do nothing so instead of chasing the car, he settled back to following it at a safer distance.

He suddenly remembered he had Miller's mobile number in his phone and called him. He smiled at the thought he was breaking the law by driving and phoning.

Miller answered immediately. "Where the hell are you?" he asked.

"Following the Audi down …" Tom didn't know where he was and tried to read the names of the side streets. "Just passed Midas Street on my left. Where the hell are the reinforcements?"

"On their way. I'm just five minutes behind you. Keep this line open and give me a commentary of your whereabouts. And don't do anything foolish!"

Tom was driving well over the speed limit in a heavily built up area, with one hand on the steering wheel and the other hand holding the phone to his ear. He thought that in normal circumstances that would count as pretty foolish. He was glad he was used to driving BMWs.

Simpson knew he could do nothing to shake the BMW from his tail. He had to get out the car before backup arrived and trapped him. At the moment there was just that damn Ashdown behind him. There was only one thing to do. He braked fast and then as he skidded to a halt he leaned across Melanie to open the passenger door. He pushed her out the car before she knew what he was doing.

He accelerated away before she had even hit the pavement. Looking in his rear view mirror, he was pleased to see his dumping Melanie had had the desired effect and the BMW had pulled into the kerb, to no doubt check on her welfare.

He drove a further half a mile then dumped the car at the side of the road on double yellow lines, next to the entrance to the tube station. He threw open the door and once again belied his size with the speed he moved. He cast an anxious glance back down the road but there was no sign of any approaching police cars, only the sound of sirens. He didn't like leaving such an obvious pointer to where he was headed but felt he had little choice.

He hurried down the steps hoping that a train would be along very shortly. He swiped his oyster card and joined the platform heading north. If the platform was suddenly swamped with police, he was trapped and stood willing a train to arrive. The platform quickly filled with a mixture of people, a number of them carrying shopping bags. Others were dressed for a night out on the town, which didn't surprise him as the tube headed very much into the centre of the London night life scene.

He breathed a huge sigh of relief when after waiting what seemed an eternity but was less than five minutes, a train finally arrived. He had never been so happy to see the doors on the carriage close and the train pulled away into the tunnel.

Tom saw the Audi slow and Melanie deposited on the pavement. He braked so fast the car behind hooted vigorously and only just missed crashing into his rear. Tom was out the car in a flash and reached Melanie just as she regained her feet. He was thankful she looked dazed but unharmed.

"Are you ok?" he asked, reaching out to support her.

"Fine," was the response as Melanie ran her hands through her hair, trying to improve her rather dishevelled appearance. "We need to get that son of a bitch!"

They both turned at the sound of the approaching police siren. The car pulled in to the side and Miller shouted through the open window, "Are you both all right?"

"We're okay," Tom replied. "Simpson is a couple of minutes ahead of you."

Miller turned back to his driver and the car pulled away at speed with its back wheels struggling for grip.

"Come on," Melanie said, hurrying to Tom's car. "You can drive."

"Where are we going?" Tom asked confused.

Melanie smiled. "Don't you want to know if they catch him?"

Once seated beside Melanie he gave her a questioning look. "You sure about this?"

"We're wasting time," was her response.

Tom knew it wasn't the sensible course of action but it didn't stop him pushing the accelerator hard to the floor and speeding away in the same direction as Miller had gone.

They had only driven a short distance when they spotted both the police car and Simpson's white Audi at the side of the road. Tom pulled over and as they emerged from the car, they could hear the sirens of at least two other police cars approaching from some distance away.

"They must have taken the Tube," Tom explained, pointing at the steps leading down into the station. A sign over the entrance announced it was called Gloucester Road.

Melanie didn't wait for a discussion and headed straight for the station entrance, closely followed by Tom. They descended the steps two at a time and found themselves in an open area which housed the ticket office. Although not overly busy there were a few others milling around looking at maps on the wall and passing through the barriers, which led down an escalator to the platforms.

Tom purchased two travel card tickets that would allow them to travel anywhere within London, as he didn't have a clue where they might actually be going. He wasn't convinced they should be purchasing any tickets or trying to follow Simpson and Miller anywhere but he knew Melanie well enough by now that her mind was set and there was no point in arguing.

Now Tom had the tickets, he was faced with the decision of which direction to take. The station served three different lines, District, Circle and Piccadilly. Each of them then went in two directions so they were faced with a ridiculous six options.

For no good reason, he decided to start with the Piccadilly line and called Melanie to follow. They headed to the left and he handed her a ticket and she followed him through the automatic barrier and down the appropriate escalator. As they reached the bottom they could go left or right.

He took a quick look at the left platform which was relatively empty. Then he looked to the right which was heading north via Green Park and Leicester Square. The platform was busy, suggesting everyone had been waiting some time for a train. There was no sign of Miller or any policemen for that matter. It was impossible to see if Simpson was on the platform without closer inspection. Melanie was looking at him waiting for his decision.

Miller hurried down the steps into the tube, followed close behind by his driver. He headed straight for the nearest escalators and flashed his badge at the man standing guard by the ticket barrier, telling him to let them through. He could see the signs saying he was heading for the District and Circle lines. He was reasonably familiar with the line and his first thought was that Simpson might head clockwise, trying to get to one of the mainline stations such as Paddington or Euston.

At the bottom of the escalator, he told his driver to check the anticlockwise platform while he took the clockwise platform. There were quite a number of people on the platform and he went first to his right and made his way along the platform checking for Simpson. He went carefully because Simpson was armed and he didn't want a bloodbath. Then he went back past where he'd joined the platform and continued to check along the remainder of the platform. There was no sign of Simpson and he returned to meet his driver whose face and negative nod, told him immediately he had also been unsuccessful.

Miller was suddenly worried the car at the top of the station entrance had simply been a decoy. Simpson was a clever bastard. But there was still the chance he had taken the Piccadilly line. Miller told the driver to get outside the station and direct the first officers to arrive to join him on the Piccadilly platforms. If they weren't armed officers, they should tread carefully. Subsequent backup should start searching the immediate vicinity in case Simpson was on foot. And get a helicopter in the air asap.

Miller then started running back along the platform to where he had seen the exit indicating access to the Piccadilly line. He shouted for people to get out the way but still had to push aside one surprised man who hadn't heard him. The man swore at him and others followed suite, telling him to be careful. Miller shouted sorry but didn't stop. He was rushing towards the Piccadilly sign but doing so with no great optimism. He realized that even if Simpson had taken the Piccadilly line, it was very unlikely he would still be on the platform.

Miller was through the exit and at the bottom of a huge escalator. He started running up the escalator but he had to slow halfway. As he neared the top he was breathing heavily and his legs felt like jelly. He cursed the fact he wasn't as fit as he used to be and slowed to a walk.

Tom and Melanie had joined the Piccadilly line platform at one end and started to slowly work their way along looking for Simpson.

"Remember he's got a gun," Tom warned.

"I remember," Melanie almost shouted, having to compete with the sound of a train emerging from the tunnel and arriving at the platform. She took an involuntary step back despite not being particularly close to the edge.

They looked at each other uncertain what to do. All the passengers had suddenly congregated at the front of the platform, ready to board the train. It made it impossible to move further along the platform.

"Can you see him?" Tom asked.

They were both desperately searching the faces boarding the train but it was a long platform and they could only see halfway along.

"Do we get on?" Melanie asked.

Tom didn't respond. He had his eyes fixed on someone who had just boarded. The man gave a furtive glance around as he stepped onto the train. Tom only saw him for an instant and was far from certain it was Simpson.

The door on the train started to close and Tom thrust his body in the way. For a second the door pressed on his body trying to close but then the sensors detected his presence and the door slid back open again. He held out his hand to Melanie and pulled her through the door before it closed behind them. A couple of passengers standing by the doorway looked at them and smiled at their last minute attempt to get on the train.

"Did you see him?" Melanie asked excitedly.

"Not sure," Tom answered uncertainly. "I saw someone. It could have been him but I don't know. I only saw him for an instant."

"Where the hell is Miller?" Melanie asked.

"No idea." Tom had been thinking the same thing.

"Oh well don't worry if he isn't on here," Melanie beamed. "I always wanted to ride your underground system."

Tom laughed at the thought someone would take such pleasure from riding the tube. As far as he was concerned it was a dirty, hot, cramped means of travel to be avoided if at all possible, especially in the rush hour.

The couple standing close by them were still smiling and the man was whispering in his partner's ear and then looking in their direction. Tom realized they must have recognized Melanie. With everything that had happened, he had completely forgotten about her superstar status. He pulled her closer to him so she had her back to most of the carriage. The last thing they needed was all her fans asking for autographs.

The train was coming to a halt at the next station. As the doors slid open he leaned out and could see that very few people were getting off, so he was able to be sure that Simpson wasn't one of them. Then again he probably wasn't even on the train. However, someone he did recognize had got off the train and then got back on again.

Miller was walking fast in the direction of the Piccadilly line. He had given up any further attempt at running. He was halfway along the pedestrian tunnel when he could hear the train arriving up ahead. He swore to himself and broke into a trot. He emerged onto the platform just as the electronic doors were closing and swore again out loud. Then suddenly the doors reopened and he knew he had a few seconds to make the train, before they would shut again. He threw himself through the nearest doors just in time. He was on the train but was Simpson?

He hated not being able to communicate with anyone above ground. He had no idea what was going on. The sooner they invented a way you could use your mobile underground the better.

Miller worked his way along the carriage looking at the passengers to make sure Simpson wasn't among them. At the end, he looked through the glass window into the next carriage but there was no sign of Simpson.

As the train pulled into the next station he descended onto the platform and looked at the few others getting off. Not seeing Simpson, he moved quickly to the next carriage and got back on the train. He walked the length of the carriage looking for Simpson but again without success.

He was feeling quite despondent. If Simpson escaped them now, he would be very difficult to ever find. His experience in the security service would have taught him how to prepare for just such an eventuality as this and he could have fake passports, money and everything else he needed stashed away.

The train pulled into Knightsbridge station. Miller moved quicker this time. He jumped from the train and walked quickly along the platform. He was able to check both that Simpson hadn't left the train and that he wasn't in either of the next two carriages.

He looked at the tube map over the doors of the carriage as they closed, which reminded him that the next stop was Hyde Park Corner. That would probably be quiet but then it would be Green Park, which connects with a couple of other lines. After that it was a succession of further stations all normally very busy and connecting to other lines. Damn he could do with some help.

Tom's spirits had soared at the sight of Miller. He still didn't know if Simpson was on the train but was very pleased to know they weren't alone. He had been giving thought to what they would do if they spotted Simpson leaving the train at one of the earlier stations. In theory they would have followed him but what if Simpson had seen them. He realized the idea of the two of them following an armed and very dangerous man was actually sheer madness.

Tom had been clear with Melanie that they had to hang back if they did see Simpson and once above ground they could call Miller to let him know. That was the best result they could achieve. He had to believe that Simpson wouldn't start shooting at them with numerous witnesses around but he didn't want to put the theory to the test.

The train pulled into Green Park station. Tom was keen to let Miller know they were on the train but not in any way that would attract everyone's attention. He put his arm through Melanie's and they stepped onto the platform. Miller was still half a dozen carriages away but he should be able to see them.

Melanie gasped as she spotted Simpson hurrying from a carriage halfway down the train. Tom had also seen him and immediately turned into Melanie and kissed her, hiding them from Simpson's view if he should happen to glance in their direction. For an instant he thought to just keep kissing and forget the idiocy they were embarked upon but he couldn't resist checking on Simpson.

Quite a large group of people had left the train and most were headed in the direction of the Victoria Line exit from the platform. The passengers were funnelling through a narrow exit at no great pace and patiently waiting their turn.

Tom considered it safe to follow and joined the back of the now quite small queue. There was no sign of Miller and he wondered whether he was up ahead or still on the train. As they emerged on the other side of the exit they joined one of the two escalators heading upwards.

At the top, they headed left following the Victoria Line signs. They found themselves in a tunnel, following the passengers heading in the only direction possible, towards the Victoria Line.

Tom accelerated his pace as he knew Simpson wouldn't be hanging around and he also hoped to find Miller. Melanie linked her arm in his and they looked like any ordinary couple in a hurry.

They overtook several slow walking passengers and then twenty five meters ahead, Tom caught sight of Miller. Melanie had also seen him and squeezed Tom's arm. Miller seemed unaware of them and Tom wondered if he had also seen Simpson leave the train and was following him. Miller was moving at quite a fast pace and they wouldn't be able to close the gap on him without running, which would potentially make Simpson aware of their presence, so wasn't an option.

Miller had alighted from the train at Green Park, planning to search the next couple of carriages, when he saw Simpson hurry from the train and head for the exit to the Victoria Line. Miller hung back out of view as he didn't want to challenge Simpson in such an enclosed space, with so many members of the public around. He didn't fancy Simpson taking further hostages. There was also the minor matter of him not being armed and in no position to apprehend Simpson without help.

A crowd formed around the exit and Miller noticed Simpson pushing himself to the front. Miller followed discreetly behind. He followed Simpson up the busy escalator but stared at the adverts on the wall rather than in Simpson's direction.

As he followed Simpson along the tunnel towards the Victoria Line, he was surprised that Simpson didn't look behind at all. He obviously thought he was safe and Miller hoped that over confidence would make him careless. He descended a flight of steps to the platforms and momentarily lost sight of Simpson, as up ahead he turned onto the actual platform.

Miller was concerned about his next move. If Simpson had chosen to stand on the platform right by the entrance from which Miller would emerge, then he might find himself walking right into him. He hung back a second and then, as a middle aged couple joined the platform, he followed close behind using them to obscure Simpson's view. He glanced nervously to each side and could see Simpson ambling down the platform to his right seemingly still unaware he was being followed.

At the same time a train was approaching from the left. Miller quickly turned to look at the oncoming train in case Simpson also turned and thus he would now only have a rear view of Miller. As the train came to a halt Miller risked a glance in Simpson's direction and saw him boarding the front carriage. Miller hurried down the platform a little to get closer to Simpson and joined the front of the third carriage.

The train was packed and he stood crammed up against an assortment of people. He had about three minutes before the train would arrive at Victoria and he knew from past experience that on arrival, virtually everyone would make a sudden rush for the exit that led to the escalators, which took you up to the mainline station. As one of the last on the train, Simpson would be one of the first off. In the mass exodus it would be easy to lose Simpson and he would have to be on his guard. At least he too would be one of the first out of his carriage.

Once above ground he would be able to call on reinforcements and was confident they would then run him to ground. They just had to be very careful not to give him the chance to take any further hostages and ensure members of the public weren't in the line of fire.

Miller had another thought, which was why had Simpson taken this rather scenic route to Victoria? At Gloucester Road when he started his journey, he was just three stops from Victoria on the Circle line. Then again it had been a smart move which had almost succeeded in him escaping. If the train had come a minute earlier he would have done. Miller recognized he had been lucky. And maybe Simpson had only decided once on the train, where he was going and plumped for Victoria. Why Victoria though? Where was he going next? He didn't have time to dwell on the thought as the train was arriving at the station.

As the doors slid open, he stepped backwards onto the platform and pretended to adjust his clothing while keeping his back to anyone exiting the first carriage. Then after a few seconds he turned and could see Simpson joining one of the escalators that ascended to the tube station concourse. Swamped by people around him he headed in the same direction, buffeted on the way by someone with two large suitcases.

He nimbly skipped by a large woman holding a young girl's hand, who was getting in the way of people who were in a hurry. Simpson was near the top of the escalator as Miller joined it and he decided he needed to walk up it, rather than just ride it, in order to close the gap a little.

As Miller jumped off the end of the escalator, he could see Simpson walking up the steps directly in front that lead to the mainline station. Miller reached for his mobile and called Taylor.

"Where the hell are you, boss?" Taylor asked.

"I've just come up out the tube at Victoria station. Simpson is about thirty meters ahead of me, looking at the departures board. Get some men here fast and lock everything down. But we have to be careful. Simpson isn't worth any member of the public getting killed."

"Will do," Taylor agreed. "Be careful boss, he's not going to come quietly."

"I know," was all Miller said before ending the call.

He was thankful he had taken the weapon from his driver when he sent him back above ground. The last thing he wanted was a Wild West style shootout but he doubted Simpson would just give up whatever the odds. He had been keeping his eye on Simpson throughout the call with Taylor. He saw him move to the specific ticket kiosk at platform thirteen, where the only ticket you can buy is for the Gatwick Express. So he is hoping to skip the country Miller thought.

He watched Simpson use his new ticket to pass through the barriers and walk about halfway down the platform before joining the train. Miller glanced up at the departure board and saw there was ten minutes until the train was due to depart. He needed more time. The train needed to be delayed. He called Taylor again and told him what he wanted him to do.

Tom and Melanie had joined the tube train at Green Park a few carriages further back from Miller. They assumed Simpson was also on the train, probably nearer the front but they hadn't seen him board. At Victoria they were carried from the train by the rush of people flocking towards the escalators. They had to wait their turn to join the bottom of the escalator and could see no sign of either Miller or Simpson.

Tom was secretly quite pleased that the danger seemed now to be well ahead of them. In the last few days he felt both he and Melanie had seen enough trouble to last a lifetime. So far luck had been with them but he didn't feel like tempting fate again.

He knew every corner of Victoria station as it was the main London terminus from Brighton. As he emerged from the tube onto the busy hub of the station he took out his mobile, thinking to give Miller a call. He looked around the open expanse of the station but couldn't spot either Miller or Simpson.

"Do you want a coffee?" Melanie asked, pointing to the nearby stand.

"Why not. I'll have a Latte please," Tom answered smiling. "I could do with warming up."

Melanie searched in her pockets then smiled apologetically. "Sorry but could you lend me some money to buy them only I don't have any on me? I think I left my bag at the hospital."

Tom had to laugh. Melanie Adams was asking if she could borrow money from him. He found ten pounds in his wallet and handed it over.

While Melanie joined the short queue, Tom looked around the station. It was reasonably busy with people returning home after a night out. He was about to call Miller when he realized it might not be the best idea. At the worst it could even alert Simpson to Miller's presence. He returned the phone to his pocket. He would call him a bit later if he hadn't heard anything. After their coffees, he would suggest they head back to the Imperial again where they were planning to spend the night.

Tom spotted Taylor first as he strode across the concourse towards the ticket barriers, accompanied by three other men. Then he saw Miller emerge from some shadows to greet them. They conversed in a huddle and Miller pointed towards the Gatwick Express platform. It was a train Tom knew very well, as for large parts of the day, the Gatwick Express ran fast to Gatwick airport and then carried onto Brighton. It was normally the fastest train link between Brighton and London. He glanced up at the departure board and saw the next train was showing as delayed. He wondered if Simpson was on the train and Miller and the others were going to close in on him.

Tom turned in the direction of the Coffee stand as he heard a small commotion. He could see a handful of people gathering around Melanie and it was obvious she had been recognized. He watched how she smiled and chatted with both men and women, completely at ease. Not a trace of her superstar status. After a minute she picked up the two cups of coffee and rejoined Tom.

Simpson joined the train and took an aisle seat. It was surprisingly busy and a number of people were eating burgers and other takeaway food that filled the carriage with inviting aromas. He was starving and remembered he hadn't eaten all day. Now he was safe, he knew the rumbling in his stomach was indicating hunger not nerves. He glanced at his watch. Only five minutes to departure time. Then he heard the announcement over the train's speaker system apologizing for the fact the train would be delayed ten minutes waiting for a driver to join the train. He wasn't too bothered as he wasn't in any rush.

He had decided earlier in the day that he had had enough of being at the bidding of the damned Irish and it was time to retire. He had gone to Jones and announced his desire for early retirement, which was well received, as Jones had a need to reduce headcount and considered Simpson a bit of a dinosaur. He had outstanding holiday and it was agreed he could go away immediately and Human Resources would work out the details while he was abroad.

Simpson had then booked two flights. First he bought a ticket to Geneva early in the morning under a false name. He also booked a flight to Lanzarote under his own name early in the afternoon. If everything went according to plan he would take the Lanzarote flight. If anything went wrong as it had, he would take the early flight to Geneva, pay a visit to his safe deposit box and be ready to start a new life. There were sufficient funds in his Swiss account and the deposit box to pay for a comfortable retirement somewhere far away. Miller would be checking airports and would soon find his reservation for Lanzarote. He would probably lay in wait for him but by then he would already be in Geneva.

As he sat watching everyone eating, he remembered the Burger King just by the barriers and decided the delay afforded him plenty of time to get some much needed food. Although he enjoyed fine dining he also was perfectly happy with a large burger meal from time to time. Tonight it would be double portions of everything. He left the train and retraced his steps towards the ticket barrier.

A train had arrived at the next platform and the passengers were tumbling off and also heading for the ticket barriers. As he neared the exit he noticed a group of men on the other side of the barriers huddled together engrossed in conversation, right in front of the Burger King. He was through the barrier as the group split apart and he immediately recognized Taylor. Then he spotted Miller.

He spun on his heels and started walking away from the group towards the underground station. Where the hell had they come from? Did they actually know he was here or were they just checking all the stations? Fortunately, others were walking in the same direction and at least partially shielding him from Taylor and Miller's view. As he walked, he expected to hear his name called and be ordered to stop but no challenge came. He accelerated his pace. He was outnumbered and knew he couldn't outrun them. If they saw him he was dead. Gradually the distance between him and the danger increased. He was starting to feel a sense of euphoria that he was once again going to escape their clutches.

Tom looked back in the general direction of Miller and the others. He didn't want to join Miller and interfere with whatever he was doing. He sipped on his coffee and turned back to Melanie. With a huge sense of foreboding, he then looked back again in Miller's general direction at the man who had just come through the ticket barrier and was now heading in his direction. He was certain it was Simpson. Why the hell hadn't Miller seen him? They were so engrossed in conversation no one had noticed he was slipping right past them.

"Don't turn around," Tom cautioned Melanie, "but Simpson is walking straight towards us."

Tom could see Melanie was fighting the urge to take a look. He half turned himself so that he wasn't clearly visible. He held the coffee cup to his lips as Simpson came near. There was nowhere really to hide. He was bound to see them shortly.

Tom spotted the moment when Simpson realized who he was approaching. He was about fifteen feet away. The revelation caused Simpson to stop mid stride and at the same time look behind, checking no doubt on the location of Miller. Melanie could tell from Tom's look of concern that they had been spotted and turned to face Simpson.

Tom let out an enormous shout of "Miller" that was heard by everyone on the station. People nearby immediately started to move away to avoid him.

The scream seemed to confuse Simpson for a second. He looked back and locked eyes on Miller. Then he started to run.

Tom saw him drawing the gun from inside his jacket. Melanie reacted first and threw her coffee at the approaching Simpson catching him fully on the chest. The impact made the protective top fly off and hot coffee splashed all over him. A fair amount landed on his face and caused him to swear.

He raised his gun in Melanie's direction and it was Tom's turn to throw his cup. His aim was true and the cup hit Simpson fully on the chin and covered him in scolding coffee.

Simpson shrieked in pain and used both arms to desperately wipe the coffee from his face.

Tom could see Miller and the others running at full speed in their direction.

Simpson turned and fired wildly in their direction, causing them to throw themselves to the ground. The atmosphere in the station suddenly changed. The public panicked at the realization of what was happening. Some dived to the floor. Others ran away screaming. A few just stood with open mouths uncertain what to do, perhaps not believing the scene unfolding before their eyes.

In the midst of the chaos, Tom watched Simpson turn back towards him and Melanie. There was a look of pure malice in his eyes and Tom was sure he would happily kill them both. Simpson raised the weapon to fire and Tom threw Melanie to the ground, covering her with his body. He heard a single shot but felt no pain. Then he heard further multiple shots. He clung tightly to Melanie until the firing stopped but didn't look up. He heard the sound of running feet approaching.

"You know you can get into trouble for that sort of behaviour in public," Tom heard Miller say.

"Very funny," a very relieved Tom responded and climbed off Melanie.

Miller held out his hand and helped pull Melanie to her feet. Tom reasoned he wasn't going to get the same assistance so scrambled to his feet without help. He felt huge relief that once again lady luck seemed to have been on their side but he didn't think he had many lives left.

A few feet away on the ground was the bloody body of Simpson. Tom knew it could easily have been him lying there. A crowd had started to gather and the police were keeping them at bay and telling them to go on home but they were standing transfixed by the sight of the dead body on the ground.

Taylor walked up to the dead body and covered Simpson's face with his jacket. Tom turned away. Given the circumstances, he was glad Simpson was dead. Miller and his men had had no choice but to shoot him and it was just as well for Tom and Melanie their aim had been accurate. Tom didn't understand what had made Simpson become the man he was but he had saved Tom's life in Richmond Park and so couldn't have been all bad.

"I have no idea what you two are doing here but thanks for your help," Miller said. "You stopped him getting away."

"Glad to be of assistance," Tom responded smiling.

With hindsight Miller couldn't believe how close Simpson had come to escaping. What the hell had made him get off the train? Perhaps having the train delayed set an alarm bell ringing. Whatever the reason, Miller recognized he should have been watching more closely. There would be no disguising that fact in his report. Questions would be asked but Miller wasn't unduly bothered. Retirement was just around the corner. And nothing could take away the sense of satisfaction he was feeling. He was quite certain Brian Potter would be waiting to greet Simpson in the afterlife.

Miller laughed, "You are both deadly with a cup of coffee."

"Years of training," Tom retorted.

"Please don't take this the wrong way," Melanie stressed, "but I am getting fed up of meeting you."

Miller smiled. "I don't blame you."

"You know I used to think England was a far safer place to live compared with back home. Every time I see Gwyneth, she goes on about what a great place London is to bring up a family. It hasn't seemed so great the last week!"

"I know what you mean," Miller concurred. The last week had indeed been mad. Fortunately it wasn't atypical. He liked Melanie Adams he decided and Ashdown was okay also. He had shown a lot of courage more than once. He wondered if they would make it long term as a couple. He hoped so.

He would have to get one of her films out on DVD. They weren't the sort of thing he normally watched but he reckoned Mary would enjoy it and he was definitely curious now he knew her, to see her acting.

"Can I get you some more coffee," Miller offered.

"Actually," Tom cut in, "I don't know about anyone else but I need something a lot stronger then coffee!"

"I'm sorry," Miller apologized. "But you will have to make do with coffee for the time being. I need to get statements from both of you. It's going to be another long night."

CHAPTER THIRTEEN

Tom was both excited and nervous about the day ahead. He had been looking forward to it for over a month and as it came closer so his excitement had built. But now as the plane landed in Miami, he was also extremely nervous. The flight had gone well and he had enjoyed his first experience of flying first class.

He had almost forgotten he was on a plane, as he sipped champagne and enjoyed great food, while the cabin crew attended to his every wish. He had spotted one of his favourite female singers sitting across the aisle and they had exchanged pleasantries. She was doing some serious damage to the free champagne but he was taking it far easier. He didn't want to arrive with a hangover. He had a big weekend ahead of him. He laughed at the absurdity that he now found it almost routine to be meeting a famous singer. His life had certainly changed dramatically since meeting Melanie.

This was his first visit to anywhere in the USA except Las Vegas and then he had spent most of his time in a huge hotel playing poker, with little time for sightseeing. As he left the aircraft cabin and stood at the top of the aircraft steps, he was hit by the warm temperature of the air. It felt almost tropical and the brilliant sunshine made him blink to adjust to the brightness. It was February and he had left behind a cold and miserable UK. There had been a scary few days leading up to his departure when snow had disrupted flights, leading to many cancellations and threatening to spoil his trip but thankfully he had taken off on time.

Tom went through passport control and collected his one large bag, purchased new for the occasion. The whole process took nearly an hour and then he was walking out of arrivals. He glanced around trying to spot his lift, which he had been assured would be waiting to collect him and there was his name being held aloft on a board.

He waved at the man and walked towards him. The driver was wearing a grey suite and a peaked cap. He looked every bit the chauffeur. He asked if it had been a good flight and Tom happily accepted his offer to take charge of the large suitcase. He followed the driver to the car park as he pulled the case behind him. The driver asked if it was his first visit and was generally amenable.

"Are you on holiday or business, Sir," the driver asked pleasantly.

"Definitely holiday. I'm here to see the Super Bowl."

"You got tickets?" the driver enquired not hiding the surprise in his voice. "They're like gold dust."

"I have," Tom answered. "A very good American friend of mine is taking me."

They spoke a little more about the upcoming game during the drive to the hotel. The driver didn't hide his jealousy when Tom admitted it would be the first ever game he had seen.

"Who you gonna be supporting?" the driver asked.

"The Steelers. My friend is a huge fan and she got me the tickets."

"Well enjoy it. It don't get much better than a Super Bowl."

They stopped outside the St Regis hotel and a bell boy came to take his bag. The taxi had been prepaid and the driver waved away the suggestion of a tip as Tom reached for his wallet.

Tom was shown to his room. It had a balcony and a view out to sea. It reminded him of Melanie's suite at the Imperial, where they had first met properly. What if he had done the sensible thing and taken the train back to Brighton and never bothered to hang around in that coffee shop, hoping she would return his call? He doubted he would be here now. He glanced at his watch. In two hours he would see her for the first time in a month. He was excited to see her but nervous. Would she still feel the same about him?

After Simpson's death they had spent a few memorable days

together over Christmas and New Year. They had gone racing, sightseeing and spent time at the bedside of a much improved Colin. They had also spent a lot of time making love. Life had been as good for those few days as he could ever remember. She had stayed for his birthday on the tenth of January and his present from Melanie, was a trip to see the Super Bowl a month later.

Two days later, Tom had driven her to Heathrow. It was a difficult moment when they said their goodbyes. He didn't want to go in with her and anyway she would get the VIP treatment. They stood and kissed, then embraced with neither wanting to be the first to let go but eventually Tom had let her leave. He watched her back all the way to the terminal. She turned and waved one last time. He went back to his empty house and sank several large bottles of beer.

For the next few days everywhere he went, he was reminded of Melanie. The Hilton where they had spent so much time in bed, his house, all the sights of Brighton were reminders of good times.

He had been back once to his coffee shop in Patcham, where Rafiq had greeted him like a returning celebrity and refused to hear of him paying for his breakfast. All Rafiq could speak about was the time Tom had taken the wonderful Melanie Adams to his coffee shop. Tom remembered it well. They had sat quietly in a corner talking of the future over coffee. After about twenty minutes a buzz had gone around the place and it was obvious she had been recognized. Rafiq had emerged from the back to welcome her and ask for a photo of her in his café. Then others had wanted pictures and autographs. Melanie obliged everyone and as usual everyone seemed to love her. Tom had the feeling he would always be extra welcome in Rafiq's café in future.

Even his betting shop only served to remind him of Melanie. She had visited for a second time towards the end of the day and after the other staff had left, they had gone to the back office and she had sat astride him only half undressed and frantically and noisily enjoyed him. Now each time he went in the office, the images of their love making were overpowering.

These were the places he spent his days and Melanie was still there in his memories. They had swapped messages and a few calls but the time difference and her hectic schedule since returning to the States had largely kept them apart. He had gone from spending a large part of each day with her to not seeing her for a whole month. He couldn't help but be worried that now she had returned home, she would settle back into her normality and gradually forget about him.

He heard a knock at his door and went to open it, expecting to see room service with the brunch he had ordered. At first he thought there was no one there but then Melanie appeared from the side of the door. She had a huge smile and looked stunning. She was wearing a beautiful red lace sheath dress that fell to her knees and hugged her body. The lined part reached from her breasts to her knees but the long sleeves and round neckline were a delicate sheer pattern. He didn't know one designer from another but didn't doubt the dress must have cost a fortune and was worth every penny. He was mesmerized by how she looked.

"I had the taxi firm call me the minute they dropped you here, as I couldn't wait to see you," she explained. "Aren't you going to invite me in?"

Tom was shocked by her sudden appearance. He had thought he had two hours to prepare. He was still in the same clothes he'd flown in and needed to freshen up. He stepped back into the room and she followed. He kissed her on either cheek in greeting.

"Is that the best you can manage," Melanie joked. She reached up to him and kissed him slowly on the lips. Her tongue darted inside his mouth. He responded and pulled her closer. They held each other tightly and kissed for a long time. He knew she could feel how pleased he was to see her.

"I desperately need a shower," he said, breaking the embrace. Then added, "It's so good to see you."

Melanie pinched her nose with two fingers. "I wondered what the funny smell was," she joked. Then she gave him a huge smile. "I've missed you too," she sighed.

"I didn't know a month could be so long," Tom replied. He was beginning to relax. Melanie was here and she was pleased to see him.

"By the way, how's Colin doing?" Melanie asked.

"He's doing great. Doctors say he will make a complete recovery. He said to say hello."

Colin was now at home recuperating and being doted on by Liz. Tom had visited several times and was surprised to find that Liz had been very welcoming each time. If she blamed him for Colin's getting shot, she wasn't bearing a grudge. And Maxwell had negotiated a further payment from the newspaper for Colin, Tom and Janet to tell the story of the events on the night Colin was shot and John killed. Tom had asked for his share to be divided between Colin and Janet but not to tell them what he'd done.

"Don't know about you but I'm feeling terribly nervous," Melanie said, as she moved to the window to look at his amazing view.

"So am I," Tom agreed. "It's been over a month and I wasn't sure you'd still feel the same."

Melanie turned slowly and stared at him. "I'm nervous about the big game you idiot. My feelings for you weren't ever going to change. Now how about that shower? I think I'll join you."

The Chief had been out down the pub for a few drinks. It had been a difficult three months but he'd come through it and at last he felt under less pressure. The mess in London had been cleared up and though he'd lost Jones as a source, things were slowly getting back to normal.

The backlash from the capture of his Operations man hadn't been as bad as anticipated. Maybe he had been selective in what he chose to tell the Cops. The fact he was talking had been enough reason for them to change everything about how they did business. It was a pain but necessary. Anything that could potentially be revealed and put them at risk was amended. Income had dropped sharply for a month but was now getting back to normal.

The talk about his leadership had gone from outright criticism to barely a whisper. Nobody was willing to put their head above the parapet and openly challenge him. So he'd decided to go for a few drinks with the boys to celebrate.

It had been a good evening. A band had been playing a good mix of pop and then played some traditional songs before finishing with Dunlavin Green, which was one of his favourite ballads. It reminded him the fight had been going on for over two hundred years. They had all joined in and it had been a grand atmosphere. He'd decided to call it a day at two in the morning, although the pub would be open most of the night. He was getting too old for all night sessions. And anyway the younger boys could let their hair down better when he wasn't around.

He was enjoying the fresh air as he staggered the half a mile back home. He was a bit uncertain on his feet but the pavement was well lit by street lamps and it was a cool rather than cold night. In truth he'd had a good few pints and was feeling a bit the worse for wear.

He was thinking about getting a sandwich when he reached home. He was feeling peckish and a ham sandwich with an ample covering of mustard would be just what he needed before going to bed.

He'd have to be careful though not to wake the wife. She had a terrible temper on her when he disturbed her sleep. He smiled at the thought that maybe he would disturb her sleep properly after his sandwich. It had been a while since they last did it.

He walked under the bridge that he had known since his childhood. It was dark and something in the shadows caught his attention. There was a blur of movement out the corner of his eye. He started to turn but he was slow to react and the blow to his head knocked him to the ground before he knew what had hit him.

He lay stunned on the ground. He tried to shake his head to clear his senses. He put his hand up to where he'd been hit and felt blood running down the side of his head, mixing with his hair, confirming someone had delivered him a huge blow.

The alcohol had clouded his normal sharp sense for danger. Had they been buying him drinks with the intention of getting him drunk, just so he wouldn't be in a fit state on his walk home? Were they still back in the pub raising a glass to his misfortune? A figure emerged from the shadows.

"Do you know who I fucking am?" The Chief asked angrily.

The man who had hit him was dressed in dark clothes and The Chief couldn't distinguish his facial features. Then he realized it was because he was wearing a balaclava covering his face.

The Chief saw him raise a large club like weapon and it came crashing down on his leg before he could move out the way, breaking his shin bone. He let out an enormous wail like a wounded animal. He tried to pull himself back from his assailant. He was sweating and in terrible pain.

The man spoke for the first time and through his pain, The Chief recognized the voice.

"You murdering bastard. Did you think I was just going to let you get away with killing my children?" Pat Murphy spat the words out with a terrible anger.

The Chief was scared but also saw a glimmer of hope. This wasn't just some random assault by a Loyalist stranger intent on revenge. He'd known Pat Murphy all his life. Surely he could reason with him. "But Pat I told you it was nothing to do with me. It was those Real bastards he joined."

"I'm not fucking stupid. I know Connor was over there. I know how you think. I know how he operates."

"Pat, we can sort this out."

Murphy seemed not to hear The Chief. "And even if they killed my son why would they kill Samantha? She was my baby girl. I loved her more than anything. More than any fucking cause."

The Chief was looking around. Why hadn't anyone come to his aid? They must have heard him scream. The pain was intolerable.

He knew what was coming when he saw Murphy raise the club again and immediately started to scream. The blow struck his other shin and the Chief heard the sound of smashing bone at the same moment he felt the unbelievable pain.

"She was a beautiful lass," Murphy continued. He seemed oblivious to The Chief's pain and screams. "And my son was a good boy. Wouldn't ever do anything that would knowingly hurt your fucking cause!"

The Chief was lying on the ground, his body was broken and shaking but his mind was working. He reasoned if he could keep Murphy talking someone was bound to come to his aid. It was only a matter of time. He thought about shouting out for help but that might provoke Murphy into further attacks.

"I have kids Pat. I know how you feel but it was nothing to do with me," The Chief struggled to keep an even voice, wanting to sound sympathetic. "Samantha was just unlucky. It was some English pervert did for her. I wouldn't have hurt her. She was one of us. It was nothing to do with me or Connor," he pleaded.

Inside, he was regretting not seeing this coming. He'd thought Murphy was okay with his explanation it was the Real boys that were responsible for his son's death. Now he was faced with a demonic madman.

Murphy wiped his forearm across his mouth. He pulled the balaclava from his head. "Shouldn't have harmed my lass," he said with conviction. "The missus is in a terrible state. I promised her I'd set things right. Enough chat. I need to get this done. Make your peace with God."

The Chief saw the look in Murphy's eyes and was terrified. "You fucking eejit," he suddenly shouted. "No wonder your kids were so fucked up with you as their father. You don't understand fucking anything." Anger had replaced the pain he was feeling. "You think this is going to make everything better? You've just made it worse."

Murphy raised his club one further time. He straddled The Chief's body. "Maybe but I know if it wasn't for you my kids would still be alive. This has to end."

As Murphy brought the club crashing down on The Chief's head, he started to scream and tried desperately to move away but it was impossible with his broken legs. He lifted his hands to protect himself but it was useless. The first blow silenced the scream but not the whimpering that immediately followed.

Murphy hit him several more times in quick succession until the features of the face could no longer be distinguished. It was just a mangled mess of skin, bone and blood. Murphy had tears running down his cheeks. He was panting from the effort of delivering the blows.

He threw the club to the ground and looked up at the sky. He made the sign of the cross and said out loud, "I'm sorry my children. I failed you but I've revenged you. Rest easy. Your mother and I will be with you soon." Then he cast one last glance at the body on the ground and walked away.

###

Read Bill Ward's second thriller Encryption.

In a small software engineering company in England, a game changing algorithm for encrypting data has been invented, which will have far reaching consequences for the fight against terrorism. The Security Services of the UK, USA and China all want to control the new software.

The Financial Director has been murdered and his widow turns to her brother-in-law to help discover the truth. But he soon finds himself framed for his brother's murder.

When the full force of government is brought to bear on one family, they seem to face impossible odds. Is it an abuse of power or does the end justify the means?

Only one man can find the answers but he is being hunted by the same people he once called friends and colleagues.

ABOUT THE AUTHOR

Bill Ward lives in Brighton with his German partner Anja. He has recently retired from senior corporate roles in large IT companies and is now following a lifelong passion for writing! With 7 daughters, a son, stepson, 2 horses, a dog and 2 cats, life is always busy!

Bill's other great passion is West Brom!

Connect with Bill online:

Twitter: http://twitter.com/billward10bill

Facebook: http://facebook.com/billwardbooks

Printed in Great Britain
by Amazon